Please

Olive

GW00832656

THE SEVENTH STONE

THE SEVENTH STONE

Eric Poyner

The Book Guild Ltd
Sussex, England

This book is a work of fiction. The characters and situations in this story are imaginary. No resemblance is intended between these characters and any real persons, either living or dead.

This book is sold subject to the condition that it shall not, by way of trade or otherwise, be lent, re-sold, hired out, photocopied or held in any retrieval system or otherwise circulated without the publisher's prior consent in any form of binding or cover other than that in which this is published and without a similar condition including this condition being imposed on the subsequent purchaser.

The Book Guild Ltd.
25 High Street,
Lewes, Sussex

First published 1992
© Eric Poyner 1992
Set in Baskerville
Typesetting by APS,
Salisbury, Wiltshire
Printed in Great Britain by
Antony Rowe Ltd.
Chippenham, Wiltshire.

A catalogue record for this book is
available from the British Library

ISBN 0 86332 763 X

1

Deafening though the roaring of the mountain was during its times of activity, always above it could be heard the scream, and always the same scream. 'El-car-o,' it seemed to say, 'Elcaro,' over and over again until the roaring faded and all was peaceful once more.

Each time the mountain roared, the highest peak of Mount Tarara glowed with a brilliant white light as a beacon shining in an otherwise evil domain.

The people of the plains to the west had always regarded the glowing peak as being the 'Elcaro' to which the haunting scream was directed and legend had it that the one who screamed was none other than the mighty Haon, the evil ruler of the mountain realm.

Haon had been in existence for as long as historical records could show, and down through the ages he had always been a threat to the peace of the plains. How he had survived no-one could tell. Where he had come from no one knew, for there had never been any form of contact between the plainsfolk and the ruler of the mountains.

The thundering of the mountains always struck fear into the hearts of those who lived in their shadow. Though more often than not no harm came to them, there was always the risk of a great devastation. It had happened in the not-so-distant past and the legend, passed down from generation to generation, told of other massive destructions of the plains over the centuries. It had long been accepted that Haon was the cause of all the trouble. He had grown to be so powerful that he could make the mountains themselves roar.

That Elcaro alone stood in his path was firmly accepted by the people of the plains but when the great devastations came, even he could not thwart the intentions of the evil old man. And so they lived in dread of the effects of Haon's power, yet at the same time they fostered a hope that one day Elcaro would finally overcome him. They were an intelligent and hard-working people who, throughout the years had rebuilt their towns after each devastation, hoping that it would never happen again. Nevertheless the youth were not allowed to be in ignorance of the Haonic threat. They listened to the stories until they knew them by heart. The occasional roaring from the mountain and the glowing of Elcaro served to add sub-stance to the tales of the great destructions. Haon and his massively evil Haonic power were very real in the minds of all who lived on the plains to the west.

It was after an unusually long period of relative calm, during which generations of plains people had been able to recover from the last devastation, that their towns and cities, now rebuilt once more, matched the elegance and beauty of the people themselves. They were a fine generation who had greatly benefited from the scientific, cultural and artistic heritage of their ancestors and had developed into an intelligent and capable people. But, intelligent as they were, there always remained the fear of the unknown power behind the roaring mountains to the east.

At this time there lived a remarkable family by the name of 'Androphine'. The parents were scholarly people who had been blessed with four children of outstanding abilities. There were three daughters and one son, all of whom had displayed great gifts, and widely differing interests.

Yma was the oldest of the girls. The boy, who was rather grandly named Omar Jason, but always affectionately known as 'Oj', was the youngest of the family. Yma, a tall, graceful girl of twenty had large dark eyes set in clear-cut, regular features. Her dark brown hair had a tinge of red in it in certain lights and she wore it long, to fall just below her shoulders. She had the figure and bearing which enabled her to look elegant in whatever she was wearing, whether it was her favourite tom-boy outfit of well-worn trousers and jacket, or her long black evening gown with its restrained embroidery acting as a foil to the beautiful earrings her parents had given her on her eighteenth birthday. Yma had always loved the out-door life and ever since she was a little girl had revelled in any opportunity for adventure. Often she had to be restrained from taking unnecessary risks but now that she was twenty and had reached that age without serious injury, her love of the outdoors had concentrated upon sailing. The sea was not a great distance away and the family boat, an eight metre coaster, solidly built and very stable, was moored close inshore during the summer months. Whenever the opportunity arose she either crewed with her father at the helm, or took the helm herself with her younger sister, Lekhar, acting as crew. These were exhilarating excursions and afforded Yma the excitement and yet at the same time, the relaxation that she needed.

The other great love in Yma's life was music. From the earliest days when she was just a baby in her cot she had reacted to rhythm and melody in a most surprising way. Music had made her bubble with joy and she would sway and beat time with her arms even before she could walk. Since those days she had displayed musical talents which could only be described as those of a genius. The flute and 'cello were her favourite instruments but she could turn to other forms of musical expression, should the music demand it. Those who heard her play were transported as it were into another world; a beautiful world of harmony and rhythm. Her own compositions had already gained public acclaim largely because of her unique ability to express widely-ranging emotions from the primitive to the ethereal.

Yma's sister Lekhar, who was just eighteen and nearest to her in age, almost matched her in height and to a large extent shared her love of the outdoors and revelled in the adventures they had together as they grew up. Lekhar however, was much more organised than Yma. She always wore her beautiful copper-coloured hair severely brushed back from her face and either plaited or secured in a pony-tail over the nape of her shapely neck. She kept her room neat and tidy with her precious books carefully stacked on the shelves her father had made for her. Her dressing table was more of a desk than anything else. True, there were the usual brushes and combs, pots of this and tubes of that which serve to enhance a girl's beauty, but Lekhar kept them all in their place, leaving her plenty of room for her studies. She was often to be found poring over some scientific tome, completely absorbed in the problem of the moment and thoroughly enjoying it! Since childhood she had shown an outstanding grasp of mathematical processes and her razor-sharp logical mind had, even at the comparatively tender age of eighteen, assimilated a considerable amount of modern scientific knowledge. It sometimes worried her parents that Lekhar was so dedicated to her studies but they knew she gained much pleasure from them, and her health did not seem to be affected by her intense powers of concentration. It was a good thing that she and Yma were able to enjoy each other's company. Perhaps this was because they were so different in temperament, and also because they shared a love of the outdoors. When they were sailing together they were both completely happy but it was always Yma who took the helm, with Lekhar as crew, content in these conditions to be told what to do, and both finding complete relaxation in their joint battle against wind and sea.

It was during one of their sailing expeditions that they saw in the distance, the summit of Mount Tarara begin to glow. They knew what would happen and sure enough, in a short while the characteristic sound as of thunder came from the mountain as if the very peaks themselves were shaking in fury because Elcaro was shining out so brilliantly over their slopes. It had been some years since the mountain had stirred and the girls were scared that this present activity might be the prelude to something worse to come; but after a while the roaring ceased and Elcaro's light gradually faded. Nevertheless Yma went about and headed as quickly as possible for the shore. They moored the coaster and were soon pulling for the slip-way in the little rowing boat they used to ferry themselves to and from the mooring. They lost no time in stowing the boat in the rack provided for the purpose at the sailing club headquarters and were home again within the hour. They found that the usual atmosphere of calm had been somewhat disturbed by the mountain's activity and the whole topic of conversation was the 'noises off' and the strange Elcaronic light which seemed in some mysterious way to be connected with Tarara's rumblings. People were talking to each other in the street and discussions were taking place in the town square as well as in the more intimate family circles.

As always, when the plains people had experienced the activity in the mountain to the east, the question was being asked, 'What on earth is it that makes the mountain come to such potentially dangerous life? – Can it be that there is truth in the old story that a demonic old man called Haon has lived there for so many, many years and that it is he who has the power to control the behaviour of the very mountains themselves?' Wherever the truth lay, it was certain that no government nor yet any individual had ever deemed it advisable to journey to the east to find the answer.

This time there seemed to be an added urgency to the debate. Life on the plains was very agreeable and only the oldest amongst the inhabitants could remember hearing at first hand from the survivors, the vivid descriptions of the after-effects of the last devastation which had come so suddenly and catastrophically from the mountain. It had taken many years to rebuild their towns, and restore their standard of living and this recent disturbance naturally was of great concern, because it might be that it was the forerunner of another cataclysmic attack from the menacing mountains which dominated the eastern horizon.

Yma and Lekhar, now joined by their sister Ecila, and Oj, their young brother, listened again to the story of Tarara, Haon and Elcaro recounted by their father and mother; a story now coloured by the fear of the possibility of more destruction to come.

'If only contact could be made with Haon,' their father said, 'if indeed he exists at all. Perhaps, with all our own knowledge of science and our ability to understand more fully than ever before the secrets of the natural world and to put them to good use, we could find ways of controlling these frightening characteristics of the mountain. Then we could live in greater security than we do at present. What is more, even the old devil Haon might find a more pleasant and peaceful life-style,' he added with a wry smile on his face.

Later that day, the children's parents, as two of the leaders of the community, were called to a meeting to discuss the latest turn of events. So the four young ones found themselves together in a strangely artificial atmosphere of reserve. Each one's thoughts were turned towards what their father had said about finding out how to control Haon and it was young fifteen-year old Oj who couldn't contain his impatience any longer and burst out, 'Why can't *we* do something about it? Here we are, four healthy, strong, pretty talented people. I'm sure we could at least have a good try!' His eyes sparkled and his enthusiasm was infectious.

9

He was quite tall for his age and powerfully built. His round face with its beaming smile and twinkling brown eyes was topped by the reddest of red hair. His body, though muscular, was lithe and his hands were already those of a capable craftsman. Even though he was still only fifteen he had developed into an intelligent young man whose skill in things practical was of an extraordinarily high standard. His mechanical talents were supplemented by an insight into the properties of the materials with which he worked. In this respect he could match even Lekhar's scientific knowledge. In fact, it was Lekhar who had taught him a good deal of what he knew, and a close bond had grown up between the two of them.

'Why not?' they responded, all three together, and Yma added, 'At least we could make an excursion into the foothills and maybe go even further.' So without any further debate, it was agreed that they would set off early the very next morning.

When their parents returned they found four very excited young people, bubbling over with eagerness for their proposed adventure the next day. Father and Mother were naturally apprehensive about the idea of their four children setting off towards the east and the great mass of Mount Tarara, but nothing concrete had come out of their meeting with the other leaders of the community and so secretly they were proud to feel that their own four offspring had cut through all the red tape of committee discussion and decided to take the matter into their own hands. Why not let them go at least into the lower slopes of the mountain? They might just find some clue there, as to why, periodically, the mountain became so frighteningly agitated. They might even find some evidence of the existence of the old man Haon, who, tradition had it, was the cause of it all.

'We'll take every sensible precaution,' Yma assured her parents, 'and no doubt we shall only be away one or two days. The weather is beautifully dry and warm, so it won't hurt us to sleep under the stars for a night or so.'

Feeling more reassured, their parents gave their consent to the expedition and preparations got under way at once.

'You'll need to wear sensible shoes,' said mother. 'And comfortable clothing too,' she added.

'Yes mother,' drawled Oj – 'what about our flannel vests!'

'Don't be cheeky,' retorted his mother and they both burst

10

into laughter. 'Now, get on with your preparations and I'll pack up some provisions for you,' and she pushed him playfully out of the door.

Oj went up the stairs in his usual way, two or three steps at a time and nearly bumped into his little sister Ecila. She was just a year older than Oj but much smaller. She pressed her petite figure against the bannisters to prevent herself being carried along in Oj's slipstream.

'I wish you'd look where you're going,' she cried.

'Sorreee,' came the reply as Oj disappeared into his room at the end of the corridor.

The danger past, Ecila opened her own door and climbed up the three stairs which led into her 'studio' as she called it. It was a fair-sized room and served as a bedroom, a study and above all a retreat, where she could be alone with her pastels and paints. Ecila had from an early age shown a quite uncanny artistic skill. She herself was almost fairy-like in build, being slight and only just five feet tall with shiny, straw-coloured hair streaming to below her shoulders. 'Her thatch,' Oj called it, much to Ecila's annoyance. Her features were clear cut, almost aquiline and completely symmetrical; her ears small to suit her face, and her sparkling hazel eyes set slightly farther apart than you would have expected in a face the size of hers. The net result was that, viewed directly from the front one saw a beauty in the making, whilst in profile one was reminded of a playful pixie. In temperament she was more effervescent than her sisters Yma and Lekhar and she had great difficulty in keeping still. She was for ever picking things up, turning them this way and that, and then putting them down again. Her eyes darted everywhere looking, looking, always looking and making mental notes of the forms, the shapes and colours of the things she observed. Apart from when she was asleep, the only time she could really be said to settle in one place for long was when she was at her easel, putting on paper or canvas the shapes, forms and colours she had stored up in her memory. Most of her creations were painted 'inside my head,' she would say. – 'My fingers only translate them into a form that other people can see.' There was no doubt that Ecila had been blessed with an artistic sense and talent very much out of the ordinary.

As she now flitted around her room gathering up pencils and crayons and a sketch pad to take on her journey the next day,

Oj called to her from along the corridor.

'I hope you don't expect me to cart your easel along with us tomorrow, Ecila. Travel light, that's what I say.'

'And don't bring your workshop with you!' she retorted sarcastically.

They were almost inseparable friends and this sort of bantering had only served to cement their happy relationship more and more as they had grown up together.

Since they had made the decision to explore the approaches to the mountains, they had become extremely excited at the possibilities the journey held for each of them individually. Ecila knew that the landscapes she would find there would provide much material for the paintings she would do when they returned, hence her decision to take the necessary equipment for making sketches and notes. For Lekhar, the new terrain promised fresh sources for observation and measurement. So amongst her belongings she would certainly pack her pocket computer, her treasured portable laser analyser/synthesiser and her small, yet powerful electronic binoculars.

For Oj the choice was straightforward. His pocket knife was a first-line set of tools in itself and he thought that he would be fully equipped with that in his pocket, but for some reason or other he also decided to pack a ball of the special string which he had acquired a few days ago because he had thought it might come in handy some time. It was a recent invention and, though made of a new fibre, it had the properties not only of common or garden string but was a good conductor of electricity as well.

From Yma's room there was no sound of packing. She was sitting on her bed with the flute to her lips, lost in the melody she was producing. For her the flute was a 'must' if they were to be away for a day or so. She couldn't bear to contemplate life without a musical instrument and the flute was much more portable than her 'cello or her piano!

And so their various preparations were made. Next morning they would be off on what promised to be a great adventure for a few days. Not one of then could begin to guess what lay before them and what experiences were to come their way.

2

Full of confidence and with their eyes sparkling with excitement and anticipation they waved goodbye to their parents who had brought them as far as they could by road and when they could no longer see the receding car, they turned their faces towards the east and the mountains.

Oj had taken charge of the pack of provisions their mother had prepared and as he heaved it onto his shoulders he feigned weakness and crumpled under the weight.

'I should think Mum's put enough in here to keep an army for a week, let along the four of us for two or three days,' he said jokingly.

Ecila came to tease him by attempting to help him to his feet and said, 'She knows your capacity for food only too well. She didn't want her little boy to fade away!'

Oj tousled her straw thatch and retorted, 'Enough of your cheek, little one!'

Laughing together they set off in pursuit of the others who had already covered about thirty metres.

For some time they made good progress as the ground sloped gently towards the steeper hills beyond. It was a gorgeous day and their spirits were high. Little Ecila, bubbling over with energy would flit from side to side of their path, peering at this flower and running her slender fingers over that boulder, feeling the beauty of the smoothness and recoiling from the roughness according to the nature of the surface. Sometimes she would be some way behind the rest because she had paused to sketch the approaching mountain. Invariably Oj would hang back and wait for her to catch up, teasing her all the while for being a slow-coach.

By midday they were beginning to climb in earnest. The gentle slopes had given way to much steeper inclines and, more and more, the mountain towered over them. Earlier they had enjoyed views of the plain where they had said goodbye to their parents but now the slopes and cliffs shut off their homeland from their sight and seemed to engulf them. At first they were all thrilled by the magnificence of the scenery, but as time went on they became increasingly apprehensive. They could no longer make out the path they had taken that morning and the way ahead was certainly getting more difficult. At one time Lekhar even suggested they should consider turning back and calling the whole expedition off. She was disturbed by a growing feeling of becoming trapped.

Her logical thought-processes rejected the idea as impossible, but, even so, she blurted out, 'We must stop this. There is something happening which is beyond my understanding. Don't you sense it too? Something inexplicable is influencing us and directing our footsteps!'

They all stopped short at her words and the looks which passed between them showed they shared Lekhar's feeling that they were being caught up in some unseen force.

Breaking the spell Oj said, 'Let's eat and rest a while – I expect we're just hungry. After all, we have been travelling for a long time over unfamiliar ground.' And so they sat down and made a good meal from some of the provisions in the packs which their mother had provided. The sun was still high in the sky and, as they rested, their spirits rose and when Lekhar posed the question, there was unanimous agreement that they should forge ahead. There could be no possibility of giving up now.

The way became steeper and more rugged and at times they had difficulty in finding a suitable route. All their energies were needed to make progress but gradually they climbed higher and higher, and still Mount Tarara continued to tower over them and the upper slopes seemed never to get any closer. Stops for rest became more frequent and when they were in danger of becoming despondent, Yma would put her flute to her lips and, by her superb music, woo them all back to a happy state of confidence, and at these times she would lead them away from their resting place, and upwards they would go without even a passing thought of going back.

For three days they travelled thus without even mentioning their home on the plain. Already they had been away much longer than they had originally planned but to them time seemed almost irrelevant. Even their recollections of home were becoming more and more dim. All that mattered now was the struggle to go further and further into the heart of the mountain. It was as if the four travellers had passed from one time scale into another where they were now inextricably trapped. At night when they stopped to rest under the stars Yma would play to them, while Lekhar busied herself trying to work out how far they had travelled and Ecila was occupied in getting some sort of order into the sketches she had made en route and in re-writing the notes she had made. Oj, more often than not, just lay on his back with his hands under the nape of his strong neck, with his eyes closed. He slept very little. When he closed his eyes he concentrated on his thoughts, trying to remember what they had done that day and the days before, since they had started out. For all of them, memories of home had, in a strange way, almost faded from their minds and yet they knew even more clearly what they were trying to do.

This particular evening Oj started from his reverie and surprised them all by saying, 'It's Haon, isn't it? – It's the old man of the mountain who is leading us into the heart of his kingdom and if we're not very careful he will confuse us so much that we'll never be able to find our way out. I shouldn't be at all surprised if he isn't at this very moment laughing his head off at our predicament!'

'Don't talk such utter nonsense,' retorted Lekhar. 'There's no logical reasoning in your argument. I, for one, cannot accept the idea that this so-called Haon has the ability to influence our behaviour at a distance. The supernatural, and that is what you're suggesting is affecting us,' she emphasised, 'has no place in my philosophy. There must be a straightforward reason for the situation we find ourselves in.'

Yma laid down her flute and joined in the conversation. 'Well,' she said, 'if you ask me, logic or no logic, supernatural or no supernatural, there are some pretty funny things going on in this mountain. We came here for the express purpose of seeking out the old man, Haon, and though we haven't seen the slightest sign of him yet, I myself have felt a weird presence surrounding us and luring us on. I'm with Oj on this and I would counsel extreme caution from now on. There's only one thing we can do and that is to press onwards until we make some sort of contact and then perhaps we shall be able to enter into a dialogue with whoever or whatever it is we call 'Haon'.

As the oldest of the party her word carried considerable weight and though Lekhar was still pretty sceptical, she admitted that particular care was essential from now on. Ecila said nothing. Of all of them she seemed least affected by their situation. She was completely absorbed in the beauty of the scenery, with the towering cliffs and the multicoloured rock formations all around her. She seemed quite content to sketch and make her notes and let the others worry about what they should do and in which direction they should go. Part of the reason for her detachment was her complete faith in her brother Oj who was always on hand to look after her and keep her out of trouble. She knew he wouldn't let any harm come to her.

Ecila's main contribution was to infect the others with her own enthusiasm for the beauty of their surroundings. When the sun rose each morning over the eastern heights she danced with ecstasy at the beauty of the dawn. She would observe excitedly how the brilliance of the sun picked out the ridges on the mountain ranges and how the flowers which grew on the slopes came to colourful life as the sun kissed their petals. Her obvious enjoyment helped the others throw off the worries they had and they laughed and joked with each other as if nothing else mattered beyond the joy of their own company.

The scenery was breathtakingly beautiful, but always there was Elcaro, the tip of the mountain, towards which their eyes were drawn and which brought them back to the reality of their quest. Somewhere, up there, was their goal and when they looked directly at Elcaro they became more and more determined to seek out and find the secret of the roaring mountain.

Thus they travelled up and up for several days, wondering if ever they would find the place where old Haon lived. On one day, when they had tramped over a particularly difficult section of the mountain and were feeling especially weary, they suddenly, all together heard a strange sound. It seemed to be saying, 'This is the way, come here to me . . .' But the trouble was that they all four thought they heard the call from different directions. For the first time they found they could not agree. They were being pulled apart by the strange voice which beckoned them along varying paths.

'This way,' called Oj as he plunged through a gap between two rocks. 'Follow me.'

'No,' – cried Ecila, 'not that way, Oj. The path turns to the right towards those trees. – Come with me.'

Lekhar would follow neither of them. 'Straight ahead,' she said. 'The path is clear for a long way ahead. We must go straight ahead.'

Yma, the oldest, was inclined to another direction completely and even moved as if to lead the party that way. However, she suddenly stopped short in her tracks and shouted, 'Stop it! – Stop it! Come here to me. Don't you see we're being got at? Something is trying to split us up. We must stick together or we are lost!'

Now Yma never, or hardly ever shouted, so the other three were stunned into immobility by the shock of her words. They turned towards her and reluctantly at first, and then with more speed, they raced to gather round her, realising the awful truth of what she had shouted at them. The incident had left them extremely scared and they knew they had had a lucky escape from some influence which had tried hard to separate them from each other. So after that they stayed close together talking to each other and trying to regain their composure.

It was then that it happened. Their voices were drowned by a roaring and a shaking of the very ground on which they stood. The mountain was coming to life again and this time they would be able to hear and see what actually happened. It wasn't very long before the top of the mountain began to glow and their whole attention became riveted in that direction. The differing instructions they had had a short while ago were forgotten and they waited with bated breath for what they all felt was sure to be a most extraordinary experience.

At this distance the light from Elcaro was almost too bright to bear and the roaring from under their feet threatened to throw them to the ground. But the four found that, together, they were able to stand, to watch and to listen. Eventually a new sound came floating down towards them but they didn't actually hear anything. Rather they absorbed new thoughts straight into their minds. It was as if all the questions they had asked themselves about the various things they had encountered along the way were being answered. Understanding was permeating their whole beings.

But before they realised what was happening to them, there stood the old man Haon with his arms upstretched barring their way. 'STOP!' he bellowed. 'This will not do. I alone am Lord of this mountain and no-one is allowed to know the secrets of Elcaro but me.'

The young people shrank back in horror and dismay at the appearance of Haon. They had always hoped that their meeting with the old man might be a friendly one but here he was glaring and shouting at them, towering over them with eyes blazing through the terrifying mask which covered his face. He was frighteningly tall and was clothed from head to toe in a robe coloured and patterned even more garishly than his mask. Never before had they seen such a figure nor had they ever met such a seething display of anger or hatred. Instinctively they shrank together for protection. No chance would now be afforded them to go forward to discover the secret of the mountain, or so they thought. 'Return from whence you came,' thundered Haon. 'Go back to the plains and live as your ancestors have lived for thousands of years. I alone will rule this mountain and I will stay here until I have at last discovered from Elcaro the secret of life itself.'

Then looking towards the summit of Elcaro he shouted, 'What is life, O Elcaro? Tell me your final secret before you sleep again.'

But nothing came in answer to old Haon's plea.

Again he shouted, 'I have lived here for all these centuries. I am powerful and know almost all there is to know, and with this knowledge I am able to control those feeble people of the plains. They are scared of me because they are foolish and do not understand all the things I understand. Give me the secret of life and I will have them completely under my control and they shall serve me until the end of time.'

Then amazingly Elcaro spoke in clear and unmistakable words they could all understand. The sounds came rippling down the mountain slopes and seemed to enter directly into their minds. – Soft sounds, yet decisive and authoritative.

'You are indeed full of facts, old man. You have worked hard on this mountain over the years, you have reached a point where you think you are ready to take over the world. Not yet, old man! As you have been allowed to pry and to probe into the depths of understanding you have completely missed the

18

point of it all. Why, these young people are wiser than you at this very moment and, look behind you, there are yet more of them!'

Sure enough there were two more of about the same age as the other four standing on the other side of Haon and listening to all that was going on. Now these two young people had experienced the same urge as our first four, to try to meet the old man of the mountain and to talk with him. They came from the plain on the other side and their people had also lived in the shadow of Mount Tarara and had never dared until now to approach near enough to discover the secrets of the mountain.

Haon whirled around with his arms flailing in a desperate attempt to intimidate all six of the young intruders into what he considered his private and exclusive domain. He looked at them venomously and snarled, 'These puny creatures, wise? What do you mean, O Elcaro? Who is there in the whole universe wiser than I, who have solved almost all mysteries and wield almost unlimited power? It is I, Haon, who am the wisest of all and I demand the answer to the final question which will make me all-powerful and able to bring all people under my sway, so that I may rule the plains and the whole universe until the end of time . . . WHAT IS THE SECRET OF LIFE!?'

'That you shall never know,' said Elcaro, 'unless these young people choose to tell you when they themselves have found the answer . . . if they ever do.'

'These fools, these weaklings?' fumed Haon. 'How can they ever expect to learn all that I have learned, and then to go further than I have gone?'

Much more quietly, Elcaro spoke again. 'They do not "expect" anything, old man, but in observing the evil way you have used all the precious secrets you have discovered, there has been born in them a germ of a vision of what life should be like, and one day perhaps they will show you just how much more powerful they are than you can ever become, with all your ranting and raving. Now, be off with you, back to your fortress and do not molest these young people any more.'

But Haon was not yet ready to obey the mighty Elcaro and he flung himself at the six, hoping to wipe them off the face of the earth. They had been standing quite dumbfounded listening to the exchanges between Haon and Elcaro, but with the quick reactions of youth and with the timely intervention of Elcaro they were able to scramble to safety in a nearby cave. With a flash of lightning Elcaro wrenched the slopes with an ear-splitting crack and a great chasm appeared, across which Haon's fury could not reach. The young ones were safe for the moment. With terrible threats couched in the most vicious language Haon continued to pour scorn on the notion that anybody could become more powerful than he. But eventually his force was spent and he retreated to the inner recesses of the mountain and left the six young folk cowering fearfully in their cave.

When all had become quiet and their courage had returned, they ventured to peer out of the mouth of the cave. Their first impression was one of chaos and confusion but then they noticed that the tip of Elcaro was glowing even brighter than before. They all stared in wonder and listened. It was then that Elcaro spoke once more.

'Children of the world, your individual talents and your combined efforts have, for the moment overcome the power and evil intentions of Haon. But do not be deceived into thinking he has given up the struggle; for it surely is a struggle in which you are involved. Now you have come this far, you must continue the search for the truth about life. But beware the powers of Haon which stretch far and wide beyond his headquarters. You will find it necessary to do battle with him many more times before you are sure of the truth. I will help you all I can but most of the time you will have to rely on your own abilities and understandings. Try to keep together because therein lies your greatest strength. When you are ready to give me the answer to the question, "What is the secret of life?", come back to me here and we shall see what we shall see. Just one more thing; each of you pick up the stone by his or her right foot. It is a gift from me to you. Not only will it help you each to remember me but, when held in the palm of the hand it will glow, and as you peer into the glow, you will find an answer to the problem confronting you and your resolve to go on searching for the answer to the great question will be strengthened. Never be without it. You cannot tell when and where you will need "Elcaronic power." May you all find what.you seek. Goodbye until we meet again.'

They all stood for some time peering at the top of Tarara

until the brightness of Elcaro faded and eventually went out altogether. No more rumblings were to be heard and there was a great silence. At last, at the same instant, they came back as it were from a dream. Automatically they stooped to pick up the stones by their respective right feet and, as they held them on the palms of their hands, they felt courage and confidence surge back into their very beings.

Everything had happened so fast and dramatically that there had been no time for introductions when the other two had appeared from the other side of the hill. But now they were together as one group, quite naturally they began to chatter to each other. The oldest of the four took the initiative. 'We are the Androphine children,' she said. 'I am Yma, this is Lekhar, this Ecila and this our brother Oj. Oj is the practical one of the family. His real name is Omar Jason, but we call him Oj for short. Ecila is the artistic one, while Lekhar solves all our mathematical problems for us. I myself love music above everything. So you see, we are all different.'

The older of the other two held out both hands to Yma in greeting. 'My name is Aggorine Daviet,' she said, 'and this is my brother, Shimah.'

Shimah, though only just sixteen stood out as the tallest of the group. He had a fine physique and moved with the ease and grace of an athlete. Aggorine was obviously very proud of her younger brother, she being just over a year older. When she was introducing him to the others she was quick to point out that athletics and sports were not Shimah's only attributes; he had excelled at Mathematics at school and was destined to be a budding scientist of note. Shimah was quite embarrassed by Aggorine's glowing account and hastened to make light of what she had said.

'I'm just an ordinary sort of chap,' he said, 'but it is true, I do enjoy life in lots of ways. It's jolly nice meeting up with you,' he added, and shook each of them by the hand.

His firm grip told his new-found friends a great deal about his character. They all seemed to sense that Shimah was a young man of integrity. His expressive dark brown eyes conveyed the message of sincerity too, and they all felt that in this young man they had found a friend who could be relied on through thick and thin. He came to Ecila last of all and somehow his face became even more radiant and his hand held hers for just that bit longer than he had held the others. He obviously found her very attractive. But he broke away and came back to Aggorine's side and put his arm round his sister's shoulder. 'Here you have my aged sister, Aggorine,' he announced playfully. 'She is at least fifteen months older than I am, and, as you see, much smaller!'

Aggorine's face broke into a smile while at the same time she shrugged off Shimah's arm and gave him a none-too-gentle cuff on the back of his head. She was used to her brother's teasing and she knew it was almost always in fun. They had grown up together, not just as brother and sister, but as good friends who enjoyed each other's company. Shimah had outstripped her in build over the past three or four years but they were both equally striking in appearance. His deep brown eyes, set beneath a broad brow topped by curly brown hair gave his face a rugged, handsome look while Aggorine's features had developed from the chubbiness of childhood into the outstanding beauty of a fine young woman. She too was dark-eyed and dark-haired. Her large eyes, set in a perfectly defined face seemed able to change from a misty dreaminess to the clear gaze of an authoritative leader as and when the situation demanded. She wore her hair fairly short and with its natural curl it seemed never to be out of place.

Shimah, recoiling from the affectionate cuff around his head went on to say, 'Seriously though, my sister is a pretty good sort, most of the time! – The only thing is, she bosses me about! I suppose I have to admit that she is almost always right and that she has all the hallmarks of a born leader. She is not unintelligent either,' he continued. 'Again I have to admit she beats me hollow at languages.' He hesitated and then added, 'Oh, and at cooking and sewing!'

All six now burst out in spontaneous laughter, and this despite the fact that only a short time ago they had been through a most frightening experience in their first encounter with Haon.

The introductions over, it wasn't long before they were telling each other all they could about themselves and by the time evening came they were well on the way to becoming firm friends. They shared what food they had left in their packs and Yma played some delightful music on her flute. Before long they were all curled up and fast asleep inside the cave which had been their salvation against the onslaught of the evil Haon.

All was peaceful when they awoke but the mountain-top was cloaked in a silver mist and it seemed impossible that the startling events of yesterday could have been more than a dream. Was it only yesterday? ... Perhaps it was longer; a week or even a month. What was certain was that they had all been there together in the same experience. If it had been just a dream, they had all shared it. It was as if they were from now on to be so closely associated with one another that they would share a common purpose in life. Together they had faced the evil powers of Haon and had experienced at first hand the forces of Elcaro which had given them courage and confidence to withstand Haon and all his works. But Elcaro had been quite explicit in his warnings to them. Haon was by no means defeated by this first encounter; there were to be many more battles to be faced and, if possible, won in the future before the young people could hope to give Elcaro the answer to the question 'What is the secret of life?' How were they to find the answer? Where were they to look? Would they all think along the same lines and tread the same path as each other in their quest? Was there, in fact, only one correct answer to the question?

All these queries came flooding out in the conversation they had together that morning. They sat around in an excited group, each anxious to share his or her 'dream', and when they realised that they had been together in the dream, if dream it was, they set about analysing their situation. There was no disagreement over the fact that they had all had an experience of a lifetime and were much wiser than they had been before. Previously their lives had been overshadowed by Haon because they were all afraid of him, but they had never thought how dangerous and destructive he could be when threatened. Had it not been for the power of Elcaro they would certainly have perished. They had set out in innocence to find out more about the seemingly mighty Haon and found that for all his power and all his wisdom, he was still ignorant of that which he desired to know most of all. His very ignorance was indeed the main reason for his malevolence. He could control the forces of the world but he could only do so through fear backed up by threats and brute force. Elcaro had displayed how dangerous the Haonic forces could be and in his own quiet way had impressed on the six young people of the plains that they would experience these Haonic forces in many forms, which would strive to control them and use them to further the power of the evil one in the world. But Elcaro had offered them help and hope. True, they would be free to live the lives they wished to live but the Elcaronic power would now always be at hand to guide and encourage them in their fight against Haon and all his minions.

There was a great joy in their hearts that morning as they shared each other's company and they seemed very loath to leave that mysterious hill cave where things they had never thought of before had been revealed to them.

Eventually Aggorine took charge and suddenly declared laughingly, 'If we sit around here much longer we shall turn into one of those interminable committees and nothing will ever be done! Come now, we must make a plan.'

The others took it for granted that what she really meant was that she had a plan already in mind.

'It seems to me,' she continued, 'that we have two alternatives. Either we go on or we go back. We have achieved at least part of what we set out to do. We have met Haon and felt his terrifying power and also seen how powerful Elcaro is in the face of evil. We have been promised help by Elcaro and we each have a tangible sign of that promise in our hands, which we are assured will help us when we face the evil one again. If we feel we do not yet have enough evidence of what is going on in these eastern mountains we should go on. If on the other hand we think it wiser to return to the plains to tell our story and encourage others to follow in our footsteps, then, we should go back. Personally, I must say I favour the second alternative. We could all return to the Androphine's home together and Shimah and I could then travel in more comfort to our own home. I am sure that what we have already discovered will encourage others to try to come here to find out more for themselves about the conflicting powers of Haon and Elcaro.'

There was a long pause before anyone expressed an opinion and Aggorine looked patiently from one to the other. Eventually Yma said she agreed, so did Lekhar and Ecila. Shimah and Oj both thought it was too early to say their mission was completed and were both keen to go on. However, after some further discussion it was generally agreed that the wiser and probably the most fruitful course would be to return to the plains and tell their story.

3

So it was that the six young folk set out on what they thought was to be a pleasant jaunt down the mountainside to the familiar surroundings of the Androphine's home in the village on the plain which stretched out from the mountain slopes. But hardly had they been walking for half an hour when they realised that, try as they might, they could make no progress down the mountain but, instead, were impelled by some mysterious power to follow a path which led them gently upwards and around a massive rock face which rose into the sky for several thousands of metres. The ground on one side of the path fell away more and more steeply as they progressed, until they were forced to tread very carefully for fear of plunging into a great chasm below. The strange thing was, however, that they were not frightened by the perilous nature of their surroundings. Instead all six of them were filled by an intense feeling of joy and well-being. The sheer magnificence of the huge rock face and the glorious panorama which spread before them seemed to inspire them with confidence and an intense desire to press on to discover what lay ahead.

Aggorine was in the forefront of the column which now had to travel in a line one behind the other, and Oj brought up the rear. This seemed a natural arrangement and none of the others questioned Aggorine's leadership, or the fact that Oj should be the one to see to it that they were all safely following in her footsteps.

They had been travelling like this for the best part of the morning when suddenly Aggorine called a halt. 'Listen,' she said, 'I seem to hear noises up ahead. Listen.' Sure enough, they could all hear something now. It was difficult to define just what the noises were or to decide where they were coming from, but noises they were and their source was not so far away.

'Stay here a while and I will do a bit of investigation,' said

26

Aggorine and she made her way carefully and quietly along the path which now took a rather sudden turn and opened into a sort of platform cut into the side of the rock face. She was grateful to be able to move away from the precipitous edge of the path and started to examine the cave-like incursion into the rock with increasing interest and subsequent amazement. At first she didn't notice anything out of the ordinary. The floor was rough stone, just as the rest of the cliff path had been, but as she cast her eyes around the walls she became aware that the path did not continue beyond the cave. The walls and the roof of the cave did not appear to be stone-like, as the floor was, but they had a softer texture which seemed to invite her to touch it. She stretched out her hand and, sure enough, the surface felt soft and even luxurious and, not only that, it was definitely warm and comforting to the touch. Absolutely amazed, Aggorine called to the others to join her and in a few moments all six were crowded into the strange refuge at the end of the cliff path. They were all standing gazing in a bewildered state at their peculiar surroundings, thankful to be off the narrow way which had led them to this haven, when they began to appreciate the fact they were hungry and thirsty after their journey. They had a little food left in their packs so they sat down on the floor with their backs to the wall of the cave and spread out the remains of their supplies intending to share it out fairly.

It was Lekhar, with her keen scientific and mathematical mind trained to observe and analyse, who saw it first and she cried out, 'Don't touch it! Something has happened to the food and it may not now be fit to eat! Look at that piece of bread. It looks like a stone. And that cake, it's turned into a real rock cake now!' And sure enough, all the last morsels of the food they had brought with them were now useless.

'What now?' was the question which sprang into all six minds.

As if to answer the unspoken question, Aggorine took charge and said, 'Back. We must go back the way we came. We just can't afford to delay another moment. The way is long and tortuous but back we must go, or we shall starve.'

Immediately in complete agreement, they stood up and turned to the pathway. But where was it? Was it here? Was it over there? Where is it now? The six friends were much too well-balanced and sensible to panic, but in each one's heart crept a semblance of fear. They were trapped in the cave with no way out. They searched and searched the mouth of the cave, but no pathway could they find. Their retreat had been cut off in some mysterious way and they were thoroughly marooned!

'Now, let's be sensible about this,' said Aggorine in a firm and practical way. 'There has to be an explanation, so let's sit down calmly and examine the situation.'

Feeling rather less confident than Aggorine sounded, they all agreed that they must follow her advice. Not one of them would admit he or she was even slightly scared but they all secretly felt that they would, at this moment, prefer to be down on the plain, sitting around the family table, tucking into some real, appetizing family food, than to be perched precariously in a cave on the face of Mount Tarara. For the time being, the fact that they were hungry and thirsty had become far less important than the situation in which they found themselves.

As they sat quietly together they once more became aware of the noises they had heard before they had discovered the strange cave. This time Yma became much more animated than the others. She listened intently and her face seemed to glow with an inner radiance. She got up slowly and stretched herself to her full height, raised her slim arms and fingers above her head and began to sway rhythmically to a beat she could discern in the noises which now seemed to be coming from the rear of the cave. She was obviously able to recognise something in the cacophony of sound that the others were not able to hear. The five who watched her, realising she was finding rapturous enjoyment from what, to her, was music, sat quietly while she now moved round them in a sort of ritual dance. Without appearing to make any particular effort, Yma touched first one and then another on the head and as she touched them they rose to their feet and began to move with her, following her footsteps and, wonder of wonders, hearing, not just noises any more, but a soft, soothing melody which impelled them to move in slow and rhythmical time with it and with each other.

Not a word passed between them but they were in complete unison as they found themselves moving further and further into the recesses of the cave. From the soft-textured walls came a distinct warmth which attracted them and they stretched out their hands to touch them. As they came into contact with the walls the music became gradually louder and louder and in the darkness at the back of the cave there appeared a light. It was quite dim at first but, as the music increased in volume, so the light became more and more bright. It was as if the walls themselves were glowing, first with a greeny tinge, then a golden yellow, until at last they exuded a brilliant white light which illuminated the whole of the cave. Despite themselves, the six friends were impelled towards the source of this brilliance which now seemed to beckon them from the very back wall of the cave itself. Led by Yma they moved as if in a trance towards the light and found that they were in fact passing through the actual wall itself. The brilliance of the light made it impossible for any of them to see anything of their surroundings when they reached the other side of the opening but, as they stood together in a huddle, the music faded and gradually they all regained their awareness and somewhat self-consciously unlinked their hands. They were silent for a space of a few minutes and then, as if by a signal, they all started talking together.

'What has happened?' ... 'Where are we?' ... 'How did we get here?' ... Questions with no immediate answers. All that the six friends could be sure of was that they were still together, and that they were apparently unharmed. They could remember the cave and the path along which they had been forced to travel. They even had a vision of a strange encounter they had had on the mountain before they set off for home ... 'Home? What was that? And where, if anywhere was it?' Not one of the six could recall with any clarity what they had been doing on the mountain nor where they had come from before that.

It was after the first burst of bewildered chatter and questioning amongst themselves had subsided into a bemused silence that Yma, who had led them from the cave and its precipitous entrance, held up her hand. It was not a signal for them all to pay attention to her but nevertheless their eyes all turned in her direction. There in her right hand she displayed something which looked just like an ordinary pebble but which had an aura or a glow around it. She had, in fact, been grasping the stone given to her by the mighty Elcaro and immediately they all remembered the words which came to them as it were from the tip of Mount Tarara. 'Try to keep together because therein lies your greatest strength,' and 'The Elcaronic power in the glowing stone will help you solve the problems confronting you.'

4

Their new and strange situation did indeed present the six friends with all sorts of problems. Not the least of these was hunger! They were all in need of a good meal but it was Oj with his tall and muscular body, used as he was to eating at least as much as his three sisters put together, who was suffering the hunger pangs most of all! So it was he who first broached the mundane matter of food.

'What is there to eat?' he said. 'We must solve that problem before we can put our minds to anything else!'

It was such a down-to-earth statement that it broke a sort of spell that had enmeshed them all up to that point. They even laughed out loud, and the sound of their voices, combined in merriment, helped to bring them all back onto an even keel once more.

By now the brilliant light which had led them from the cave had moderated somewhat, or was it that they were getting used to it? In any event they were now able to see more of their surroundings.

The place on which they were standing was like a platform or stage. It was covered with a soft and definitely warm substance, as was the great rock face through which they had passed to reach this safe haven. Whoever or whatever had led them here had ensured they would not be cold. But what about food? Again it was Oj who first noticed the silver ball-like substances which seemed to be growing out of the warm green walls. Impelled by his great hunger Oj took one in his hand, smelt it and without consideration or hesitation popped it into his mouth. The taste was good and, as he swallowed, a feeling of well-being spread throughout his body. He was no longer hungry but felt completely satisfied and as strong as he had ever felt in his life before.

It was not long before all the others had followed his

example and eaten one of the mysterious silver balls and were provided with all the sustenance they needed. In fact they all felt so refreshed and invigorated that they forgot the fact that they were apparently cut off from the outside world and imprisoned inside the mountain. But what of that in any case? Here they were warm, they seemed to have food enough and to spare and with all their varied talents they felt able to meet any circumstance which might arise and deal with any problem which might confront them. They were lost in a euphoria of contentment. What is more, as they took stock of their surroundings, they found them becoming more and more to their liking. How it happened, they could not tell, but they seemed only to have to think about a particular thing and it was provided; not always in the way they had expected, but certainly to their complete satisfaction.

Yma yearned for the haunting music they had heard before and which had guided them away from the peril of the outside cave, and there it was again for them all to hear and for their combined enjoyment.

Ecila, little Ecila with her straw blonde tresses and her elfin figure darted about from one part of their new abode to another, intrigued by the greens of the walls and the silver of the food balls they had eaten. She liked the colours she saw but longed for the whole canvas of the spectrum to add to the monochromes around her. And there they were! As the glare of the brilliant light faded even more, Ecila was able to discern colours of every hue, some near at hand, some farther afield. They seemed at first to be disembodied, just colours, but as she looked more intently she made out forms. Some were like trees standing in the foreground of a landscape which she could see stretching out before her. Beyond the trees were huge splashes of colour, like fields and hills of red, green, yellow and purple brush strokes across the panoramic canvas which was opening up to her as every moment passed. Ecila was entranced and longed for her own easel, canvas and paints to try to capture the magical sight in front of her.

All she could do was drink it all in, registering it in her artist's mind for use when the opportunity arose. 'When will that be?' she wondered. She didn't know when or if ever it would be possible for her to record on canvas the magnificence of the scene before her but she promised herself that one day it would happen. Then it would be her masterpiece. Of this she was certain, for never before had she seen such beauty nor had she been so emotionally affected by a landscape. It was as if she was already part of the scene; as if her whole being was responding to some unknown attraction within the strange land in front of her. She had been smitten with a feeling akin to love and she wanted only to be for ever part of that land with its peculiar yet beautiful forms and colours.

The other five could only dimly share the view Ecila had excitedly pointed out to them and they were not so emotionally affected by it as she was. Nevertheless they all realised that for Ecila, what she saw was the ultimate in beauty, and they too wished it were possible for her to have her paints and canvas so as to capture that beauty for herself and for all who would come to share it with her. Yes, to share it with her . . . But why should she share it with all and sundry; even with her brother, sisters and friends? Ecila suddenly became very possessive of her artistic talents and felt she wanted all this beauty for herself.

'Go away,' she blurted out. 'Leave me alone!' and she ran away from the rest as far as she could go.

'What on earth has got into Ecila?' gasped Shimah, who had come to look upon her as a very special person and one to whom he could become very attached. But now, what had happened to make her seem so utterly different? Whereas before she was kind and considerate, now she had become belligerently selfish and had shown quite clearly that she didn't want any of the others to come near her or to share in whatever it was she was experiencing. It had all happened in a twinkling of an eye. One minute Ecila was her normal, sweet-tempered, artistic self and the next a totally different character, independent and unfriendly.

Shimah went towards her where she stood alone, apparently quite oblivious of anything else except the beauty of the scene which stretched before her.

'What's the matter?' he said tenderly.

'Nothing, nothing's the matter,' came her sharp reply. 'Nothing that you can do anything about anyway. I just want to be left alone. All the company I want is out there,' and she spread her arms out to the magnificent scenery she could see before her.

Shimah was taken aback by her rejection of his attempt to befriend her but he still persisted. 'That's all very well,' he blurted out. 'I'm sure you can see more in it than I can. All I can see is what appears to be lots of coloured rocks and a few peculiar bushes and trees . . . all very pretty I'm sure, but . . .'

Ecila turned on him and stopped him short. With eyes blazing she cried, 'Pretty? Pretty? It's nothing short of magnificent. You must be completely blind if you can't see how wonderful it is.' She turned away from him and her mood changed. In a voice charged with emotion she simply breathed, 'I must have it. I must make it part of me. I must, I must, I must.'

Spreading her arms again as if to enfold all the scenery before her she started to move forward, slowly at first and then more quickly. Soon her feet seemed not to be touching the ground. A wide pathway opened up and she was gone! Speeding to the very depths of the beauty, she was absorbed into it and soon was lost to sight.

Shimah stood rooted to the spot, unable to move, unable to understand what was happening. All he could do was to reach out towards Ecila as she sped away from him and the rest of the group, shouting her name, 'Ecila, Ecila, come back, come back!'

But she was gone.

For what seemed an age, Shimah stood staring into the distance into which his friend had disappeared, though it was but a moment. Aggorine was by his side.

'Where is Ecila?' she asked.

There was no answer from Shimah who appeared not to be aware of her presence.

She touched him on the shoulder. 'Where is Ecila?' she repeated. 'I thought you came to fetch her.'

After a while all that Shimah could say, and that only in a whisper was, 'Gone . . . gone.'

'What do you mean, "gone"! Gone where? We saw her here with you only moments ago and now you say she has gone,' said Aggorine rather testily. 'She can't have gone far. There isn't any way off this plateau.'

Shimah, gradually coming to himself, looked around him and then at Aggorine and all the others who by this time had joined them.

'She's gone,' he said. 'She just stretched out her arms to the view in front of her and found her way out.'

'This is all very silly,' said Aggorine in her best matter-of-fact tone. 'There must be a logical explanation. She can't just have vanished into thin air!'

She had noticed that the others were looking quite bewildered and she felt, born organiser that she was, that it was necessary to reassure everyone, though, if the truth were told, she herself felt just a little nonplussed. There didn't seem anywhere for Ecila to hide, but nevertheless they all ran about looking into every corner, sure at first that they would find her but eventually having to admit that Ecila had, indeed, vanished into thin air. At last, realising that their sister was lost, Yma, Lekhar and Oj clung together, weeping quietly.

The five friends at last sat down in complete silence when the fact of Ecila's disappearance finally had to be accepted. Their feelings were a mixture of grief at their loss and fear of the unknown circumstances surrounding the whole incident. There was not a sound to be heard. The lovely music, which had so entranced Yma earlier, had stopped and the uncanny silence bore down on them and added to their depression.

They sat there not knowing what to say or do. The situation seemed quite hopeless. At last, as if they had all thought of it at once they each thrust a hand into their respective pockets and withdrew the Elcaronic stone which had been given them after their strange and frightening encounter with the vicious Haon on Mount Tarara. Elcaro had told them that it would help them solve any problem which they may be called upon to face. Well, they certainly had a problem right now and perhaps the Elcaronic power would point them towards a solution. As if they were forced to do so, they all stretched out their hands holding the stones until their fingers touched and their arms formed the spokes of a wheel. There was still no sound but, after a while the stones began to glow and, though no words were spoken each of the five friends experienced a sense of inner confidence which had been so lacking before. Gradually they became aware of the fact that silently, yet very clearly, the voice of Elcaro was implanting a message into their minds.

'Take heart,' it said. 'You have just had a great shock, but you must realise that the normality you all experienced on the plains, before you attempted to climb the mountain and confront Haon, just does not obtain here. He tried crudely to destroy you on the mountain path, so I brought you inside out of physical danger, at least for the time being. In this place you are, however, still subject to Haon's evil influences and he will take what opportunities he can to overcome your good intentions and your purity of heart. He has been able to gain considerable power through his ruthless tactics and his utter disregard for the well-being of members of the human race. This place is what one might call the "womb of the world". You have a complete life-support system, warmth, food and drink and an atmosphere to sustain you. Within this place you will be able to experience all the same sensations you knew before you came, but you will find that sometimes they are larger than life. You will be confronted by all sorts of problems, most of which have been created by the greed and avarice of the human race over the centuries and capitalised upon by old Haon until he now holds the whole population of the world to ransom. Make no mistake, the Haonic power is immense and capable of widespread destruction. Haon himself realises this and has not been backward in using it when it meant that his evil influence would spread even wider. There is only one thing that Haon lacks and it is the understanding of the secret of life. He can only destroy. He does not know how to create. His greed and evil intent have blinded him to the real purpose of the existence of the human race. Over the centuries he has sought the answer but to no avail. Elcaronic power has stood in the way of his complete domination of the human mind and soul. Now he has reached the threshold of the final conflict. If he is so inclined he will wipe out all that exists in the world and the secret of life will be lost, not only to him, because he will destroy himself as well in the final explosion, but to all mankind. Desolation will return to the Universe and life itself will lie dormant for eons.'

As if to allow the five friends time to absorb this devastating prospect, Elcaro remained silent for a while. Imagine the turmoil into which their thoughts had been thrown by the message from Elcaro. What was to be done? ... How was Haon to be thwarted in his evil designs? ... Was it up to them and was it for this very reason they had been guided to this place?

36

Then, with these questions still bewildering the five friends, the voice of Elcaro came again, intruding into the thoughts of each one of them . . .

'It is indeed for you young people to stand in the way of the evil one. I will help you, but I alone cannot defeat him. Haon himself represents all the worst characteristics of the human race down the ages. Only when confronted by a human power more effective than the material power he wields will there be any chance of his being overthrown and the shackles with which he has enslaved mankind be broken. Your selfless friendship for one another is the essence of that power and it is something that Haon can never understand because of his selfishness, his pride and his greed. So, again I say, "Take heart". Go from here in search of your lost friend and rescue her from the temptation by which Haon has ensnared her. Her love of art and her skill in all things artistic were responsible for her being caught off-guard when Haon spread before her the prospect of capturing what seemed like the ultimate in beauty and colour. She is at this moment in an ecstasy of enjoyment surrounded by beautiful things and she is revelling in the joy of seeing and being able to record for herself the most magnificent shapes and forms and colours she has ever seen. Every facility is afforded her to create her own masterpieces and in her excitement she is at the moment, quite oblivious of the fact that she is being watched by the minions of Haon. They are under instructions to observe her every move and to wait for the time when she shows signs of becoming so saturated with the beauty around her that she will begin to become dissatisfied with it all. Then will be the most dangerous time of all for her because Haon will know that she will be at her most vulnerable. He will then show Ecila a different sort of beauty; the beauty of self-indulgence, power over the elements and other people and the greedy satisfaction which comes from possessing all the things that others need and cannot afford. If Haon succeeds in corrupting her in this way he will have scored a great victory, and never again will human beings be able to appreciate the intrinsic beauty of the things around them and the world will become grey and uninteresting for them.

'Your first and pressing task therefore is to locate Ecila and woo her away from the evil influences into which she has been ensnared. The way will not be easy and there will be dangers and problems for you to face. Do not always choose the obvious and well laid-out pathway and always be on your guard against circumstances designed to split you up. Haon will be aware of your progress and will make it as difficult as he can for you. He will not be able to stop you completely if you maintain your combined resolve. He has no weapon in his armoury to defeat complete friendship and selflessness. Beware of snares and attractions along the way and never forget that the awesome objective before you is to thwart Haon in his evil designs and to deprive him of the material power with which he plans finally to enslave the world. May good fortune go with you and may your resolve remain firm and constant.'

It was some little time before the five friends made a move after Elcaro had finished speaking to them and when they did 'come back to consciousness' they found that their right arms were still extended and their hands still holding the Elcaronic stones at the centre of the circle around which they were sitting, with their arms forming the spokes of a human wheel. The stones were no longer glowing, and gradually they all withdrew their arms and slipped the stones into their pockets. No words passed between them but they all knew that they had shared in the same experience and that Elcaro had placed upon them a great burden and yet one which offered a tremendous challenge. Normally they would probably have been terrified at the prospect of confronting Haon but somehow the promise of help and guidance from Elcaro bred a tremendous sense of confidence within each one of them. They knew that the task before them was indeed within their combined capabilities but the way ahead was far from clear. How to proceed was the first decision they had to make and as usual it was the innate leadership of Aggorine which came to the rescue.

'First,' she said, 'are we all resolved to accept the task set before us by Elcaro?' In the enthusiasm which by now had gripped them, they all with one accord shouted as if to defy Haon and challenge him to try to stand in their way. 'Yes, yes, yes, we will, with Elcaro's help.'

A great feeling of well-being and excitement had now engulfed them and they clasped each other by the hand and spoke of what they were about to do and what they would do to Haon when they again came face to face with him. It was as if a tremendous concentration of power had come into their midst and they all felt that if Haon had appeared then and there, wielding all the evil forces at his disposal, they would have swept him aside as if he had been just a noisy and irritating mosquito!

Again it was Aggorine who persuaded them that they should first work out a practical way to approach the problem. 'We must not forget that we are, to all appearances, trapped in this place,' she said. 'There must be a way out, so come on, let's find it.'

Behind them towering up into the sky was the sheer face of the cliff through which they had so miraculously passed some time before. They remembered that it was Yma who had been led to follow the mysterious music which had brought them all from the danger of the cliff ledge into the comparative safety of the interior of the mountain. Now, as they took more detailed stock of their surroundings, seeking a way forward on their journey, first to find Ecila and then to confront the evil Haon, it was Shimah who shouted that he had found what appeared to be rough-hewn steps in the wall. They led precipitously upwards, but that was no deterrent to Shimah. With his strong limbs he began to climb, calling to the others to wait below until he had explored the primitive stairway. Up and up he went, the others watching from below. Eventually he came to the end of the steps. He could go no further, but as he looked around him he saw what he could only describe as a dense forest with no apparent way through. However in a short time his keen eyes picked out the semblance of a pathway. 'This must be our way ahead,' he thought. 'Elcaro told us the journey would not be easy, so here must be the start of our quest.'

Though the others found the climb to join Shimah at the top extremely difficult, they all managed to reach him with only a few scratches to show for their effort. They stood spell-bound surveying the scene in front of them, miles upon miles of forest with only the suggestion of a track leading down to it, but nevertheless a track they knew instinctively they had to take. What lay within the forest and what they might find beyond if they ever reached the other end, they knew not. It seemed that a sense of urgency developed within each one of them so that they immediately made preparations for the descent into the unknown. It would be wrong to give the impression that they were not afraid. Never before had any of them been confronted with such a journey and such an undertaking, so it was quite natural for them to be apprehensive of what lay ahead. There was no question of retreat and Aggorine knew that they were all resolved to proceed, now they had found the way forward.

'Shimah, you take the lead,' she said, 'and the rest of us will follow, keeping in close order. Oj, bring up the rear and help any of us who get into difficulties. Let's go!' And off they went into the unknown.

The way down from their vantage point proved to be not as difficult as they had at first feared, and it was not long before they were cracking along at a good pace towards the edge of the forest which seemed to fill the whole of the plain beyond the mountain whichever way they looked. On the way down from the steep pinnacle which had provided them with a way out of the rock cavern, Shimah, and for that matter all five of them, had time to reflect on the strange happenings of the past few hours. But Shimah in particular, because of his great friendship for Ecila and because he had heard what she had had to say about the scene she could see, which was so much more than all the others could see, realised she had come under a great emotional influence which had transported her from the ordinary plain on which they all lived to an infinitely more exciting and alluring one. Forces had been at work on Ecila's mind which had been so powerful that they had taken her physically away from her friends in such a dramatic and frightening way. Where was she now? Was she really still alive? Was she really being treated well? The wily Haon was certainly at the back of her sudden disappearance and this realisation made Shimah all the more apprehensive about her welfare.

There was some comfort to be had, however, from the fact that Elcaro had told them they must be bold and continue the search for Ecila until she was found and, if possible, rescued from the evil one. So they *must* believe she was still alive, and that it suited Haon's purpose at the moment to see that she was not harmed. It was perfectly clear that Haon had decided to use Ecila as a most effective bait to lure the others into his snare from which he undoubtedly had no intention of their ever escaping.

These thoughts and many more like them grew into an obsession in Shimah's mind until he could contain himself no longer ... 'STOP!' he yelled. 'We must stop and consider what we are doing and where we are going. We must have a plan of action. We may, in our innocence, be doing just what the evil Haon wants us to do.'

5

By this time the five friends had reached a small level area very close to the forest. It was somewhat higher than the land around them and from it they could see in all directions. They were all glad of a rest and Shimah's command, for it was just that, a command, that they stop and consider the situation, was more than welcome.

Shimah paced across and around the plateau in an agitated frame of mind. The others took advantage of the soft warm grass to sit or lie full length and relax, for they were physically tired after their long trek. Shimah, powerfully built Shimah, shrugged off his weariness and while he paced around, he cast about in his mind what he could do himself to rescue Ecila. He felt he could face any danger and overcome any opposition which he might encounter in normal circumstances, but these were not normal circumstances. There were powers and forces at work in this strange place which presented problems of a very different character.

So, holding himself unnaturally in check, he too sat down and repeated what he had said when he had brought them all to a halt, 'We must have a plan of action.'

Naturally Aggorine was first to respond. 'The problem,' she said, 'is that we haven't yet considered on the one hand what we are up against and on the other what we possess jointly and individually to deal effectively with whatever is facing us.'

She paused for a moment and then continued, 'The facts – what are the facts? Number one: Ecila has been spirited away and may at this very moment be far away as a prisoner of the evil Haon – on the other hand she may be quite close to us and unable to communicate. In either case we are confronted with a situation which not one of us has met before and which therefore needs to be examined in great detail. Number two: the very physical characteristics of this place are strange to say the least. We seem to have been transported into a world where the natural rules do not necessarily apply. Number three . . .'

But before Aggorine could get to fact number three Lekhar butted in. 'But Aggorine, wait a minute,' she said. Her mathematical and scientific knowledge and talent usually demanded a quiet, almost reverential attitude of mind in which she would analyse the evidence surrounding a problem and step by logical step seek a solution. Her clarity of thought was always a source of amazement to her friends and they all looked towards her as she interrupted Aggorine. 'I agree,' she began, 'that Ecila's disappearance and the strange land we find ourselves in are extremely important and demand careful analysis within the whole strange situation, but I feel we must start from a different premise. I suggest we should consider first what started us all off on this journey and what influences have directed our actions and our thoughts along the way.'

Lekhar paused for a moment and then, taking their silence as an invitation to continue, she looked at Aggorine, the group's accepted leader. The smile she received in response to her unspoken apology for having stopped her examination of the facts, also encouraged Lekhar to proceed.

'We came from the plain lands beyond the mountains, where everyone lived in fear of the forces concentrated in the mountains which we believed would engulf and destroy us one day,' she said, 'and we must never forget that important fact. That is our starting point. All six of us have been endowed with certain talents in different ways and probably quite by chance we were brought together to employ these talents in the search for truth – the truth about life.' Now 'chance' was not normally acceptable to Lekhar with her logical mind. All analysis for her had to be based on observation and evidence. So when she used the word 'chance' she was accepting the fact that the process by which the six of them had been gathered together had been governed by factors at present beyond her understanding. Maybe one day she would understand that process but, at the moment, she had to have a starting point and it certainly was a sound fact that they were together as a group and that they each represented a wealth of ability in their own respective spheres.

In moving onto the mountain they called 'Tarara' they had encountered influences which did not fit into the way of life to which they had been accustomed on the plains, but Lekhar had been able to accept the strange phenomena into her system of logical thought. Step by step she recalled their progress, and she was able now to put to the group of friends an assessment of their present position and suggest how they should proceed.

'The search for truth and for the answer to the question, "What is the secret of life?" is what we are embarked upon,' she continued. 'We have had a fierce encounter with the evil forces of Haon and have survived the onslaught. We have survived by the help and guidance of Elcaro who has augmented our own determination and abilities with Elcaronic power. We have seen how, despite the tremendous control Haon has over the material world he still lacks that which he so dearly desires – knowledge of the forces and the meaning of life itself. Strange though it may seen, Elcaro has indicated that we six mortals possess that knowledge though we are not aware of it as yet. At the end of our quest and our confrontations with Haon, all may be revealed to us. But we have a long way ahead of us yet.'

Here Lekhar paused as if to collect her thoughts before proceeding but before she could, the distraught Shimah blurted out, 'What about Ecila? We must consider her rescue as a first priority!'

'I agree,' said Lekhar, 'but I must emphasise that, until we have carefully taken stock of our peculiar position, we dare not proceed.'

'We know Haon is out to destroy us, so why don't we just seek out his headquarters and take him by surprise?' responded Shimah, his eyes glistening and his fine physique exuding power and youthful impatience.

'I do not agree with your statement that Haon is out to destroy us,' replied Lekhar, 'at least not yet. I have come to the conclusion that we are physically safe, probably for some time to come. I am also sure that no material harm has come or will come to Ecila as long as she holds her ground mentally. Cast your minds back to the first of our confrontations with Haon,' she said, addressing them all. 'We witnessed not only the evil power he possesses but also his fury in not being able to understand the ultimate truth about life itself. Elcaro made it quite clear to the evil one that we six mortals together held the secret which he sought and that only through us might he share it. It is therefore clear to me that Haon will not destroy us yet, though it is equally clear that he intends to pressurise and frighten us to the point where we shall be only too glad to reveal the secret.'

Here Lekhar allowed herself a restrained smile as the other four charged, 'But we don't know the secret!'

She went on, 'I have given a good deal of thought to that very point and have concluded that the answer must be in several parts – no one person can yet answer the question, "What is life?" But, together, the six of us, possessing such a wide variety of abilities and interests, yet sharing a common purpose and friendship, may eventually be able to understand how the parts make up the whole answer.'

It was at that point that Oj, the skilled practical one of the group, whose co-ordination between mind and limb enabled him always to produce work of great quality, gave down-to-earth support to Lekhar's theory.

'The stone in itself is not the final sculpture; the tools certainly are not, neither are the skill and vision of the one who wields those tools. But bring them together and you produce the final result – the answer, in all its perfect proportions.'

'How true that is,' said Yma. 'Oj has convinced me of the validity of Lekhar's deductions. Sorry, Lekhar, I don't mean to be rude, but your argument left me wondering whether it would ever be possible to share our individual insights.' She paused and then went on: 'Oj's point can be applied to so many aspects of life. In music, for instance, the notes on the paper are not the concerto, the composer's ability and vision are not, neither the flute, the oboe, the violin nor any of the instruments, but put them together and you can have sheer beauty and delight!' She sighed, as if transported through her own thoughts into a realm where music reigned supreme.

Meanwhile Shimah had settled down with the rest and had followed Lekhar's discourse with increasing interest and growing confidence in the belief that Ecila was almost certainly still safe, at least physically.

'But,' he said to Lekhar, 'what do you mean when you say, "As long as she holds her ground mentally?"'

Before Lekhar could answer, Yma butted in.

'You are not the only one, Shimah, to find Lekhar's argument difficult to follow! We are used to her now but you and Aggorine may have a problem with her turn of phrase occasionally. I know I shall embarrass her, but I must tell you that she has a much clearer and more logical mind than most, and she reads so many learned magazines that when she is expressing her thoughts she often uses words and arguments which wouldn't normally be in everyone's daily vocabulary. I'm sure she doesn't mean to "blind us with science," it is simply that the way she puts things into words is the way her logical and scientific brain works.'

By now Lekhar actually was blushing but she smiled at her older sister and said, 'Am I really as bad as all that in explaining things? – I'm sorry if I am and I'll try to improve!'

They all made the most of her embarrassment and teased her unmercifully, but after a short while they dissolved into laughter and Lekhar was able to continue.

'You are a rotten lot!' she said light-heartedly. 'But now, getting back to Shimah's question about Ecila holding her ground mentally – and for that matter we ourselves doing the same. I submit this is the essence of the only weapon with which we can confront and finally overcome the evil Haon. It is of the utmost importance to our survival that we all resolve never to let Haon or any of his agents invade our minds and capture our thoughts, our skills, and above all our understanding and love of what we do best – Yma with her music; Aggorine with her leadership and overriding concern for the welfare of those she leads; Oj with his supreme practical ability; Ecila with her artistic vision and skill; you, Shimah, with your control of your physique and the humility with which you temper your athletic superiority; and finally myself who seems to have been endowed with a degree of mathematical and analytical talent.'

'I see,' said Shimah, 'so you really feel that Ecila is still alive and that there is a good chance of us finding her again?'

'Yes, I do,' replied Lekhar. 'But, and it is a great "but", it all depends on her never surrendering her mental powers to the corruption and evil which Haon represents.'

'I believe she can do that,' said Shimah, 'so let's go! – We can't afford to waste time.'

'We are not wasting time,' interjected Aggorine who had been absorbing Lekhar's train of thought from the beginning.

'Lekhar has given us hope and inspiration, and I feel we

46

should be extremely grateful to her.'

'Yes, yes,' the rest shouted, their spirits now flying high.

'Yes, certainly,' repeated Aggorine, 'but can I add my little bit to the assessment of our present position? I am sure Lekhar implied the importance of the role of Elcaro in all this when she mentioned the help we had received in the early stages of our encounter with Haon. I feel that by ourselves, in our own mental and physical strength we may not – almost certainly shall not – be able to overcome Haon and his associates in evil, but with the almost supernatural help afforded by Elcaro we can face him with confidence.'

Lekhar looked at Aggorine, nodding her head in assent but with a worried frown on her forehead. There was obviously something in what Aggorine had said which disturbed her. Eventually she came out with it.

'In my scientific upbringing I have never been able to accept sequences of events based on anything other than those which were capable of being verified by logic, mathematical argument and experimental observation. It is extremely difficult for me to believe in chance and, for want of a better word, what we call supernatural. But I have to admit that our experiences on this enterprise have clearly been influenced and even directed by forces and powers which do not fit into my thought processes. But we have all been lifted out of the terrestrial framework into a region which is beyond our present ability to understand. Perhaps we shall eventually be able to come to a logical conclusion and our human understanding will be able to encompass these things which are at present a mystery. But for the moment, through our experience of them and our observation of their effects, we must accept that circumstances beyond our present abilities to control, are surrounding us and we must be prepared for the unexpected and if possible, learn how to turn the supernatural powers to our own advantage and the furtherance of our quest. – Wow, did I say that?' she cried, laughing at her own confession, 'Well it's true! – did we not receive a powerful token of Elcaro's concern for our welfare in the glowing stones we each have in our pockets? Were we not forced to desert our homeward path and climb the precipitous path to the cave, and was Yma not inspired to enable her to lead us to the comparative safety of this inner world in which we now exist, with its complete life support

47

system? And above all did we not, each one of us, simultan-eously resolve to press forward to the goal, which is to discover the secret of life itself and at the same time to defy Haon and all his evil powers?'

Lekhar's words had a deep and lasting effect on all the friends as they sat around on the small plateau which had become for them a sort of lecture theatre cum debating chamber. They all felt moved and not a little encouraged by the analysis of their position which the razor-sharp brain of Lekhar had unfolded before them. Up to this moment they had been at times bewildered, at others despondent, at others afraid, but also at others exhilarated. Now, having heard Lekhar declare that many of the things that had happened to them since they set out on this adventure were inexplicable even to her analytical mind, they realised that from now on they must expect strange influences to be at work and accept them as the norm. In doing this it would eliminate the unsettling effect their experiences had had on them up to now, and at the same time take a good deal of the sting out of whatever ploy Haon might choose to adopt against them. They would deny him the advantage of surprise by absorbing the supernatural into their thought processes, thereby strengthen-ing their defences and enabling them to meet with fortitude the onslaught which they now were convinced Haon would throw at them in an attempt to weaken their resolve and to capture whatever secrets of life they each possessed. They were all much more confident now, that the evil one would not prevail against them and even more resolved to proceed against him.

'But what about Ecila?' Shimah asked almost accusingly. 'She is in danger at this very moment, and we seem to have forgotten that fact. We *must* make her rescue our first priority in any plan we may adopt in our battle against Haon.'

Aggorine answered him, as she now felt they had reached a point in the discussion when she could take charge of their movements again.

'No, Shimah,' she said, 'we have not forgotten Ecila and you are quite right that her plight must always be in the forefront of our minds. I agree, and I think we all do, with Lekhar's analysis of Haon's objective and that it means both Ecila and all of us are in little or no danger physically from his evil forces. It is our minds he is after. So, though we all want to

48

release Ecila from Haon's grip we must not act too hastily and run the risk of failure.'

This cautionary approach, sensible though it was, was difficult for Shimah to accept, being a man of action and confident in his own ability to overcome all opposition by the strength of his arm. But he looked at Aggorine and, accepting her wise leadership, he had to admit that she was undoubtedly correct. 'Of course, I am sure what you say is best for all of us including Ecila, but please, let's get on with it!'

'But not before we've eaten, please! I'm starving.' It was Oj of course! 'But what do we eat?' No sooner had he asked the question than he spied a whole patch of the silver balls they had eaten before. They had again appeared as if by magic and still tasted good and very satisfying.

6

It was clear that all five of them shared Shimah's desire to 'get on with it' but it wasn't immediately clear how they should proceed. There was no doubt that by staying put they would achieve nothing, but the period they had spent in appraising their situation had, in itself, been a great advance and had clarified their ideas and at least provided the basis of their future strategy. It was Oj who now suggested the direction they should take. He had a craftsman's eye for detail and accuracy and, while he had attended closely to the discussion, he had, at the same time, been searching the terrain around them for a possible route.

At first he had only been interested in the great forest of trees which lay in their path. He was somewhat of an expert in wood. He knew most of the different species which grew on the plains and understood how important they were to the climate and ecology of the area in which they grew. He also had a feel for types of wood which could or could not be used by a craftsman when he had a particular job to do. So he was perplexed by the forest in front of him which seemed to comprise just one type of tree and that of a peculiar form and colour. Admittedly the trees were green but he had not seen such a green before. It was as if they had all been painted with a matt substance of turquoise hue – or was it what his mother used to call 'eau-de-nil?' – 'A strange colour for a tree,' he thought, but it didn't at first surprise him in view of all the other strange things they had already encountered. Then he became intrigued by the fact that all the branches were attached to the trunks at odd angles – some straight out, some upwards and some hanging down. The trees were neither firs, nor oaks, nor beeches nor sycamores. Then he realised each tree was a mixture of many different types! 'That's odd,' thought he.

He knew all about the practice of producing hybrids in the plant world and he could also remember his father producing a rose bush which had red and white flowers at the same time, but he had never seen such trees before as those in the forest ahead. Could it be that they were not trees at all? He knew Haon to be capable of all sorts of devilish tricks, so perhaps, just perhaps, he had laid this tremendous obstacle in the path of the five friends which appeared to be impenetrable to their mind's eye. Was there any substance in his theory? Was there any substance to the trees in the forest? There was only one way to find out. They must go forward boldly, showing no concern or fear and exerting all their mental energies to overcome what Oj was now convinced was a psychological trick which Haon was using in the belief that such a barrier would make them abandon their journey.

When he excitedly put his ideas to the rest of the group he could not at first convince them of the possibility of the truth of his theory. But as they thought about it and knowing that Oj was not the sort to be overfanciful, being normally down-to-earth and practical in his approach to problems, they came to a common mind and determination to trust to his craftsman's expertise and accept that the forest was indeed another mani-festation of Haon's attempts to overcome their willpower and destroy their confidence.

'So,' said Aggorine, sensing that all were in agreement, 'let us go to this so-called forest and see whether it can withstand our onslaught!'

She stood up, her powerful, comely figure displaying all the defiance and confidence she could muster and, to give encoura-gement to the others, she stretched her arms outwards towards the forest and shouted, 'Haon beware! We are coming forward. We, from the plains, do not cringe before your devilish power. We will never give up!'

At first there was silence, an eerie silence, all around them. No echo of Aggorine's challenge came back to them, no sound at all. Then before their astonished gaze the forest became a blaze of colour with shapes and forms of every kind. Could it be that Ecila had, in her captivity, become aware of Aggorine's powerful message to Haon and had in her own way tried to get a message through to her friends that she too shared in their determination to continue the quest? The beauty of the colours

51

and shapes certainly spoke of Ecila's artistic talent and each of the five friends felt a surge of pleasure and excitement in the certain belief that she had in fact been in touch with them. This meant, of course, that she was still very much alive and in control of her own mental processes.

But before they could give vent to their happiness the silence was broken by a roaring and a crashing. The colours disappeared as suddenly as they had appeared and a great storm raged across the whole vast area which had been the forest such a short while ago. Out of the chaos of darkness and swirling dust came the bellowing of the enraged Haon.

'Challenge me, will you? You weaklings. Do you not realise that if I chose, I could at this very moment wipe you and all those like you on those puny plains right out of existence, and if you continue to annoy me, that is just what I will do!'

The five friends stood close together in a combined defence against the tumult and against the wrath of Haon.

It was, of course, Aggorine who again expressed their contempt for the evil one.

'Get on your way, old fool,' she cried. 'We are not afraid.'

'Old fool, old fool?' screamed Haon.

'Yes, you are a fool to believe that you can stop us coming forward in our quest for the truth, a quest in which we know we have more chance of succeeding than you have, with all your material prowess and power.'

No words can adequately express the frenzied reaction of Haon to those words. He ranted and he raved while everything around the small plateau on which the five stood seemed to erupt again in a roaring and a screaming as if all the thunderstorms there had ever been were concentrated together. But they were miraculously untouched and unharmed. Suddenly all was peace again and Haon once more retreated, no doubt to lay further plans to try to stop the progress the five friends were making into what he considered to be exclusively his domain. He held sway over his world by sheer superiority of force in the face of which no one had ever dared to mount a challenge. Yet here now were these five puny mortals standing up to him and defying his authority. The mere fact that he had not carried out his threat to wipe them out of existence proved to the friends that there was truth in their belief that they held a secret between them, as yet unknown to them too, which Haon desired above all things. The 'secret of life' was their defence and the Elcaronic power which the benevolent being, Elcaro, had given them, gave them also confidence in their ability to face up to all the difficulties and dangers of their journey. They must press on deeper into Haonic territory where they were sure they would eventually find Ecila. How they would find her and how to release her from the mesh of Haon's captivity were questions that could only be answered when they had discovered the centre of Haon's eerie empire.

As they now surveyed the scene before them, they were delighted to see that the seemingly impenetrable forest had given way to a pleasant looking countryside with meadows, rolling hills, lakes and streams. It was as if the strange trees never existed, even in their own imagination.

Delighted they certainly were, but all five of them stood, just gazing in amazement at the peaceful scene as if they had been stunned by the ferocious attack launched against them by Haon, an attack which they had, by sheer will power it seemed, been able to withstand and come through unscathed.

Shimah was the first to stir. 'I know Ecila is still alive,' he cried. 'Somewhere out there, and probably even further away than we can see, I know she is waiting for us and will be doing all in her power to withstand the wiles of her captor. The vivid colours we saw before the storm must have been an attempt on her part to communicate with us.' He looked around at his four friends. 'Come on!' he said. 'Let's make progress while we can.'

Aggorine put her hand on his broad shoulders and gave him a friendly rebuke for being too precipitate.

'We all know how you feel about Ecila, Shimah, but as I have said before and we have all agreed, our policy must be one of planned progress as far as these strange powers around us will allow. It is dangerous to be rushing off at a tangent.'

Shimah agreed, but he was obviously still anxious to go into action.

Aggorine, in her role as leader of the group called them together for a pow-wow.

'Before we talk about where we go from here,' she said, 'I feel I must warn us all, myself included, against being too confident in our own abilities to fight and conquer the evil Haon.' She paused as if she was wondering how to express what was in the forefront of her mind.

Eventually she said, 'We could not have come so far, nor achieved so much if it had not been for the strength and protection which have come to us from Elcaro. In the excitement of our quest, we forget that fact at our peril!'

Lekhar looked up at Aggorine.

'At one time,' she said quietly, 'I would have completely dissociated myself from the ideas you have expressed, but as we have journeyed and have witnessed so many strange events, I have come to the conclusion that the logic on which I based my thoughts and even my life style before, are not the be-all and end-all of things. My philosophy now has to include the acceptance that there are many things beyond the most intelligent human's ability to understand. So I have, somewhat reluctantly,' she smiled, 'to accept what you say, Aggorine. I too am sure that Elcaro has been helping us and I would go further and declare that, by so doing, Elcaro has given us a glimpse of the secret we seek to discover.'

They all looked at her, waiting for her to explain, but all Lekhar added was, 'What I mean is, that while logical argument and scientific observation take us a long way towards the truth about the physical world, there are still at present many things beyond our understanding.'

Yma, as indeed they all did, looked amazed when they heard this, but Yma's eyes in particular lit up with the realisation, probably for the first time, that in her world of music, it wasn't just the notes on paper which constituted the concerto or symphony, nor yet the instruments on which it was played. Neither was it the skill of the musician in interpreting the work of the original composer. All these things were important but there was something else inherent in the music itself which carried the inspiration of the composer into the very hearts and minds of those who performed the work and of those who heard it. There was always an intrinsic beauty in the piece which could lift the emotions of those who played and those who listened, to almost magical heights, but at the same time could be completely destroyed into discord if one or more of the instruments, the players or even the listeners did not play their part accurately, skilfully and attentively. Yma promised herself that in future she would pursue perfection in her music even more assiduously than she had hitherto. Perhaps then she might find out what musical beauty really was.

Aggorine had simply reminded them of their dependence on Elcaro, and the effect was electrifying. Each one of them was imbued with an even greater zeal to go forward to face any new danger that may be set as a trap for them. In this confident mood they cast around for their next move. Where would the next stage of their journey take them?

Oj was the first to notice that there was some sort of haze hanging over a small area in the extreme distance and he drew the attention of the others to it.

'Maybe,' he said, 'there is some form of habitation there and, if so, perhaps we ought to go in that direction. If there are people living there, it could be that we could enlist their help in our journey. They are almost certain to be under the influence of the evil Haon and may welcome the chance to overthrow him.' The other four felt just a little dubious at first but it certainly did seem to be a possibility. So it was decided to head in the direction pointed out by Oj.

At last therefore the five friends left the little plateau which had been such a sanctuary to them and where they had survived yet another of Haon's attacks and where, perhaps above all they had realised even more clearly the strength and comfort given to them by Elcaro.

The path they chose led gently downward towards an expanse of grassland with real grass and real trees dotted about singly and in groups. They felt at home here because the place reminded them of the plains where they lived. Not many words passed between them. They were all preoccupied with their own thoughts. Where and how would this journey end? When would they return to their old homes? What was happening there? All these questions were without answers at the moment. They could only trust that in due course the answers would become clear and that their whole quest would be successful.

After a while they came upon a glittering expanse of water and decided to rest for a time. The water looked inviting and it was pleasantly warm to the touch. Despite a plea from Aggorine to be careful, Shimah could not resist a swim. He plunged in and splashed about in the shallows revelling in the refreshing feeling it gave him. After having tried unsuccessfully to persuade the others to join him he headed out into the deeper water with the powerful strokes of an accomplished swimmer. Soon he was just a dot in the distance and Aggorine began to worry.

'I wish he wouldn't be so venturesome,' she said plaintively. 'He always was one to take risks when we were at home and we were for ever on tenterhooks until he returned safely. I have to admit that I can't remember any time when he failed to complete successfully the task he undertook, but this did not stop us being worried about his escapades!'

She put her hand to shade her eyes from the dazzling light above the lake and searched for Shimah in all directions but he was nowhere to be seen. When last spotted he had been heading for the edge of the lake far away to the right, where the land sloped steeply from the water.

'Perhaps he has decided to explore those cliffs,' said Oj. 'He may have seen something interesting there and have gone to investigate.'

'Let's hope so,' murmured Aggorine, 'let's hope so.'

The place on the shore where they were resting was sheltered and warm and they all became drowsy and eventually dropped off to sleep. How long they had been asleep they did not know but they were woken by an excited Shimah who was obviously bursting to tell them of his adventure and what he had found. He must have been out of the water for some time, as he was quite dry.

'I've found something,' he said excitedly, 'something which might give us a clue to Haon's whereabouts and lead us to Ecila.'

His four friends, now roused from their slumbers by Shimah's enthusiasm, leapt to their feet and clustered round him, anxious to hear more.

'I swam, as you know, far out across the lake,' he continued, 'and then, just as I was about to turn back, knowing Aggorine would be worrying about me,' he teased, 'I saw across to the right there,' and he pointed towards some rocky hills in the distance, 'what I could only describe as the mouth of a tunnel. It wasn't just a cave, it was much too regular for that. The entrance was a perfect arc and the sides were quite straight.' He paused for a moment as if to savour the effect which his words were having on his audience. 'It must have been fashioned and built by skilled hands. No cave could ever have become so perfectly proportioned by erosion alone.'

The group of friends, by now completely captivated by Shimah's story, were suddenly struck by the implications of what he had told them. It was Lekhar who voiced their common conclusion. 'This means that at some time there must have been other intelligent, skilled beings here. – Maybe they are still here!'

'You haven't heard the end of my story yet,' interrupted Shimah. 'I made my way cautiously towards the tunnel and came out of the water some hundred or so metres from the entrance. I found myself on a narrow beach of bright orange granules like sand, which was soft to the feet yet quite able to support me. Having had a good look round – for I too had realised by this time that there was a possibility of there being other people about – and seeing no traces of them, I was able to make my way towards the tunnel, pretty confident that I wasn't observed. Still, I wasn't going to take any chances, so I kept as low as I could and moved quietly from the shelter of one rock to another. The land rose steeply from the beach and there were lots of large fragments of cliff which must have fallen away and now rested on the shore. These gave me good cover as I moved towards the opening in the cliff.'

While Shimah had been describing his escapade, he had been adding to the dramatic effect it had had on his friends by adopting the sort of furtive postures and gestures he must have used when he was actually approaching the tunnel.

Now he cupped his ear with his hand and said, 'As I reached the mouth of the tunnel itself my head was pounding with excitement for I could actually detect noises coming from the depths of the tunnel which convinced me that not only had skilled hands worked on the passageway into the cliff, but they – whoever or whatever they were – were still engaged in some sort of activity which was making the sound of machinery whirring and beating rhythmically.'

He paused for breath before continuing. 'I could hardly contain my excitement, I can tell you! – I wanted to enter the tunnel to see for myself what was the source of the noise and what the creatures were like who were making the noise. I did in fact take several steps into the darkness before I hesitated and eventually stopped. The words of Elcaro came into my mind in spite of my intense desire to go it alone and confront whatever lay ahead. I knew it to be the sensible thing to do to return to you and to go together. I remembered that Elcaro had warned us that Haon would try to separate us and conquer our minds individually. He already has Ecila in his power – at least physically – and how I wanted to go ahead and find her! But I retreated and made my way along the narrow beach, back to where I had left you. It seemed as if I had been away for ages, so imagine my joy on finding you asleep just where we had all been before I went for a swim. – So here we are and thanks to Elcaro's advice and help we can now go on together.'

Automatically they each felt in their pocket for the Elcaronic stone and experienced again a surge of confidence in their ability to face a new and exciting chapter of their journey.

7

They had all listened intently to Shimah's account and were now impatient to follow him back to the mouth of the strange tunnel. But Aggorine once again very wisely advised caution.

'First of all,' she said, 'Shimah must have a rest. Strong as he is, I am sure his long swim and the return journey via the land has tired even him.'

To this Shimah declared that he was perfectly capable of proceeding straight away and was not in the least tired. Aggorine however insisted on a short breather while they took stock of the situation. Reluctantly Shimah acquiesced but couldn't quite hide his impatience. After all, Ecila was out there somewhere, and even at this very moment she might be in danger of giving way to Haon's insidious attempts to capture her mind and learn for himself the secret of the artistic temperament and skill she so fully possessed. Maybe the tunnel would lead them to the centre of Haon's headquarters, where Shimah was certain Ecila was now being held.

There was no doubt in any of their minds that Shimah's discovery was of the utmost importance, nor that their way led towards and into the tunnel. How to approach it was the question Aggorine put to them – by water or by the coast or perhaps by scaling the cliffs and dropping down to the entrance from above. Oj immediately said he could soon construct a raft which would take them easily and silently across the lake, and for a while this seemed to find favour with them all. However, the risk of being spotted from the cliffs eventually made them discard that idea even though it meant they would have a tiring journey overland instead. Shimah said he hadn't seen any obvious cliff path which would enable them to approach from above and so this second choice was rejected, even though the journey over the top of the hills with plenty of wooded cover offered the best chance of their arriving at the tunnel unobserved. So it was that they chose to retrace Shimah's steps along the shore of the lake, being careful to take advantage of every bit of cover the rocks and cliffs afforded. Now the decision had been taken they lost no more time. With Shimah leading the way, closely followed by Aggorine, and with Oj bringing up the rear they set off.

The going was easy to begin with. In fact it was very pleasant to be making their way along the shore of the sparkling waters of the lake, keeping close under the cliff, out of sight of anyone who might be on watch. Their encounters with Haon to date had impressed on the friends that, though he may be evil, he was undoubtedly highly intelligent and capable of employing his power over the material world in all sorts of strange and amazing ways. Even the logically minded Lekhar had had to add a new dimension to her philosophy and include the distinct possibility of Haon having mastered the supernatural and discovered how to use it to further his evil intentions. So, though they took all the precautions they could to avoid discovery, they were under no delusions as to Haon's ability to use means as yet unknown to them, to seek them out and set the most potent of traps for them.

As they moved silently along the side of the lake, all was so peaceful that the very existence of a being such as Haon, intent on their destruction, seemed sheer fantasy.

'Things are going well,' said Yma suddenly, 'so well that I feel I want to express the joy inside me by composing a lakeside melody in honour of this lovely place.' With that she perched on a rock and before she could be restrained she put her flute to her lips and began to play. Such was her musical skill that, try as they may the others could not bring themselves to stop her. They were all entranced with the sheer beauty of the music, which at the same time, seemed to embody the dazzling white of the surface of the lake, the gentle lapping of the water and the orange strand and the more ominous cliffs rising sharply over their heads. But above all there was a powerful peace in Yma's music and all of them experienced a deep sense of well-being. The music seemed to fill the air all around them and they were in tune with it. Suddenly, from the direction of the mouth of the tunnel great swathes of colour could be seen sweeping out and across the whole of the lake. Beauty in colour beyond their imagining was conjured up before their eyes.

'It's Ecila!' cried Shimah. 'She has somehow heard Yma's music and has found a marvellous way of letting us know she is still alive!'

Hardly had the words left his mouth than the colours were gone as suddenly as they had appeared. The scene before them changed in the twinkling of an eye. The lake lost its dazzling white appearance and became black and louring. The water was broken up into huge waves and a great wind threatened to sweep the friends off their feet. They all huddled together beneath the overhang of the cliff behind them and cowered there waiting for the storm to subside. In the midst of the storm came that ghoulish laughter which by now they knew to be Haon delighting in their predicament.

'How do you feel now, oh musical one?' he bellowed. 'Go on, play your flute as much as you will, it has no effect on me! You may think you are the only clever one, but I too can make music! Listen to this.' And out of the clouds above and the very bowels of the earth beneath them there came discordant noises, great crashes and explosions completely without form, frightening beyond words. Yma clung to her friends in terror, knowing that she had been the one foolhardy enough to provoke Haon into wrath again.

Aggorine put her arm round her and without any semblance of reproach she said, 'The stone, the stone, Yma – Elcaro will help us!' Fumbling in her pocket Yma felt the comfortable curve of the pebble and found it warm to her touch. Did Elcaro speak to her, or was it just her fancy? But she felt impelled to take her flute once more and play. This time, with growing confidence she produced as stirring a sound as had ever been composed. She moved defiantly out from beneath the cliff and in the face of Haon's wrath she played and played and played. Miraculously the sound of her single flute was amplified a thousandfold and the stirring music filled all corners of the hills, the cliffs and the beach, and spread across the waters until the harmony of Yma's composition overcame and silenced the clanging and clashing of Haon's so-called 'music'.

There was no immediate reaction from Haon or at least none the five friends could detect, but when Yma eventually laid down her flute, standing gracefully and triumphantly on the edge of the lake, once again calm and beautiful, there came from the direction of the tunnel the unmistakable voice of

61

Haon, but in a tone so soft and even friendly that at first not one of the five realised it was indeed the voice of the evil one who normally ranted and raved.

'Your music beguiles me, little one from the plains. You must play again and teach me to play also,' he wheedled. 'Do not be afraid.'

Yma smiled, realising that the beauty of her music had been a completely new experience for old Haon and that she had made him desire that beauty for himself. Just as Ecila had shown him the beauty and skill of her art, so Yma herself had now penetrated his defences. But Ecila was physically under Haon's control and alarm bells started to ring in Yma's mind, warning her that she too was within an ace of being absorbed into Haon's territory. She shuddered as if a blast of cold air had struck her and turned and ran back to her friends with outstretched hands. As she did so they embraced her and held her safe, though she was trembling with emotion. Seeing his uncharacteristic pleading was to no avail Haon burst out once more, making the earth shake beneath their feet and a shriek came to them from across the water.

'I'll get you in the end – all of you. You cannot escape!' – loud at first and then receding into the distance until all was peaceful again.

It was some time before the five friends recovered their composure. This most recent encounter with the Haonic forces had set them back on their heels, but gradually, realising that in a mysterious way Yma, with her wonderful music had met and repelled the enemy, a sense of elation filled their hearts. It was Lekhar who set the seal on their new-found confidence.

'I can't explain what has happened in any logical way,' she admitted, 'but when one considers the vastly superior physical power at Haon's disposal compared with our combined human frailty and realises that with consummate ease he could snuff us out like a candle – and yet he hasn't done so – it follows that our original conclusion that he will not kill us off until he has captured whatever it is we possess in our minds, was correct. I firmly believe we can take heart from that thought and proceed towards our objective. Nevertheless we must be even more careful than before. I am sure he came close to taking Yma from us just now and it is to her credit that she resisted him so effectively and routed him so convincingly.'

Yma had been silent until now and she had tears in her eyes when she lifted her head and said, 'I didn't know what I was doing, but I do believe Elcaro spoke to me and, in a marvellous way, supported me as I stood playing on the lakeside. Without Elcaronic power I should have crumpled and no doubt, just as Haon stole Ecila from us in the early days of our journey when none of us was prepared for, or understood his awesome and mysterious ways, I would now be in his clutches.'

Aggorine's arm was still around Yma's shoulders, comforting her. 'We are still together,' she said, 'and together we must remain until we have found our dear Ecila and have dealt with Haon one way or another.' She tried to put all the confidence she could into her words, even though she too had been thoroughly shaken by what had happened.

Yma smiled. 'Yes,' she said, 'together – we must go on together.'

Oj was up and about first. He paced up and down and his face wore a deep frown showing that he was wrestling with a problem. At last out it came.

Turning towards the rest of them he burst out, 'How does he do it? How does the old devil know where we are and what we are doing, even when he can't see us?' His arms fell loosely to his side. 'For the life of me I don't understand,' he said with a little strangled laugh. 'Here we are, walking peacefully along the shore of a lake, stopping to enjoy Yma's lovely music, when out of nowhere comes, first the greatest technicolour show we've ever seen followed by all hell let loose around us.' He gave a gesture of hopelessness. 'It just doesn't make sense.'

With that he turned on his heel and walked towards the lake, kicking at the sand and pebbles as he went until he was standing at the water's edge looking out towards the place where Shimah had said he had found the tunnel.

Lekhar got up and followed him until she came up to him at the edge of the lake. She didn't speak for some while but just stood silently close to Oj as if she just wanted to let him know that she too shared his bewilderment. Eventually she spoke.

'You are absolutely right to bring this problem into the open, Oj,' she said kindly. 'I am sure we are all as much perplexed as you, and it would be good for us to talk about it. Come back to the others and let us share our thoughts.' So together they rejoined Yma, Aggorine and Shimah who they found had also taken up Oj's remarks and were already well into a discussion they had sparked off.

'Well, have you solved the problem?' said Lekhar teasingly as she sat down on a nearby rock.

'No, of course we haven't,' replied Shimah, a little petulantly. 'How can we solve a problem when we don't have the experience to help us understand what is going on?' He put out his hand palm uppermost as if offering his own limited experience to the rest of them. 'The question is simple enough,' he said. 'How does Haon know what we are doing and where we are doing it – and also by what means is he able to command such material forces as he has already displayed to us?'

'Simple the question may be,' said Aggorine, 'but how and where do we find the solution?'

Lekhar jumped down from her perch on the rock and said excitedly, 'I think Shimah has said something very important. He said the question was a simple one, but he has actually posed two questions and if we can separate the two in our minds we might find it easier to understand them.' She held the stage and they all looked at her expectantly. '"How does Haon know where we are and what we are doing?" is the first question and "How does he wield such material power?" is another,' she said. 'Let's put our minds to the first one and see what we come up with.'

'He must have the most efficient spy system in this world – or in any other come to that,' interjected Oj, trying to be very practical about the whole thing. 'Perhaps there are listening bugs all over the place and Haon's minions are sitting in their H.Q. tuning in to the ones along our route.' He paused. 'The trouble is, I don't even believe that story myself!' and he gave a little helpless laugh.

Lekhar turned to Oj with a questioning look on her face and suddenly she clapped her hands and shouted, 'Well done, Oj, well done! – bugs it could be, but what sort of bugs, I ask myself? Wherever we are, Haon seems to be able to locate us, even if we are not making any noise or even talking to one another. But we can't stop ourselves thinking! – Are we, – are our minds with their active thoughts, the source of Haon's information? Could we, by just thinking, be sending messages which he has the ability to receive and interpret, a sort of

64

selective and amplified telepathy? I can only remember the most elementary facts about this sort of thing,' she continued, 'but I know there is a good deal of research being done on the function of the human brain. One thing I do remember is that we all produce so-called "brain-waves", or, more scientifically, "beta rays" when we think and it is possible to detect the radiation which is given off from the head as a result. We all know that Haon is a highly intelligent, if devious, character and it is possible that he and any minions he may have working for him, have been able to pick up these waves at a distance and use them as a direction-finding device to locate their source. I can't believe that he can gain any specific information about what the person is thinking, but it is much more likely that he can learn that the person transmitting the brain waves is such and such a distance away in such and such a direction. – Very useful information in itself when you want to prepare a reception of one sort or another for the approaching person.'

'Well, well,' said Oj. 'I'd never have believed it! Fancy everyone being a walking bug!' – and he laughed out loud ignoring the fact that they had to proceed as quietly as possible.

'Keep your voice down,' said Aggorine sharply. 'You may be overheard.'

'What does it matter if we are?' rejoined Oj. 'The old devil Haon knows all about our position anyway, so until we can find a way of de-bugging our heads we might as well shout as loudly as we want to!'

Once again, Oj, the practical one, had come straight to the nub of the problem – what practical steps could they take to deny Haon his 'brain wave' information?

By this time all five of them were convinced that Lekhar's theory was not only plausible but almost certainly correct and they began seriously to consider what counter-measures could be taken. It was Oj who eventually suggested a solution.

'I expect,' he said, 'we have all played around with radio and television sets at one time or another and have found the reception vary from place to place. This is due to the receiver being screened from the radiation in some way and the best screen of all is one made of metal. I remember we had a metal garage at home and that the car radio wouldn't work inside the garage. So if the receiver can be screened from the radio waves, why can't the transmitter? If the theory is correct, and our heads are giving off radiation stimulated by our thought processes, we ought to be able to stop the rays at source by sticking our heads into some sort of metal box!'

They all laughed now. The picture of them all walking around with tin boxes on their heads was too funny to be taken seriously. In any case they hadn't a tin box between them, let alone one each.

'We shall just have to put up with the fact that Haon can locate us whenever he wishes,' said Yma. 'If what we believe is true, that the six of us – and I'm including Ecila – have in our make-up that very thing that Haon desires, we are in no mortal danger. True he can, and no doubt will, make it pretty hot and frightening for us in the hope of learning our secrets, but hopefully he will not destroy us.'

'Let's hope you're right,' interjected Shimah, 'but you all know by now how I feel about the old devil Haon. He's got Ecila in his power and if we don't watch out he will pick us all off one by one. I'm all for a determined attack on his headquarters before he has worn Ecila down and captured her artistic spirit and skill for himself. If that ever happens we can be sure we shall never see Ecila again. She will be of no more use to Haon and he will have no compunction about killing her off. So, as far as I'm concerned, brain waves or no brain waves, the sooner we get moving the better.'

'Calm down a bit,' said Oj. 'It's no good thinking we are going to be able to beat Haon at his own power-crazy game. We've got to adopt a much more subtle approach. I, for one, was most impressed by the way Yma was able to stand up to him when he tried first to entice her into going with him on the pretext of wanting her to play for him and then, when that failed, to stand against his fury. It shows that Haon is not as all-powerful as he thinks he is. I believe he has begun to realise that all the control he has over the material forces of the world only gives him the ability to destroy and not to create in the way Yma showed she can with her musical ability. Perhaps this realisation, even though it is stimulated by envy and a greedy desire to possess the creative powers himself, shows that there may even be hope for Haon becoming a more reasonable being than he is at the moment.'

'Not in a million years!' burst out Shimah. 'Haon, become more reasonable? – never! He is evil! evil! evil! – and we must destroy him!' His eyes flashed and his fist clenched tightly as his gaze turned towards the mouth of the tunnel he had discovered earlier, and it was some little time before he regained his normal composure.

Yma came close to him and put her hand on his arm. 'Ecila will be all right, Shimah,' she said. 'We must be as patient as we can under the circumstances. If we try to make a frontal assault on Haon's headquarters we would almost certainly provoke him into destroying her and us in his fury, in spite of the fact that we believe he thinks we hold the answer to the secret of life and that he too desperately wants to know the answer. So let's keep to our plan to go forward as a group in the hope that, with Elcaro's help, we can get Ecila safely away from him and perhaps at the same time turn Haon himself away from his evil ways.'

Calmer now, Shimah turned to Yma and, though he said nothing, it was clear that he accepted the wisdom of her words and his eyes thanked her for understanding his particular concern for Ecila. They smiled at each other and made their way back to the others whom they found sitting close together apparently playing the old children's game of cat's cradle with the ball of string which Oj had brought with him.

'What on earth are you doing?' asked Yma, her eyes sparkling with mirth. 'Are you hoping to catch Haon in a fishing net?' – and she laughed out loud.

'No,' said Aggorine without reflecting Yma's merry mood. 'This is something which might prove much more effective than a net to catch him in – rather a net to enable us to hide from him!'

Both Yma and Shimah were intrigued and wanted to know more about the possibility of a 'magic' net which would render them invisible.

'No, not invisible,' Lekhar said, 'at least not in the optical sense. When we were talking about the possibility of Haon having the ability to detect the beta radiation we emit when we are thinking, we all laughed at the prospect of walking around with our heads in tin boxes to screen the radiation at source. Well, Oj has suggested a possible alternative to the tin boxes – which we don't have in any case. With his usual foresight in being prepared for any eventuality he not only brought along his 'first-line-tool kit' – his 'wonder-knife' as he calls it, but he also popped into his bag a roll of this new material which, as you see, looks and behaves like very strong string but also is a good conductor of electricity. What we are doing is trying to make hats for us to wear like the old-fashioned hair nets. Both Oj and I are convinced that a net of conducting material of about two centimetres mesh will be just as effective a screen for the beta rays as a complete tin box would be. – At least we feel it's worth trying. – Come on now, see whether or not you can qualify as a maker of hair nets!'

It wasn't as easy as they had at first thought, but eventually it was Aggorine who produced a basic design and in due course they were all sporting their new and quite exclusive headgear.

'There's no easy way of proving experimentally whether or not these things will do the trick,' said Oj, 'so we shall just have to hope that our theory is correct.'

Lekhar agreed with him but added that Haon himself might provide evidence of their effectiveness as they approached closer to his lair. His reaction – or non-reaction – to their presence would show whether or not his beta ray amplifier was picking up signals from them or not.

'It's a pretty risky way of proving a theory,' she said ruefully, 'and one which I wouldn't normally recommend, but we have no choice, I'm afraid.'

'The sooner we start, the sooner we shall know the answer,' came from the impatient Shimah, already on his feet and raring to go.

8

With Shimah leading and Aggorine at his shoulder they set out again along the shore towards the tunnel which they could now see quite clearly in the face of a cliff which ran sheer down into the lake some kilometre from them. Keeping close to the cliffs to minimise the chance of their being spotted by any sentry Haon might have posted, they made good time towards their immediate objective. Aggorine, as leader of the group, was cautious even though she felt Haon might rely more on his device to detect their 'brain waves' and not feel it necessary to have a guard outside the tunnel entrance. Nevertheless she kept Shimah gently in check and guided him away from the open beach, even though it would have provided easier going.

When they had reached a point approximately two hundred metres from the tunnel entrance they called a halt to make a careful examination of both the tunnel and the cliffs above the entrance. These cliffs rose sheer to a height of at least a kilometre but around their base was a great mound, even, one might call it a fair-sized hill of rough rock and other soil debris. This they presumed had been the result of the excavation of the tunnel and they could tell by the thick covering of vegetation in between the bare rocks that it had been many years since the work of digging out the tunnel had been done.

The five friends listened intently for any sound of the activity which Shimah had reported after his swimming expedition. Sure enough, as if from the depths of the mountain, there came a regular buzzing sound, the source of which could easily have been something like electric generators or even a crowd of people whose conversation at this distance would have resolved into a general buzz, especially with the tunnel acting as a guide for the sound, the source of which they were now certain was deep within the mountain.

Nothing stirred in the whole of the landscape nor in the

seascape which they could survey, nevertheless Aggorine insisted on a very careful examination of the cliffs and clifftops which towered above them. It was only after some ten minutes or so of searching that Oj raised his hand and pointed to an area near the top of a ridge which was not as rugged as most of the rest of the mountain.

'Look there,' he whispered excitedly, 'there, where that knife-edge borders on that more rounded area. Do you see it or is it just my imagination? Is there not a sort of haze over the smoother rock, the sort which is caused by heated air when light shines through it? There, look now, I'm sure I'm right!'

They all followed his pointing finger and one by one they all agreed there was certainly a difference in the appearance of the atmosphere above the smoother rock than elsewhere.

'There must be a vent for hot gases somewhere there,' said Lekhar,' and she couldn't help adding a simple scientific explanation. 'The hot gases produce a variation in refractive index as they billow from the vent and this bends the light rays a little, this way and that, causing the hazy effect!'

'Yes, yes,' interjected Aggorine, 'I expect we all remember a bit about that phenomenon from our elementary science lessons. What is more important now is to discover what it is that is causing the haze.'

Shimah immediately jumped in and volunteered to climb up and investigate and was all but on his way before Oj said he would go with him. Aggorine, with her natural caution thought the climb too risky but had to admit that it was important for the group to know what was going on up there. Reluctantly therefore she and the other two girls agreed that they would stay put on the shore while the boys scaled the cliffs.

'Try to keep in sight won't you?' said Aggorine. 'And if you find the way impassable, don't take unnecessary risks. We don't want to have to mount a rescue operation. And remember, Elcaro has warned us about getting separated. So do be careful.'

The three girls settled down to make themselves comfortable in the warmth of the afternoon, with their backs to a boulder so that they each had a good view of Shimah and Oj as they set out. The rocky spoil at the base of the cliffs slowed the boys up somewhat and when they reached the cliff itself, it looked as if they had already come to the end of their attempt. The cliff seemed to offer no footholds nor any crevices up which they could progress and it meant that they had to move along towards the tunnel entrance as they searched for a suitable route. At last when they were within not more than fifty metres of the entrance, Shimah noticed what appeared to be a staircase cut into the face of the rock which had been hidden from their view previously. In no time they had their feet on the stair and were climbing steadily. Every now and again they looked back towards the place where they had left the girls but it was not until they had made about two hundred metres of height that they caught sight of them again. All seemed to be well with them and the boys could see that the girls had spotted them on the cliff.

They had reached a small platform which had been hewn from the solid rock in much the same way as the staircase had, and they were both glad of a rest. Strong as they were, the two hundred metres' climb which, in their excitement, they had scaled far too rapidly, had certainly made them puff. So now they spent some minutes getting their breath back and surveying their surroundings. The platform commanded a fine view on all sides. In the direction from which they had come they could see a great distance over the lake and to a further range of mountains beyond. To right and left the cliffs rose steeply and offered little or no foothold but they could now see that in their forward direction there was a definite track leading upwards towards a much smoother hill top and sure enough, there was the heat haze they had seen from the shore.

With a wave to Aggorine, Lekhar and Yma and, after indicating that they were intending to proceed towards their objective, the two boys set off again. This time the path led slightly to the left and they reckoned that, if the tunnel ran directly into the mountain, they were climbing right above it. After a further half hour they came upon a pleasant grassy area which sloped gently upwards and which afforded them a clear view of the summit. There was the haze, much nearer now and it wasn't long before they could feel the heat from the gases as they streamed upwards from a point just beyond the top of the slope.

Oj laid a restraining hand on Shimah's arm and suggested they didn't rush impulsively to find the outlet in case of danger from the gases themselves or in case there was a sentry posted to guard the area, assuming that Haon now knew there were intruders in his territory. So they skirted around the top of the hill towards the right and, gaining height by climbing a jagged rock peak, they were able to look down on what was no more than a circular opening in the bare rock from which the hot gases rose. They could now also discern the same sort of whirring noise they had heard coming from the mouth of the tunnel, so there was no doubt in their minds that the chimney top they were looking at was in fact the opening of a vast air-conditioning system serving what must be a huge cavern below. They were intrigued by what they saw and heard and speculated as to the significance of what they had found.

'It must mean that somewhere below us is a town, maybe even a city which, being underground, needs to be air-conditioned. But why underground, when it so easily could have been built out in the open amongst these towering mountain peaks?'

Shimah expressed both their thoughts and Oj added, 'Could we have stumbled on Haon's headquarters, or is this just one of his outposts or satellite towns?'

'More likely to be an outpost, or perhaps an industrial area,' said Shimah. 'I reckon Haon's lair is far away in the safety of the highest of the peaks of those great mountains,' he added.

'We'd best be getting back to the girls,' Oj said. 'We are not visible to them from here and they will be getting worried since they must have lost sight of us when we came to these smoother slopes.'

So the boys retraced their steps carefully and in a short while had reached the platform where they had rested on the way up. They were relieved to see the girls still waiting where they had left them. Aggorine was in fact peering in their direction, shading her eyes against the light. She was obviously delighted to catch sight of them again because she waved furiously and ran to the others to bring their attention to the boys who were waving in return.

In about half an hour they were all reunited and the two climbers were soon recounting what they had discovered. The girls agreed that all indications pointed to the fact that there was some sort of living community inside the mountain and that the tunnel entrance must lead to it. There was no doubt in their minds that their own way led into the tunnel and that it was important to their quest that they should make contact with whoever or whatever lived within the mountain. So, cautiously, they picked their way over the piles of rock and spoil, retracing the route which Shimah and Oj had taken earlier. Eventually they reached the stone staircase which had enabled the boys to climb up the side of the tunnel entrance but this time they were not going that way. Instead, keeping close to the cliff face they inched their way towards the opening itself. They only had about fifty metres to go and this they covered in a very few minutes without incident.

As she reached the opening, Aggorine, who was in front, raised her hand to bring them to a halt around her. 'Listen,' she whispered, 'what do you make of that sound?'

The whirring they had heard when further away, now took on a more distinctive rhythmical character. True there was a general noise level above the rhythm, but quite clearly they could now discern this more regular 'beat, beat, beat'.

'Machinery,' whispered Oj, 'heavy machinery. Could be a generating station. Haon is bound to require power for his headquarters, so my guess is that inside the mountain we shall find that source of power. What fuel is used and how the power is fed out to the other areas of Haon's kingdom is a mystery at the moment, but if we could get close enough to see the actual plant, we might be able to turn the discovery to our advantage.'

'How do you mean, Oj?' asked Yma.

'Well, first of all, the system of power generation will give us an insight into Haon's standard of technology and secondly, if, by some means we could control, or even cut off the power supply, we should be able to cause old Haon some discomfort, to say the least.'

Lekhar was following Oj's argument intently and nodding agreement.

'Let's waste no more time,' she advised. 'Haon may at this moment be preparing some other sinister delaying tactic for us.'

'I wonder if he knows where we are?' said Yma. The others looked at her in some surprise. She went on: 'We haven't heard from the old man for some time now, ever since we've been wearing these metallic hair nets, in fact. The boys have been exploring on the mountain and we have all been pretty exposed as we made our way along the shore towards what we believe now to be one of Haon's important outposts. Yet there has been no violent reaction from him. My guess is that the theory of the beta rays, or brain waves produced by our thoughts being screened by the metallic mesh is correct, and that for the time being at any rate, Haon has lost contact with us.'

Aggorine jumped in quickly to advise caution. 'If that is so, and it certainly seems a distinct possibility,' she conceded, 'it means we shall have to be extra careful to try to avoid detection by any other device Haon may have. If we can get near enough to examine the machinery inside this mountain without Haon or any of his minions knowing, it will be a tremendous advantage to us. So let us be on our guard and use the little bit of initiative we have gained to good effect.'

As if to add point to what she had said, she shepherded them all into a recess just inside the tunnel mouth. While speaking she had automatically scanned the surroundings over the lake and upwards to the mountains beyond and the sky above. She had certainly seen something out of the ordinary and now as she concentrated her gaze from the shelter of the cavern entrance, she saw it again. It was only a tiny speck of intense light moving across the sky at high speed. First it was going to the left and then to the right, backwards, and forwards and yes, it was getting gradually larger which meant it was coming closer to them.

'Look,' she said, 'what do you make of that?'

The others crept forward so that they also could see what Aggorine had observed. It was Lekhar, when she had taken a good look, who pulled them all back to the shelter of the recess again.

'It could be some sort of observation satellite,' she whispered, 'and who will it be looking for but us?' We must stay hidden for a while before we venture further into the tunnel itself, where we should then be quite out of range of that spy of the sky.'

She had hardly finished speaking when the walls of the tunnel entrance became illuminated, dimly at first and then with a very bright yellow light. The five friends held their breath in anticipation of being discovered by whoever or whatever had been piloting the bright object to and fro across the sky, for it was now clear that it had come to rest quite close to their hiding place. No sound could they hear as they waited, frozen into immobility. No footsteps, no voices – nothing came to their ears. They only knew that the 'something' was hovering or maybe had even landed outside the entrance to the tunnel. They waited for what seemed hours but in reality was only a matter of about two minutes and then, to their intense relief the light began to fade and in next to no time was gone altogether.

'Wow, that was close!' exclaimed Shimah as they all relaxed their tensed limbs, and he moved gingerly towards the opening of their refuge to see if the coast really was clear.

'There's no doubt in my mind,' said Lekhar when they had all followed Shimah's beckoning arm, 'no doubt at all that our recent visitor was some sort of robot designed to send back messages to Haon's headquarters. If we hadn't had the good fortune to find that hidey-hole in time, we would most certainly have been discovered. Haon must suspect that we might have found his secret tunnel and sent out his robot spy to investigate. Hopefully the information he has received back is negative, which will enable us to go along the tunnel without him knowing that we are anywhere near it. Incidentally, the mere fact that he has used this method of searching for us is pretty conclusive proof that our metallic headdresses have cut off his beta ray bugging system.'

'It's time to move,' said Aggorine, 'before Haon tries any more of his tricks. We may have stolen a march or two on him but we can't expect him to leave us alone. He is certainly too interested in what Elcaro has told him we possess and which has eluded him up to now. He will continue to harass us until he captures our very minds.'

9

With Shimah leading and Oj bringing up the rear they moved slowly into the darkness of the tunnel. As far as they could tell it ran directly into the mountain with very little, if any, deviation. The floor was smooth but not slippery, though the walls were rough hewn, so they had to be careful not to graze their limbs as they felt their way along. Eventually it was too dark to see even a metre or so ahead and it was then that Lekhar remembered she had packed her electronic binoculars. Ferreting about, she found them wrapped carefully together with her pride and joy, her laser analyser-synthesizer. The binoculars worked on the old established principle of a stream of electrons being directed onto an emitter which was thereby excited into giving off a narrow beam of one of several frequencies, depending on the needs of the user. Lekhar was familiar with the dial settings and chose a visible wavelength in the green area of the spectrum. Putting the binoculars to her eyes she was able to receive the reflected beam from any objects in her field of view and focus the image in the way in which ordinary binoculars are focused. The other four could dimly make out the rather ghostly green beam as it struck the rocky sides and roof of the tunnel but could not see shapes and forms as clearly as Lekhar could using the binoculars, so they had to rely on her descriptions and instructions.

'I'm sorry,' she said, 'but I can't make the illumination any brighter. This is, after all, only a portable, and therefore a low-powered instrument, but you can all take turns to have a closer look in a moment.' After a short while she continued, 'We are not at the end of the tunnel. It seems to extend for some distance yet. See what you make of it, Aggorine.'

Aggorine put the binoculars to her eyes and peered into the distance.

'I can't make out anything in the form of an obstacle for

some way,' she said and passed the viewer on to the others.

They too agreed that the way ahead was clear. So with Lekhar now leading with her binoculars and acting as the eyes of the group they moved ahead in line astern with Oj as usual as the guardian of the tail.

The now familiar whirring and beating sound was gradually increasing and eventually was so loud that they felt they must be very close to the source and yet could still not see anything remotely resembling machinery. Lekhar suddenly reported a blank wall about one hundred metres ahead and advised caution. The dim green glow from her binocular's beam had been providing the others with enough illumination to enable them to grope their way along, but now she switched the device to infra-red, invisible to the naked eye, as an extra precaution against their being discovered.

Naturally they came to a halt, closely bunched up behind Lekhar, for they had to keep in physical contact with each other in the pitch darkness. Lekhar surveyed the area in front of them with great care. At first there was nothing but the blank wall they had seen in the green light, but as they approached very cautiously, Lekhar led the way towards the left-hand corner. She whispered that she had detected another source of infra-red radiation besides that reflected by the beam emitted by the binoculars and it was coming from the area towards which she now guided them. Suddenly, without warning Lekhar lost her footing and would have fallen if it had not been for Shimah who had been second in the column and had had a tight grip on her belt. In the confusion they all tumbled against each other and it was a few moments before they found they were at the top of a flight of steps leading downwards into the very bowels of the earth. They could hear the noise of machinery even more distinctly now and became increasingly determined to discover the source, so, this time with Shimah leading, using the infra-red binoculars, they made their way down and down.

At first the steps spiralled their way down and there were convenient hand holds in the rock, but when they had descended some two hundred steps they came upon a straight section which continued downwards, but less steeply. In the distance, some hundred metres away they could all now see a faint glow and as they got nearer, Shimah was able to switch off the electronic binoculars and proceed in the light coming from the end of the stairway. Excitement was running high as they neared their objective and it was all they could do to stop themselves rushing forward to discover the source of the noises which were now loud and clear. But this time it was Shimah who advised caution.

'You four stay here a while,' he said. 'I'll creep forward and, if the coast is clear I'll beckon you to follow. You'll be able to see me against the light.' So forward he went until he reached a point where he could see beyond the end of the stairway. What a sight met his eyes! There before him was a vast cavern stretching some two hundred metres in the way he was facing and about one hundred metres across. As they had all suspected for some time, the sound they had heard was that of power generators but they had not expected to see such a huge array of machinery as Shimah now gazed at. He wanted to explore further but his first task was to discover whether it was safe to call the others so that they then could go on together.

The cave was not brilliantly lit but it was light enough for Shimah to see quite clearly, not only the generators, but the walkways and stairways which criss-crossed the machinery and were evidently there to enable the maintenance of the generators to be carried out. The astounding thing was, however, that, search as he may, he could not see a living soul anywhere, and the thought passed through his mind that the workmanship in the machinery must be of the highest standard for them to be able to function with a minimum of surveillance or even none at all. At the far end of the underground chamber he could just make out something which looked like a cabin and he presumed that it was there that any engineers who were on duty would be based. But close at hand he could see no human activity; not even a solitary sentry.

'Old Haon must be pretty confident that no intruders could find this place,' he thought. 'What a surprise we'll give him!' And he smiled to himself in anticipation.

But now he beckoned to the others to join him and soon they were reunited and were all suitable impressed by what they saw. With no apparent danger of being seen, let alone overheard, they were able to have a short discussion to decide tactics. Shimah was for making their way towards the cabin in the distance where they might find out who or what was in charge of the magnificent array of machinery. But this would, in Aggorine's opinion, risk discovery, confrontation and almost certain capture.

'I'm intrigued,' said Lekhar, 'as to what is the source of energy which is used to drive these huge machines. It must be nuclear. I can't think of any other fuel which could do the job in such a confined space. If that is so, then the heat generated by the nuclear reactor would probably be used to provide steam, which in turn means an adequate supply of water. The vent into the atmosphere which Shimah and Oj found when they climbed the mountain is certain to be stationed over the reactor to take away excess steam and at the same time to act as the outflow of the air-conditioning system.'

'Could the water come from the lake, d'you think?' said Oj. 'It seems logical that water could be piped from there, probably along the tunnel we came through. We couldn't see much when we were there, and even if we had been able to see more clearly it wouldn't have helped because the pipe would most certainly have been buried beneath the floor.'

'Don't let's worry about that now,' interjected Aggorine. It's much more important for us to press ahead, avoiding detection if we possibly can.' She sounded a little annoyed. 'Come on, don't let's be side-tracked into proving your scientific theories and risking everything we've done, by getting caught. There must be a way out of this place which could lead us to Haon's base. After all, if there are custodians of this power complex, and they are up in that cabin, they must have means of getting to and fro. They couldn't just live here all the time.'

'You're right,' agreed Shimah. 'We seem to have forgotten the fact that Ecila is a prisoner of the old man of the mountain and that our first task is to find her and make every effort to rescue her. After that, if somehow we can overcome the evil one, there may be time for further examination of his organisation.'

Shimah's words brought them all up short and not only did their thoughts turn to Ecila and her plight but instinctively they each put a hand into the pocket containing their own personal stone, the gift from the benevolent Elcaro. As soon as their fingers felt the comforting smoothness of the stones, a sensation of well-being and confidence came over them. No longer did the prospect of confronting the evil Haon seem to be such a mammoth undertaking, fraught with insuperable difficulties and dangers. They believed that, with Elcaro's help they could and would succeed in their quest. What the outcome of it all would be they could not even begin to guess but what they did realise as they stood, five comparatively tiny mortals in this huge, pulsating power base, was that come what may, their goal was to find, confront and overcome the one who ruled in these mountains and who caused such fear and havoc to those who lived on the plains.

10

All these thoughts came flooding back into their consciousness and gave them a great urge to get on with the job. Keeping a wary eye open for any signs of life and using all the cover they could, they made their way along the wall of the cavern which, judging by the direction in which they had entered, was the eastern side. Aggorine calculated that the exit for the power and for those who maintained the machinery, must be to the east, towards the further depths of the mountains and that it would be there where they would find the Haonic community and no doubt Haon himself.

Shimah was again in the lead and under his guidance they moved swiftly and silently. Just once he stopped suddenly and the rest followed suit. There was an open area up ahead which they had to cross and it was clear that anyone in the cabin, to their right now, would be able to see them, if in fact, they were looking in their direction. Very gingerly Shimah peered around the end of the large turbine which had been giving them adequate shelter from prying eyes. They were near enough to the cabin for him now to be able to see quite clearly that there were about ten people inside. Several were sitting at a control panel and luckily had their backs to them. The other three or four were sitting at tables and seemed to be intent on whatever task it was they had before them. There was only one who faced directly towards them and from whom there seemed to be the greatest risk of their being seen as they crossed the open area to the shelter of the next turbine.

'What can you see?' whispered Aggorine.

'I can see about ten figures in the cabin,' he breathed in reply.

'What are they like?' Aggorine queried.

'Tall and human. What were you expecting? Demons? Dragons? Robots or what?' he replied with a grin.

'Well,' she said, somewhat hurt by Shimah's sarcasm, 'this is the first time we have actually seen any Haonites. I'm glad at least that they are not much different from us.' Regaining her composure she went on, 'Is it safe to move on?'

'No, not yet, there's one facing this way. We shall have to wait until he moves, or find some other way.'

While the five friends were considering what to do, the person in the cabin facing them got up and walked towards the control panel to talk to one of those working there.

'Now!' said Shimah, and they all, as one body, sped across the danger zone and waited with bated breath for any sign from the cabin that they had been discovered. Nothing happened, and in a few moments Shimah peered cautiously round the edge of the machinery and happily was able to report in a whisper that all was as before. No-one in the cabin seemed at all excited and they were all working as they had been when he had first observed them.

He now beckoned them to proceed and with every step they put the operators in the cabin further behind them. It was after they had covered about one hundred and fifty metres from where they had entered the cavern, that they came to what they assumed to be the exit. A tunnel, very similar to that by which they had entered, ran at right angles to the cavern wall. This time, however, there was some illumination and when they looked into the tunnel they could see a widely-spaced string of electric lights suspended from the roof and stretching as far as they could see into the mountain. This tunnel was not more than three metres high but much wider.

Along one side there ran huge insulated cables and along the other side ran a pathway. In the centre a single rail was laid, which was obviously for a monorail system of transport. There was no carriage to be seen, so they assumed the next journey would be from the other end towards the power station.

It was a tempting thought that they might wait for the arrival of the carriage and somehow stow away on it and hitch a lift to the other end, and it was equally tempting to set off on foot along the pathway. But again, Aggorine's cautionary advice prevailed.

'We must wait, not only for the carriage to arrive but for it to set off on its return journey,' she said. 'If we go along the path now, we risk meeting the relief train on its way in and as far as I can see, there is little or no cover we could use as it passed us. We would almost certainly be observed by those inside the carriage. So we must wait for its arrival and find a secure hiding place while we wait.'

'Let's hope we don't have to wait long,' said Shimah, and, as if in answer to his remark, above the noise of the generators, they became aware of a sort of hissing or whistling sound coming from the far end of the tunnel.

'Quickly!' called Aggorine. 'We shall have to make do with that turbine,' and she indicated where she meant them to go.

Fortunately no-one stopped to argue or to suggest an alternative retreat, for no sooner were they hidden from view than a cigar-shaped conveyance slid to a halt close to where they had just been standing. It wasn't long before the replacement team of ten people had disembarked and started to make their way, chatting to each other, into the centre of the generator complex. As soon as they had disappeared from view, and despite Aggorine's attempt to restrain them, both Oj and Shimah made a dash towards the stationary vehicle which had brought the new group of Haonites a few moments previously.

There was no-one left inside, so the boys assumed one of the team drove the device or, what was more likely, it travelled automatically. Not only were they intrigued by the design and function of what, to them, was a novel form of transport, but both of them were hoping to find a way for them all to hitch a ride in secret.

It was Oj who noticed there were large freight compartments at either end and he soon discovered the outer door which was, as may be expected, firmly locked. At first the boys were frustrated by this set-back but on trying the passenger door, they found it opened easily. The crew had obviously never contemplated the possibility of there being alien stowaways near at hand, and had not bothered to secure the door.

By now the girls had joined the boys and with hearts pounding with excitement and in fear of the imminent appearance of the crew going off duty, they all poured through the door, not knowing what they meant to do, once inside. Lekhar was already examining the control panel and she soon declared that its operation seemed quite straightforward and if it was their wish, she could soon whisk them off into the unknown.

83

Yma and Aggorine, on the other hand, lost no time in finding an inside door to one of the freight compartments and were delighted to find it unlocked.

It seemed hours since the monorail had arrived and the new crew for the generator complex had moved off to replace the others in the cabin, but in point of fact, no more than four minutes had elapsed. Now the five friends were faced with a vital decision. Should they commandeer the conveyance and risk possible capture at the end of the journey or should they play safe and hide in the rear compartment? That was the choice before them and a decision had to be taken pronto. Lekhar's fingers were itching to set things in motion but she was finally persuaded that it would be more prudent to take advantage of the comparative secrecy of the freight area. Even this mode of travelling was fraught with danger. How were they to emerge when they reached their destination without being observed? What if the returning crew had to bring back a quantity of luggage and stores? The compartment was quite large but the five of them would take up a fair proportion of the space. Strangely enough, they had given no thought to the safest way to travel, namely along the path on foot. No doubt they all felt the thrill of adventure in travelling with the unsuspecting Haonites and also they were all anxious to see what they expected to see, the Haonite city.

As it happened, they had plenty of time to arrange themselves amongst the few crates which the freight compartment contained and conceal themselves quite effectively from both entrances. The returning crew did not appear for nearly a quarter of an hour. They no doubt had a debriefing or handover session with the new crew. But now they were coming. They could be heard chattering together as they boarded. The five friends could not make out what was being said, but it was clear that their presence was not suspected.

Within a few moments following the slamming of the outside door, they were off. Whatever personal kit the crew were carrying they had obviously taken into the passenger area. No freight or large luggage had been loaded, for which the five friends were most relieved. It was difficult to estimate the speed at which they were travelling but they were all impressed by the lack of noise. Just the swish or hiss they had previously noticed was all that could be heard. The impression was, however, that this was a very high speed vehicle. Lekhar was timing the journey, mainly out of curiosity, but statistics, however simple, were one of her interests and time and again she had had cause to be glad she had certain facts at her finger tips. It could be that the length of this journey would enable her to come to some conclusion as to their ultimate position and, who knows, it might be useful information for their return journey, if in fact, they ever did return.

Just twenty-eight minutes had passed before they felt the brakes go on and had to brace themselves to absorb their forward momentum and stop themselves being thrown towards the door leading to the passenger compartment. Very soon all was still and the crew could be heard disembarking. Shortly Oj stirred and stretched his cramped limbs.

'Not yet,' whispered Aggorine.

'I'm only going to find the door,' replied Oj, equally quietly.

'Be careful then,' she retorted.

It was pitch dark in their hiding place and they could see nothing.

'Wait,' said Lekhar, and she got her electronic binoculars out of her pack. Setting it to 'visual' and switching it on, she was able to produce the pale green beam she had so successfully used in their journey from the lake to the power complex. In the glow, Oj soon found the door, but where was the means for opening it? He soon realised that the opening mechanism could only be operated normally from the outside and, try as he may, he could find no way of budging the door.

'What about the other door?' said Yma anxiously, fearing, as they all did at that moment, that they were trapped until someone opened the compartment from outside. Before the words were out of her mouth, both Oj and Shimah were at the door leading to the outside but again, no visible means of opening the door could be found. They were indeed trapped, and now the real prospect of discovery and capture loomed large in all their thoughts.

Aggorine took charge of the situation. 'Let's sit down and consider what course of action we should adopt,' she advised in as confident a voice as she could muster. 'As I see it we can either continue our efforts to force open one of the doors or we can wait until a loader comes to put something in or to take these crates out. In order to take advantage of the open door we should have to overpower whoever it is who comes. Either way, we would draw attention to ourselves and Haon would undoubtedly learn that we had been able to penetrate his kingdom as far as this and he would certainly conjure up something very distasteful for us.'

'We shall have to risk discovery, I'm afraid,' said Lekhar quietly, 'and we shall have to risk it soon. This compartment, though quite large, only contains enough oxygen to keep us going I guess for another half hour. There isn't even a key-hole through which air can pass. So speed is essential if we are to get out alive, let alone without being detected.'

These words had a significant impact on the group of friends and there followed a moment of silence when all were conscious of their hearts beating faster than normal in their bodies. Very soon Oj and Shimah sprang into action.

'We must be able to smash our way out,' Shimah said impetuously and the two boys began casting around the compartment for a suitable implement. They weren't going to be beaten by a silly door!

By now however Yma had felt in her pocket for her Elcaronic stone. Its smooth surface felt comforting in her hand. She it was who had experienced the strength and confidence which Elcaro had given her as she played her flute on the shores of the lake and enabled her to confront the wrath of Haon and withstand his power. Now again she was sure a solution to their situation lay with the promise Elcaro had given them to help solve their problems.

She was standing near the door leading to the passenger compartment and as if in a dream, she took her flute from her bag, put it automatically to her lips and made as if to play. But no melody came out. Her fingers seemed out of her control for she played just a single note very softly and then another and another, each higher than the previous one until she was shaken out of her trance by the door suddenly springing open.

'An acoustic lock!' exclaimed Oj. 'I've heard of those before. They were in the early stages of development, as I remember.'

But no-one wanted to hear more of what he remembered. They were only too grateful to see their way of escape so magically appear and it was all they could do to stop themselves shouting for joy.

With but a moment's hesitation they made good their escape from the freight compartment, thankful that they were no longer trapped within it, but equally thankful for the secrecy it had afforded them in their swift though cramped journey from the power base. In order not to show themselves to any sentry who might be posted outside, nor to any casual observer who might be passing, they went down on all fours and crept along the gangway between the seats, with Shimah and Oj leading. Poking his head over the arm of the last seat before the exit, Oj was able to get a clear view of the immediate area outside the compartment. What he saw was quite encouraging. The monorail had come to rest in a covered bay, very similar to the railway stations with which they were all familiar. It was apparent that this shuttle which plied backwards and forwards to the power complex had a special bay to itself.

Beyond the low platform Oj could see several other platforms which were probably for the trains which served other parts of Haon's kingdom. While he watched, a train made up of several coaches such as the one they were themselves in, pulled in to one of these other platforms and people, lots of them, got out and equally lots more then boarded the coaches.

There were people milling about all over the station, some just strolling aimlessly, probably waiting for their train and others much more purposefully striding away from the platforms towards what Oj presumed was the main exit.

'What do you see?' breathed Aggorine in Oj's ear and, retreating to the comparative safety of the floor of the gangway, Oj told them what the conditions outside were like.

'They all look just like us,' he said, 'and they all seem to be behaving very much as we do on a railway station. The only thing about them that's different, is that they are all wearing very similar clothes to each other and in fact it is difficult to see which are male and which female. There seems to be a national uniform they all wear. If we tried to mingle with the crowd we'd stick out like sore thumbs.'

At this Lekhar wriggled her way back into the freight area and started examining the boxes which had so conveniently provided them with cover on their journey. Soon there came a muted cry of triumph from her.

'I thought I'd caught a glimpse of this package in the dim light from my binoculars when we were trying to find our way out,' she said. 'It was squashy and as I tried to support myself on it, it gave way and felt soft to my touch.'

Quickly she tore the package open and sure enough it contained clothing. No doubt it was part of a consignment of stores for the power station which simply remained on board until needed.

'If we wear these things,' she said, 'we could mix with the inhabitants of this place and no-one would be able to tell us apart. We would be able to travel about undiscovered and yet ourselves observe everything going on around us.'

There was no need to persuade the others of the sense of her argument. They were soon sorting through the contents of the package to find uniforms which fitted, and in about five short minutes they were transformed into inhabitants of this strange mountainous country, – or at least into very passable look-alikes. They all felt much more confident now in their ability to explore the world outside the train compartment and after some little discussion decided that the safest thing to do was quite casually to walk out onto the platform as if they had every right to be there and without haste to make their way towards the station exit. The generously-cut caps which formed part of their rig, quite easily covered the metallic hair nets they were still wearing and which they were now absolute-ly convinced had prevented Haon's electronic wizards from homing-in on the beta radiation produced when their thought processes were particularly active. Since they had been wear-ing them, they had had no contact or visitation of any sort from the one they still referred to as the 'evil old man of the mountains.'

11

Within the capacious pockets of their new clothes they each managed to stow the few things they had previously carried in their packs and then the packs themselves were stuffed back into a remote corner of the freight compartment where they hoped they would lie undetected for some time. Their own clothes they retained, not only because they felt they might need them again if circumstances demanded it, but also because it looked considerably colder outside than it had been on their journey until now. The locals looked cold as they hurried about and the conclusion about the lower temperature was justified as soon as Shimah slid open the door. He had spent a moment or two walking purposefully along the gang-way between the seats towards the driver's control panel, as if to give any casual observer the impression that he had every right to be there and in fact was possibly a maintenance mechanic doing a routine check of the apparatus. His real purpose was to see if the coast was clear for the group's departure.

There was no sentry on duty and the passengers on the other platforms seemed totally uninterested in the special little shuttle which obviously plied quite regularly between the city and the power base. No doubt they were used to seeing it standing idle in its own small bay. So Shimah signed to the others that they should now make good their escape and one by one, as casually as their pounding hearts would allow them they stepped out and with only a glance around they made their way singly and silently towards the exit, which now came into view as they moved along the short platform.

No-one seemed to cast more than a cursory glance in their direction and they became more confident that their disguise was effective and that they were safe to walk with the crowd and yet be undetected as the aliens they were.

So many strange and sometimes inexplicable things had happened to them since they had started to climb the lower slopes of Mount Tarara that memories of their lives before that were often rather dim. The station with its noise and bustle wasn't a big station by comparison with the one or two city termini they knew on the plains, but nevertheless it brought back to all five of them a much more vivid picture of their homeland than had been in their minds for some time. Perhaps it was being with people again or maybe it was the town itself, as they stepped out into it from the forecourt of the station which stimulated their memories. Whatever it was that made them think of home, it certainly caused a degree of homesickness to well up in their hearts. However they each knew they could not allow anything to deflect them from their avowed intention to find and rescue Ecila and if possible to get near enough to Haon to discover what sort of a creature he really was. Their only previous encounters with the old man of the mountain had developed rapidly into violent confrontations, with Haon ranting and raving with all the venom at his disposal. Surely, if only they could create a situation where he would be prepared to talk to them in a more rational way, they might be able to convince him that life held more for him and all mankind than the mayhem and destruction which the indiscriminate use of power brought in its wake.

When out of earshot of the nearest person they gathered together as a group once more and Yma gave expression to these thoughts. They realised what a close affinity there was between them as they had all been thinking along the same lines. True, Shimah felt far more angrily disposed towards Haon than the rest because he was holding captive his dear friend Ecila, but he too admitted to being just a bit homesick.

Once more it was Aggorine who broke the spell and brought them back to earth.

'We can't hang around here,' she said. 'We've got a job to do and the sooner we get on with it the better. In any case the longer we stand idle, the more conspicuous we shall become. We must act as normally as we can and use our eyes and ears to gather information.'

From what they could see of it, the place they were in was not much more than a small town. They had expected it to be of city proportions and were rather surprised to find it to be otherwise. The streets were of moderate width and the pavement wide enough for them to be able to walk five abreast. They noticed at once that there were no vehicles on the roads except unusually shaped and quite long bus-like contraptions which almost always were filled to capacity with members of the local population. This seemed to be the only means of getting from one part of the town to the other except by foot along the pavements. Very few people ventured onto the roads themselves except to board the buses and for a very good reason too. The buses travelled at speed and almost silently. So it became a risky business to cross from one side of the road to the other unless it was at designated crossing points. The locals were obviously well disciplined and followed the rules to the letter.

The whole impression was one of efficient drabness. The few shops there were were stocked only with essential items as far as could be seen. Nevertheless there seemed to be a plentiful supply of those types of goods. But there was no gaiety about the place or the people. As may be expected, all the signs and names printed on the shops and the goods inside them were in a language quite foreign to the five friends and, not being able to understand what the words meant, this added to their growing feeling of isolation amongst the bustling activity.

As they strolled through the town, they said little to each other, their main preoccupation being the town itself and its inhabitants. They each instinctively took it for granted that they should not risk being overheard speaking in their own tongue, so when a word or two passed between them, it was when they were out of ear-shot of the nearest townsfolk.

Aggorine, who it will be remembered was extremely good at languages, was the first to notice that some of the shop signs and the names of the goods in the windows bore a distinct resemblance to one of the languages she had herself studied. Her brother Shimah used to tease her about that one in particular, saying it was a dead language and couldn't possibly be of any use in this modern world. But secretly he was very proud of Aggorine's proficiency in the several languages she spoke fluently. She used to defend her interest in the dead language by pointing out that though it was no longer spoken, nevertheless it formed the basis of many of the words and expressions in the various languages of today.

91

As she looked around she became more and more excited because, with a little common sense, coupled with her natural flair, she was soon able to understand the meaning of some of the words and eventually the sentences on the various signs. If only she could get hold of a dictionary, she felt she could soon gain a reasonable mastery of the local language. But she could see no possibility of that happening in the near future so she had to content herself with translating what she could see on the signs and hoardings about her.

While Aggorine was so engrossed, the rest of the group were taking stock of their surroundings and were soon even more convinced than they had been at first that this town was too small to be the capital of the mountain kingdom. They had been walking for no more than a quarter of an hour when they came to a square which was quite clearly the centre of the town. Again, the general look of the place, like the streets leading to it, was very drab with little or no colour anywhere. A large building stretched the whole length of one side of the square and Aggorine was able to tell them that the notice indicated that it housed the civic offices. A queue of some thirty people straggled along the pavement from the main entrance and they were being controlled by six men in military style uniform who, rather grudgingly it seemed, let one or two at a time from the head of the queue pass through the door into the building.

The soldiers, for that was what they appeared to be, were much taller and more powerfully built than the rest of the population, very similar in fact to those who had made up the maintenance teams at the power station.

By their domineering attitude to the people in the queue, it began to dawn on the five friends that the soldiers were part of a military police force based in the town to control its inhabitants and to protect the power supply to the rest of the country. While they watched from the other side of the square there was a commotion in the centre of the queue. Two of the soldiers had waded in and in no time at all had extracted one man, rather taller than the rest, whom they considered to be the cause of the pushing and shoving and quite brutally had beaten him about the head and body and pitched him into the gutter. It was some time before he was able to struggle to his feet again and make good his escape from the soldiers who still stood menacingly nearby.

This unfortunate individual scrambled across the square straight for the bench where Aggorine and Lekhar were sitting. The other three had chosen a seat a little further on in order not to give the impression that they were together as a pack. They had all witnessed the scene outside the civic offices with considerable distaste and not a little anger. It was as much as Shimah and Oj could do not to rush to the aid of the victim of the soldiers' brutality. All would have been lost if they had done so and, as it was to turn out, much more good was to come out of the incident than would have done had they acted on impulse.

Bleeding from a wound on his forehead and holding his arms tightly around his waist the poor wretch just managed to reach the bench before slumping in pain right next to Aggorine who had, with the others, watched aghast, yet helpless, the whole sordid affair. Here was a problem indeed! Aggorine's heart went out to the injured person sitting now so close to her that she could not contemplate not offering him help and comfort of some kind. She wished so much for the support of the other four but she knew it had to be done by her and her alone so as not to risk showing a concerted effort on behalf of the poor fellow, which might attract attention and further action by the soldiers. Aggorine knew she couldn't involve the others at this stage but she remembered the words of Elcaro who had promised to help them solve their problems and instinctively she put her hand into her pocket and curled her fingers around her stone. It felt smooth and comforting in her grip and as she held it she sensed it was becoming warm, and her hand, then her arm and eventually her whole body tingled with excitement, her confidence and resolve both growing stronger with each passing second.

Without thinking she gently placed her other hand on the man's forearm and out of her mouth, again without any will of hers to form it, came the one word 'friend' in the local language. Her word met with a responsive though tentative glance and Aggorine knew at once that she had been able to communicate her desire to help the unfortunate man hunched beside her. Whether or not the man sensed that Aggorine was not one of the locals he gave no indication, but after a short while he became agitated and moved a little further away from her so that her hand no longer was able to rest on his arm. Later she was to learn that he moved away because he did not want to put her in danger of the same sort of treatment by the soldiers as they had meted out to him. But he had clearly been affected by her concern for his welfare and eventually, without looking in her direction, breathed two words which miraculously Aggorine could interpret as 'Follow me.'

With that he struggled to his feet and made his way with some difficulty towards the entrance to an alleyway in the corner of the square remote from their seat, where they saw him prop himself up against one of the pillars of the archway forming the entrance. He was undoubtedly in need of a rest but Aggorine knew he was waiting to see whether she would respond to his 'Follow me.'

No words were needed between her and Lekhar, sitting next to her, nor was a message to the other three needed. They all knew that whatever action Aggorine took, they too would follow. As casually as possible, apparently not in the least concerned about the injured man, she rose to her feet and strolled over to look in the shop window behind her. She lingered there for some minutes before turning to walk towards the alleyway where she was relieved to see the man still propped against the pillar. When she was within ten metres of him he lurched into a shambling walk again and was momentarily lost in the dim recesses of the alleyway. Aggorine followed and at a discreet distance, so did the others.

Though there was quite a crowd in the alleyway, it was not difficult to keep the injured man in view as he made his stumbling and erratic way close to the buildings on one side, stopping now and again, partly for any support he could find against the wall, but also to cast a furtive look behind him to make sure he had not lost the one who, in such a strange way, had declared herself his friend. And so they progressed in straggling line astern, now jostled by the townsfolk going about their business, now with a clear twenty or thirty metres across a minor square before plunging into yet another narrow passage.

At last the man lingered longer than usual at a small brown door set in the stone wall and Aggorine realised they had arrived at their destination. With a final glance over his shoulder and a longer, searching look around to check that the coast was clear, he made the smallest of gestures but clear enough for Aggorine to understand that she was to follow him into the building. Then he was gone through the entrance and the door left unlatched. Carefully Aggorine approached and the other four quickly joined her as she reached the door.

'Are you sure we should go in?' breathed Yma.

'I'm positive,' replied Aggorine. 'I'm also convinced that a new and exciting phase in our journey is about to begin,' and without waiting for any protest or argument she pushed open the door and stepped over the threshold.

Inside, the injured man was waiting for her and immediately grasped her hand and made as if to lead her into a room at the back of the house. He had so quickly closed the door behind her that the others had had no chance to follow, so she held her ground and, pointing to the door, repeated several times the three words which had passed between them earlier in the square. 'Friend – follow me,' and when she said 'me' she pointed to herself.

The man seemed not to realise that more than one had been following him and with understandable caution he repeated Aggorine's words but in a questioning tone of voice, 'Friend – follow? Friend follow?'

Aggorine nodded to answer the question in the affirmative and made to open the door but despite his injuries, he was there before her, placing his hand on the latch. As if to be thoroughly convinced, he repeated his question once more. 'Friend follow?' and pointed, as Aggorine had, to the door.

'Yes, yes,' she replied, nodding furiously, not realising that the 'Yes, yes' had come out in the local language!

This time the man was sure of her sincerity and turning to the door, opened it until he could peep through the crack. Seeing first one, then all four with worried looks on their faces, he opened the door wide enough for him to step outside. Fortunately there was no-one else in the immediate vicinity and, after a momentary look of appraisal, the man beckoned to them to enter and with what they took to be a generous welcome, he bowed low and ushered them into his house with a wide sweep of his arm. Once inside, the man put his finger to his lips and led the way into the room at the rear of the building. The whole place was badly illuminated and in a poor state of repair, but when he switched on the light, the room took on a different complexion entirely. Even though the walls and furniture were drab, there was an air of welcoming comfort. Indicating that they should sit down, and, without attempting to speak, he did his best to show them that they were most welcome and he was delighted to have them under his roof. He was clearly still in pain following the beating he had received from the soldiers and there was a large gash covered with clotted blood on his forehead just above his right eye. There seemed to be no other occupant of the building, at least not of the ground floor and the general impression was that the man lived here alone.

Realising that something ought to be done about the wound, Yma approached him and, gesturing to her own forehead and then to his, she succeeded in making him aware that she wanted to do something about his wound. He in turn put his hand to his head very gently and the expression on his face showed that, in the excitement he had momentarily forgotten his injuries. But now he led the way to a small room which served as a combined kitchen and wash room, ferreted around in a wall cupboard and presented Yma with a bottle of what she presumed was an antiseptic. The other girls had followed Yma's lead and all three now fussed around their new-found friend until they were satisfied that they had done all they could to make him more comfortable. At first he resisted their ministrations but soon succumbed, and in fact rather enjoyed being made the centre of their attention.

In the room once more with the two boys, they stood or sat for a while in awkward silence. The whole of one wall was covered by shelves on which was stacked a library of books and it was this which provided the ice-breaker. Both Aggorine and Lekhar rose from their chairs and went to examine the contents of the shelves, the man following closely. Even a cursory glance was enough to show that the owner of such a collection was a scholar of considerable standing and when a number of the books had been taken down for closer inspection, the illustrations, if not the language, revealed that there were works of science, literature, art, music, mathematics. In fact a more detailed examination of the shelves would have shown that the books covered a vast range of academic studies which could only be encompassed by a person with an exceptional brain. By the intense pleasure he showed in the interest which, by now, all five of his guests were displaying in his collection, clearly this man was such a person.

Until now they had each remained silent, content to accept the hospitality and friendly attitude of the man of the house, but examining the books loosened the tongues of the five friends and soon there was a flood of conversation as they became more and more excited when they found they could at least understand the nature of their contents, if not the detail because of the language barrier. And then Aggorine, having been frustrated in her search for a book which would help her understand the language, turned to the man with a questioning look on her face only to find his face wreathed in smiles. He came towards her and, taking both her hands in his, he said slowly but quite distinctly, 'I do not know how you got here nor why you have come, but it is a great joy for me to have you, who come from the plains, as guests in my humble house.'

As he spoke, each one of the five friends stopped what they were doing and turned towards him with astonishment written all over their faces. They just could not believe their ears. It was so unexpected and yet so thrilling to find that they could now communicate with this man who had accepted them as friends.

They all started talking at once and each wanted to know 'How?' – 'Where?' – 'When?' and 'Why?' to all sorts of questions. The man surfaced from the deluge, holding up both his hands as if in surrender.

'Patience,' he said. 'Let it be sufficient for the moment that I am lucky enough to have learned your language. I seem to have some natural facility for language and when the opportunity came to learn yours, I took it. I never thought I would have occasion to use it and in fact you are the very first live audience I have ever been able to address in plains language,' and he smiled at his own play on words. But he continued in much more serious vein. 'The people of this town are denied access to the plains beyond the high peaks. For many generations they have been a subservient race, controlled by the military and scientific might of those who live in the higher reaches of the Tarara range. – You see, I know the name your people give to this vast mountainous area,' he said as an aside. 'I also believe you call their leader by the name "Haon". Is that correct?'

Aggorine nodded her assent. She and, for that matter, the others were amazed at his command of their own language and also the revelation of the people's suffering under the forces of Haon. Surely here they had found a valuable ally in their quest to rescue Ecila and confront Haon himself. However before that could happen they would need to learn more about this intelligent man and hear all he could tell them about Haon's kingdom and in particular his apparent control over some of the forces of nature. It would also be necessary for them to lay their own intentions bare before him so that implicit trust could be built up between them. Of course, at this stage they had no idea whether or not he would agree to help them but they certainly hoped he would.

At last Aggorine found her tongue again and said rather formally in response to their host's words, 'Thank you for accepting us into your house. It is also a great joy for us to be here and to have found a person like yourself with whom we can converse. We are truly sorry to hear that the people here have for so long been at the mercy of Haon and wish you to know that we too, who live on the plains, have for generations been devastatingly affected by his wrath and by what appears to be his supernatural powers. You and your people live much more in the shadow of Haon than we on the plains do and so I suspect you have much greater knowledge of him than we have and we hope you will tell us all you can about him and his extraordinary control over this mountain domain.'

Yma interrupted her before Aggorine launched into a full-scale discussion on Haon and said, 'I think our friend deserves to know who we are and why we are here but,' – and here she addressed herself directly to the man – 'you must still be in considerable pain and discomfort after your beating. Is there not something else we could do to make you more comfortable?'

'What you have done already has made me feel much better, thank you,' he replied. 'But I agree. Let us sit down and get to know each other. We do not even know each other's names yet. I am called "Varac" and I live here alone with my books for company. You can see from the state of my rooms that I am not at all domesticated, though I have learned to look after myself adequately and I find my studies and my precious books more than compensate for the lack of physical comforts. But please, try to find somewhere to sit and tell me about yourselves.'

The obvious pleasure Varac displayed in their company and the warmth of his acceptance of them, relieved the awkwardness they had all felt in having invaded the privacy of his home and now they were able to relax. There were only seats for four in the room, so Shimah and Oj chose the floor while Varac offered his favourite chair to one of the girls. They would have none of that, of course, and insisted that he took it himself.

The five friends looked from one to the other, not knowing which one of them would start to tell their tale and for that matter, where to begin. They were still wearing the clothes they had discovered in the freight compartment of the shuttle train which had brought them from the power station to the town, complete with the caps which hid their wire mesh 'hairnets', and it was the embarrassment Oj felt in still having his head covered by a cap which provided the starting point. He put his hand to his head, took the cap off, and apologised for not having removed it earlier.

No doubt Varac was more than mildly amused by the sight of Oj's red and rather unruly locks entrapped in what looked a bit like a fishing net, so the smile which spread across his face was understandable. Oj responded with a smile too.

'I know I look daft in this hair net,' he said, 'but there is a good reason why we are all wearing one. We don't usually go around looking like this but we believe these contraptions have enabled us to avoid being traced and possibly captured by Haon. Before we made them out of this string, which is also a good conductor of electricity, Haon seemed always to know where we were. We concluded therefore that he had somehow acquired the ability to detect the beta-rays given off when our minds were active. We were acting as built-in bugging devices! It certainly seems we were on the right track because since we have worn these nets to act as screens to stop the beta-rays at source, we have had no further encounter with him.'

By this time they had all taken off their caps to reveal the hair nets each one wore and Varac, looking from one to the other smiled again and said teasingly, 'I must admit, it is a rather odd form of head gear!' And they all joined in the joke. The atmosphere between them was now one of trust and after a little further bantering, when Oj got his own back by describing the local cap as not being the height of sartorial

99

elegance, Varac begged them to tell him their story from the day they set out until their chance meeting with him in the town square.

So it was that for a long time that evening the five friends poured out all that had happened to them along the way leaving out no detail and each in turn taking up the story. Shimah was most concerned that Varac should learn of Ecila's disappearance, while Lekhar was at pains to emphasise the incidents which to them were beyond explanation, where her logical approach to the problem broke down, where something supernatural seemed to be influencing events. Yma found herself telling Varac about Elcaro and how they had been befriended by this benevolent being, if 'being' it was, and how from time to time they had experienced support and gained courage by calling on the Elcaronic power which they had been promised would always be available to them. Oj, on the other hand, as may be expected, wanted to assure Varac that wherever and whenever they could, they had tried to find a practical solution to the problems which confronted them, using the talents each one of them variously possessed. But it was Aggorine who strung the whole story together, starting from the life style of their people on the plains and explaining how periodically they were drastically affected by the violent activity of the Tarara mountain range. She wanted Varac to get as clear a picture as she could give him of the way in which the harmony of the life of the plains people was disturbed, if not shattered, by the fear of devastation coming to them from the east and how it came about that from two independent sources first four, and then two of them had set out hopefully to meet up with the source of the evil power and even to try to persuade whatever or whoever it was, to leave them in peace in the future.

By the time their story was complete, from the beginning, through their first encounter with Haon, when the 'four' and 'two' had joined forces to make the 'six', and on through every aspect of their momentous journey, the evening was well spent and they were all very tired.

Varac could hardly contain his amazement and excitement but he too, was so mentally exhausted that it was he who suggested that his story should wait until morning.

'I shall have a good deal to tell you,' he said, 'some of which may help you to understand many of the things which are mysterious to you now. But let us wait until we are refreshed and in the morning you shall hear what I have to say.'

Ever since they had entered the mysterious mountain kingdom through the sheer face of the rock, the five friends had been sustained by eating the silver ball-like substance which always seemed to be plentifully available whenever they needed it. They had never worried that the supply would fail them because their hunger had always coincided with the discovery of a fresh outcrop of the strange food. Once, when they had been confronted by a vast stretch of what appeared to be barren countryside, they had decided to pick more than they required for their immediate needs and Oj filled two or three empty pockets of his pack against the possibility of their not finding a fresh supply in time for their next meal. However, when later that day they stopped for a rest, they found the silver balls had shrivelled into small dry gains of dust and were now quite inedible.

They had been somewhat disturbed by this turn of events and immediately made preparations to move on to try to reach a more verdant area where fresh supplies might be found. But before they could even put their packs back on their shoulders, Yma had given a cry of delight, having espied a patch of the life-giving food just beyond the rocks against which they had been resting.

Since that incident they had always trusted to their finding food when required and had not again tried to carry a store with them.

Pleasant and satisfying though the mysterious food was, it was a great treat for them to share in the meal which Varac had prepared for them before they retired for the night. He apologised profusely for the lack of quantity and variety but explained that, living alone, he rarely kept a very full larder. The next day, if possible, he would make amends and introduce the travellers to much more of the local food. Despite Varac's protestations, they all thoroughly enjoyed their meal and were fully satisfied at the end. Varac would hear nothing of their profuse thanks for his hospitality, saying it was a tremendous thrill and honour to have them as guests. He insisted that the three girls used his own bedroom for the night while he and the two boys took a chair each in the living room.

So it was, that after the excitement of the day, peaceful sleep descended on the swollen household of Varac, the intellectual one.

12

When the boys woke in the morning, Varac was nowhere to be seen. The chair he had chosen as his bed had certainly been slept in, judging from the disarray of the makeshift bedclothes and the cushion he had used for a pillow. But of him there was no sign. Momentarily only, the unworthy suspicion entered both their heads that perhaps the events of the previous evening had been a clever confidence trick to get them to reveal all their secrets and that now, at any moment, the soldiers would come, directed by Varac, to take them all into custody. They were ashamed, as they realised by a single glance from one to the other, that they were thinking alike and Shimah, recalling the delight with which Varac had entertained them, dispelled their doubts. But where was Varac?

It wasn't long before their unspoken question was answered. The boys had busied themselves in putting the room back into some sort of tidy order, when they heard the street door click open and almost immediately there was Varac, beaming with a 'good morning' smile and carrying a bag loaded with provisions.

'I hope you slept well and feel ready for breakfast,' he said. 'I've been to the early morning market to collect a few things. There are not many people about at this time of day and it didn't take me long to gather a few necessities together.'

Both Shimah and Oj were delighted to see him again and were thoroughly ashamed at having had the slightest doubt about the sincerity of his friendship. When Shimah confessed to Varac that they were worried when they woke and found him gone, he nodded his head and with a sympathetic look in his eyes he said, 'Of course you were. I should have thought. After all you have been through, it was quite natural that you should consider that possibility. Please forgive me for causing you more distress. I should have woken you before leaving. Thank you for being frank with me. It shows you really do trust me even after so short an acquaintance.'

They seized each other by the hand as if to seal the complete restoration of confidence between them and no more was said. The boys knew now, even if they hadn't been sure before, that in Varac they had found the one person who would support and advise them to the uttermost and whom they could trust with their lives.

'It's about time those girls were up and about,' said Oj and he went to the door of the bedroom and gave it a thunderous knocking. Laughingly he added, 'That should rouse them!'

Sure enough, first Lekhar, then Aggorine and finally Yma emerged, all three rubbing bleary eyes and wanting to know why they had been woken so early!

'Come on, sleepy heads,' teased Varac, 'what about washing those pretty faces while we get some breakfast on the go. There is a lot to talk about and a lot to do, so the sooner we get on with it the better.'

Within ten minutes they were perched on chairs or arms of chairs around Varac's table, tucking in to a hearty meal which Varac had produced from the shopping he had done that morning.

'We shall never be able to repay you for all your kindness and all the trouble you are taking on our account,' said Aggorine apologetically.

'It's no trouble at all,' replied Varac. 'In fact I wish I could do more.' He paused and then in a more contemplative mood he continued, 'Well, perhaps I may be able to help in a less tangible way by giving you as much information as I can of the problems you may encounter when you continue your journey.'

'Which must be soon,' interjected Shimah. 'I am sure Ecila is more and more at risk the longer we delay. We must remember that she is our first priority, not only for her own sake but because the longer Haon has her in his power the more likely he is to destroy her free artistic mind and come closer to discovering the secret of life which she and all freedom-loving people enjoy.'

He turned to Varac. 'What lies ahead of us?' he asked. 'Tell us if you can.'

Varac smiled at the impetuous Shimah and sighed. 'What

lies ahead of you?' he echoed. 'I wish I knew exactly what you will find. All I can do is to tell you what I know of Haon and his people and hopefully that knowledge will help you to plan your own strategy and, with the power of Elcaro, to bring your mission to a successful conclusion.'

In the telling of their own story the five friends had described as vividly as they could, the help which Elcaro had given them and the promise they had received of assistance in overcoming problems on their journey. Yma had been the main source of information about Elcaro but for some unknown reason she had not told Varac about the Elcaronic stones each one had been given. The others had, perhaps unwittingly, taken their lead from Yma and they too had kept that part of their story secret. No doubt they all felt that Elcaro's tangible gifts to them were too precious to risk being revealed to a comparative stranger, which Varac had been initially. However Varac had been left in no doubt about the power for good which Elcaro had instilled into the very lives of the five travellers. Though he had known them for such a short time only, he felt within himself and openly confessed the view that his own life henceforth would be different due to his encounter with them. It was as if some Elcaronic influence had begun to permeate his own thoughts and had brought with it a serenity which would enable him to face the repressive regime under which he lived with even greater fortitude than before. His spirits were high as he seated himself in his chair and the others spread themselves as comfortably as they could around him waiting expectantly for Varac's story to unfold.

'I was excited to learn,' he began, 'that your people of the plains have, over the years developed a high degree of scientific and technological understanding and practical expertise. We have always been led to believe that yours was a backward system, not capable of matching the great achievements of the Haonic people. We have been starved of information from beyond the great high mountain through which you so miraculously passed, so it is no wonder that over the generations we have come to believe what our lords and masters tell us. But make no mistake, the Haonic scientists and mathematicians have made remarkable strides towards discovering and using the secrets and forces of nature. You will undoubtedly witness some of the results of their work when you reach the central complex and, from what you have told me, you have already experienced the power which Haon can wield from a distance.'

'We certainly have,' interjected Lekhar. 'From the very first time when he vented his fury on us for daring to enter the mountain range, I have been trying to find some logical explanation for what appear to be supernatural happenings, but have had to concede that they are beyond my ability to comprehend. Perhaps one day, in the not-too-distant future, I shall come to understand the basic principles of the forces which enable Haon to appear to us as the apparition of an old and furious old man, to spirit Ecila away from us into a world of blazing colour and light, to create so many strange visions and to be able to locate us so easily whenever he wishes. We have, however, had a small success against this last of Haon's powers. Our crude hair nets, woven out of highly conductive string seem to have effectively cut off his source of information concerning our whereabouts. This suggests to me that the Haonic scientists have discovered how to use the beta-radiation given off by active brains, not only as a bugging device to pinpoint the position of the people concerned but maybe also to lock into the beta beam and transmit their own information directly back into the brain of the one emitting the original beta waves. It sounds plausible but at the same time fantastically improbable. However, if something of the sort is possible, the Haonites would have the power so to control our thoughts that any images they wished us to see would appear absolutely real to us.'

'Far be it from me to argue with our tame scientist,' said Oj, turning a beaming smile of incredulity on Lekhar, 'but all that sounds too much like a fairy story to me for it to be in the least possible.'

'I'm afraid it's beyond my comprehension too,' added Yma, 'though I remember, as I stood on the lakeside and Haon became interested in my music, I experienced what I can only describe as a battle of wits which seemed to be being waged within the recesses of my mind. If you remember, it was only by the support of Elcaro that I was able to overcome Haon's insistence that I should go to play my flute for him. I should have joined Ecila as a captive, I am sure, had I not been able to withstand his insidious onslaught on my thought processes. Perhaps, Lekhar, there's more truth in your, admittedly,

106

fantastic theory than any of us can realise at the moment.'

Varac had listened intently to the conversation between these highly intelligent young people which his initial remarks about Haonite scientific achievements had sparked off.

But now, in the pause which followed Yma's contribution he continued: 'You may be much closer to the truth than you can possibly think at the moment. I myself know that for years now, the scientists of the Haonic complex have been concentrating a great deal of research into the function of the human brain. Some time ago processes were developed by which energy was produced in abundance by using the principle of nuclear fusion, as distinct from the previous method employing nuclear fission. This gave the scientists complete and safe control over the production of atomic energy and provided them with untold power through a system which was easy to maintain, and from which a great deal less waste material and fewer side-effects of a harmful nature were produced than from the earlier method based on nuclear fission. You have yourselves seen one of the power stations and have guessed correctly that the energy source is nuclear. What you won't have been able to see however, is the heart of the system itself, largely because it is much smaller than that used in the primitive nuclear plants, but also because the shield which has been developed to surround the power source itself not only completely blocks the passage of harmful atomic radiation but curtails all electro-magnetic and particle radiation of whatever frequency, including the visible band. So, when you were in the power station, not only were you safe from the deadly atomic radiation but, had you been aware of what to look for, you would probably have seen a pure white globe no bigger than this room, inside which was the heart of the power station.'

Aggorine interrupted Varac briefly by saying, 'We weren't very interested in making a tour of inspection while we were there, impressive though it was. All we wanted to do was to find our way of escape as soon as we could. We were, however, intrigued by the fact that there were so few people in the command centre of the complex. The whole thing seemed to run itself.'

Varac nodded. 'Alongside the development of safe nuclear energy has run research into control systems and, from what information I have, I understand the computer has almost completely taken over the control of such things as power complexes, transport systems and communications. But, as I have already indicated to you, the people here are no more than a slave race, being completely under the military control of the agents of the Haonites. As such they are never allowed access to any of the research centres nor to the results of the work being done there.

'There are a number of such towns scattered around the mountains and all the people in those towns have, for many, many years, been controlled mentally and physically by the seemingly all-powerful Haon. Each town is sited close to a huge excavation like the one which houses the power station you discovered and in years gone by, the people of the town were forced to do all the manual work involved in those excavations. Most of that sort of work is now finished but they are not allowed to enjoy the fruits of their labours beyond that which is necessary to sustain a basic standard of living. If any of the people rebel, they are dealt with summarily by the soldiers, and many who do so do not survive. Normally I keep a very low profile and use what intelligence I have to live the sort of life I most enjoy. As you may gather, that life is bound up in my books. I love nothing more than to study and to acquire whatever knowledge I can. The incident with the soldiers, which effectively brought us together, was caused by my frustration in the queue bubbling over in a most uncharacteristic way for me. I was lucky to get away with my life! – But I was even more fortunate in meeting with you five young people. You have brought me a measure of happiness I have never enjoyed before and with it I have experienced a strong feeling that your mission to confront Haon will not only benefit your own people of the plains but will also bring relief to the folk in this town and in the other towns like it. How you are going to achieve your objective, I have no idea but, if I can be of even the slightest service to you, I shall be delighted.'

'The more information we have about Haon the better,' said Aggorine, 'and we, too, are sure that our meeting with you will prove to be a great help to us in the next stages of our journey.'

Lekhar was becoming more and more excited as Varac unfolded his account of the scientific advances achieved by the Haonic people and she could hardly restrain herself from plying him with questions of detail, but she realised he might not be able to add much more to the broad picture he had already painted for them.

So she simply said, 'Research such as you describe has been undertaken in our country too but it sounds as if we have not yet produced such advanced results. It is true, our scientists have also mastered the safety problem in the use of nuclear energy and our material lives are largely controlled, or should I say influenced by the ever-developing computer industry. What intrigues me most of all is the work you say is being done into the function of the human brain. Could you tell us more about that? – As far as I can gather, Haonic scientists are directing their efforts towards the control of the thought processes and therefore of the behaviour of the individual, whereas the work in our country on the complexity of the brain has taken a completely different direction.'

Here Lekhar paused, as if to try to recall what she knew about the results of that work.

'Go on,' urged Varac. 'What do you mean by "a different direction"?'

'The aim is totally different,' she replied. 'In our country, work designed to discover how the human brain functions is along purely medical channels, contrary to what appears to be the purpose of that being done here. Haonic brain research seems to be directed solely towards controlling the actions of the person concerned, thereby giving the controller absolute power over the individual. In our country, as far as I can gather from reading the scientific and medical journals, the point has been reached where doctors can stimulate the brain of a sick person in such a way as to increase greatly the body's natural healing processes. As yet only some of the more common ailments can be cured in this way but the results so far are most encouraging.'

'You are quite correct,' said Varac, 'and I don't think I can tell you much more about the subject than you have so ably deduced for yourself. It is true that the major objective is to gain power over people, so that Haon can reign supreme. From what you say, your people are far more concerned for the well-being of their fellow creatures, and this illustrates a fundamental difference between your way of life and that of the Haonic race. Haon would sneer at your attitude, because all he understands is the satisfaction he gains from imposing his will on other human beings. He is in no way interested in their welfare.'

'When you say that, I can almost feel sorry for him,' said Yma.

'I was thinking that too,' added Aggorine. 'He must be a very miserable old tyrant if he can't appreciate the beauty of friendship and the joy of doing things which will please other people.'

'Now, don't let's get too sentimental,' warned Shimah. 'He's no more than an old devil to me, who has vented his wrath on people in his own kingdom and also caused untold suffering to people in our country beyond the great cliff face. And what is more, he has Ecila in his power.'

'Shimah is right,' said Varac. 'If you are to confront Haon successfully, you must remember that his intentions are always selfish and that he regards concern for other people as weakness. We, who have lived under him for generations, have never known anything other than harsh treatment. We are now no more than serfs and all hope of ever regaining our independence vanished many years ago.' He paused and then added with a smile, 'But you have brought a ray of sunshine into my life at least.'

He went on, 'Now I must tell you what I know about the Haonites apart from their scientific achievements. If you know something about them and their origins it might be of use to you when eventually you meet up with them. Their history goes well back beyond living memory. In fact the stories of how they came to settle in the depths (or heights) of the mountains are now no more than legends. As you can imagine, these stories have been embellished over the years as they have been passed down from one generation to another. Some people maintain that their ancestors were humanoid beings from another planet who were not able to get away from the earth's gravitational pull, once they had landed. Finding the atmosphere and mountainous terrain similar to that which they had left, they settled and multiplied. The advanced technology which they must have brought with them was way beyond anything then on earth and this may be why they are so advanced scientifically today. Personally I must say the story certainly does have a ring of truth about it.

'Another theory which may be just as probable is that the

Haonic race derives from a chance mutation caused perhaps by intense atomic radiation from outer space or even from an unnaturally large concentration of nuclear material in one of the mountain peaks. There have been many stories told of huge, man-like animals who used to roam the mountains and it is just possible that from their stock sprang the race of people now known as Haonites. They certainly are well-built and strong and in order to survive they would have had to adopt an attitude of the "survival of the fittest", which left them little or no room for consideration of the welfare of any other being but themselves. Of course, neither of these theories may be correct, but whatever the truth is of their origin, the fact remains that they are now as they are: strong, well-built, intelligent and ruthless.

'Fortunately for you and all those who live beyond the mountains, once they had established their frontiers on the lower slopes of the mountains and subdued all those who lived in that region, the Haonites did not seem to show any desire to move out onto the plains. They're a very self-sufficient people. I know that your predecessors have suffered devastation because of what you call the "wrath of Haon", but I believe there is a practical explanation for those happenings. There is no doubt that, in the course of their scientific research, there have been terrible accidents, the effect of which would have been felt well beyond the mountains. These experiments which went wrong were always carried out well away from the central Haonic region, which in any case would also be shielded by a field-force of great strength. It is almost certain that that is how destruction rained down on your people. Experiments continue to be carried out but the explosions seem now to be carefully controlled. Nevertheless you have still been able to hear the rumblings as far away as your own home. I am pretty certain that is the truth of the matter and I trust you and your people will never again have to suffer the "wrath of Haon".'

There was visible relief in the faces of the five friends at what Varac had told them and almost with one voice they said, 'Let's hope you're right!' – Not that they doubted Varac in the slightest, but his forecast of no more devastations was so unexpected yet so very welcome, that they were unable to absorb it immediately.

'This is terrific news,' blurted out Aggorine and she would

have poured out more expressions of relief and jubilation but Varac interrupted her.

'You mustn't take it for granted that what I have deduced from my observations and my study of the historical stories is necessarily correct nor that circumstances might not alter. From what you told me earlier about your first encounter with Haon and the exchanges with Elcaro, it would appear that he feels he now has complete control over the material world and is seeking something more, which at the moment he doesn't understand. He wants to know the very essence of life itself, and I guess that he knows full well that the path along which the work of his scientists is going will not lead to the answer to that question. Elcaro has indicated that you young people may be able to supply that answer, so, to ensure that he has a trump card to play he has taken Ecila hostage, not only to strengthen his position in his battle of wits with you, but also to ensure that you will eventually come of your own accord into his fortress. So do not lower your guard against Haon. Be prepared for any eventuality.'

'My sentiments exactly,' added Shimah and the others nodded their assent as each recognised the wisdom of Varac's warning.

There followed a long pause while each of them was busy with his or her own thoughts.

Eventually Varac broke the spell saying, 'There is still the question of Haon himself.'

'What do you mean? Is he different from the other Haonites to any great degree?' asked Aggorine.

'A great deal of mystery surrounds him,' answered Varac. 'No doubt he himself has, over the years encouraged people, his own most of all, to look upon him as a magical, all-powerful ruler. Whether what we know or have heard about him is true, no-one can say, but what is clear is that he holds complete dictatorial power in his own hands and woe betide anyone who does not comply with his wishes.

'When you were telling me about your people of the plains yesterday, you said that the story of Haon, handed down from one generation to the next, told of this old, old man who had been in existence "since the beginning". I think those were the words you used. So you won't be surprised to hear that we have a similar tale to tell.

112

'You asked if he is different from the other Haonites, Aggorine,' Varac continued, 'and my answer is most definitely "Yes." There is a great deal about him which is different and the most dramatic thing is that he has indeed been alive for hundreds of years, if "alive" is the correct term to use. The Haonites have never known another ruler. Haon has always held sway generation by generation and he is the only one who seems to possess immortality. He also possesses powers which can only be described as supernatural. Of course the information at my disposal is only secondhand but it has got the authority of time-honoured stories which have been passed down from one generation to another. There has never been any question of another ruler taking Haon's place over his subjects and, as far as we can tell, no-one has ever challenged him for the leadership.

'It is said that two thousand years ago, or thereabouts, there was a tremendous struggle between the forces of good and of evil. Great storms raged all over the earth. Lightning and thunder, floods and earthquakes threatened to tear the planet apart. All people were terrified and many perished. But eventually a measure of peace returned and it was generally accepted that the forces of evil had been defeated. However, the story goes that the cause of the cataclysm was a concentration of devilish power from outer space which had descended on earth to attempt to take it over as a base for further operations of a similar nature on other planets. When, after throwing all their venomous forces against the earth and its inhabitants, the evil invaders found that total victory could not be assured, because of the resourcefulness and courage of the people, they decided to withdraw. Now, the legend tells that besides the resistance of the earthlings, there had arisen a struggle for power within the ranks of the invaders themselves and this is where we hear of Haon for the first time. He is reputed to have rebelled against the leaders and led an uprising which was both violent and costly to the forces of evil. Eventually the uprising was crushed and Haon alone of his force escaped extermination. Finding that the last battle was going against him, Haon deserted his followers and made his escape into the mountains. Shortly afterwards, what remained of the devilish invaders left the planet earth as mysteriously as they had arrived and Haon was marooned in the mountains, destined to use his powers to carve out a perpetual existence for himself as an earthling.

How long he lived a solitary life is by no means certain, but it is believed he wandered from peak to peak and valley to valley until he eventually came across the ancestors of the present day people we now call Haonites.

'You yourselves,' continued Varac, 'have had some experience of his so-called magical or supernatural powers, so it will not come as a surprise to hear that Haon used these powers to demonstrate his superiority over these people. In a very short while they were looking to him for leadership, which he, with great cunning, at first refused, but eventually he allowed himself to be "persuaded" to take control. And so he was established at the head of a band of followers once more.

'Wherever those early inhabitants of the mountain had come from, and I have already told you that their origin is shrouded in mystery, the fact remains that they were fine physical specimens, standing almost two metres in height with the rest of their bodies in matching proportion. They were intelligent beings but lived their lives under the rule that only the fittest survived and no-one gave thought, or raised one finger to help if others appeared in need. They were ideally suited to Haon's own evil philosophy and, once he had become their undisputed leader, together they made a formidable force in the mountain country.

'Under Haon's guidance, his subjects, for subjects they were, under his complete control, ranged far and wide within the vast range of mountains and wherever they found a settlement such as this one here, they reduced the inhabitants to little more than slavery.

'Those in this town were forced to excavate the tunnel and the huge cavern for the power station. That mammoth task took years and many of the people perished during the operation. Food and other commodities were demanded to supply the Haonic overlords and this place, like the other slave towns, became impoverished and the spirit of the people was so ground down that any hope of a return to a normal way of life was lost for ever. Now that the Haonic kingdom is well established and no major project demanding slave labour is in prospect, the people are left in comparative peace, but remain under the close scrutiny of the soldiers of the Haonite guard.

No quarter is ever given if an argument arises through the frustration the people feel under the heel of the oppressor, and the luckless person involved in the argument rarely survives. I myself, as I have told you, was extremely fortunate in my confrontation with the soldiers the day I met you. There is no hope of any change, as I have said, but people have, over the years managed to keep alive the stories of their ancestors and, to a certain extent, their customs and way of life.

'Now you five young people have come, armed only with your bare hands, your extremely high intelligences and, perhaps above all, your love of beauty in all its forms and your concern for the well-being of your own people and all others with whom you come into contact. These "armaments" Haon would not even recognize as being of any worth, let alone strength and, if you ever get near enough to him, he will laugh you to scorn, should you so much as breathe a challenge to his authority and his great material strength.'

Varac ended his story there and waited for comments and questions from his young guests.

It was Yma who spoke first. 'You paint a vivid picture of our adversary,' she said, 'and I am sure it would only take a lifting of Haon's little finger to bring about our extinction. However we all believe he is not yet ready to destroy us. But he has our dear Ecila in his grasp and we know what danger she is in, if, indeed, she is still alive.'

'Of course she's alive,' burst out Shimah. 'I would know if she were dead. What is more, I have ever confidence that she is capable of resisting Haon in any attempt he may make to rob her of her love of the beauty of art. But the longer we delay, the longer she is under pressure, and so I say we must make haste to continue our journey.' He sat down, red in the face and very agitated.

'Yes, yes,' continued Yma, 'it's true, we must proceed as soon as we can, but what I wanted to say is that we must not lose hope nor underestimate our own strength. Our major source of power comes from Elcaro who has promised to help us in our quest. We also know that Haon is desperately anxious to discover the secret of life and Elcaro has told him that we hold that secret. If he destroys us he destroys his chance of ultimate knowledge and control over the earth.'

Varac had heard the young people refer to this 'secret of life' before and now his curiosity got the better of him.

'Do you in fact know the answer to that question?' he asked.

'That's the funny thing about it,' replied Aggorine. 'If you were to ask us to give a clear answer, we would find it beyond our individual abilities, but Elcaro hinted, after our first encounter with Haon, that collectively we knew more about the solution to the riddle than Haon ever would, unless we chose to enlighten him. Hence his various attempts to try to extract the information from our very minds. Our battle with Haon is not so much a physical one but rather one for the defence of our thought processes.'

'Don't let's get too airy-fairy over this,' interjected Oj. His practical mind had been stimulated into action by Shimah's insistence that they should be getting on with things. Turning to Varac he said, 'Physical battle or no physical battle, mental fight or no mental fight, the fact remains that we are here, while Haon is some distance from here deep in the mountains, and if we are to have a confrontation of any sort, either we have to go to him or in some way persuade him to come to us! What do you suggest, Varac?'

Varac paused for a moment before replying. Then spreading his arms as if to enfold the whole group he said, 'My dear young friends, the task you have set yourselves seems to me to be insurmountable. Haon holds all the advantages, save the one you have mentioned. Now, I recognise that the answer to the secret might prove to be more powerful than all the control that Haon wields over the physical world, but the risk of instant obliteration, should Haon decide, in a fit of frustrated temper, that he is not interested after all, is extremely great. I cannot propose any course of action until I am convinced you yourselves recognise the risks, and despite everything, you are determined to proceed.'

'I know I can answer for all of us,' said Aggorine. 'We do know the risks – and we do want to proceed.'

Expressions of full agreement came from the others and Yma added, 'We know the risks and we have already experienced some of them and we have also seen the powerful help Elcaro is ready to afford us in the face of those risks. Without Elcaro's help it would be another story completely but with it we feel confident that we can rescue Ecila and return to our homeland. How to set about it from this point is the big question at the

116

moment.' She smiled at Varac and added, 'You have made us so welcome here, Varac, that in one way we don't want to leave. Yet leave we must, so please point us in the direction we should take.'

Varac returned her smile and, without expressing it, indicated his joy at having them as his guests. But soon his face turned grave and he said, 'It is only you who can decide what action to take. I can only give you what information I have at my disposal and you must weigh up the alternatives. The journey from here to Haon's headquarters would be dangerous and exhausting in itself, to say nothing of the risk of being captured on the way. No member of this community has ever been allowed to make that journey, so I cannot be precise in my directions. I do know however, that your objective lies some fifty kilometres to the east and, from even a cursory glance in that direction, you yourselves can see the menacing mountains which lie in wait for any traveller on foot.

'This little town used to have several small outlying communities years ago and there were tracks which the people living there used when they needed to come into the centre. One such community was on a high plateau in the direction you would have to take. It lies some kilometres away and no doubt you could find it again, despite the fact that the paths must by now be largely lost through the neglect of ages. Little snippets of local history indicate that the site was a very pleasant one. The plateau stretched away to the east for approximately six or seven kilometres. There was a lake there and the settlers were able to be almost self-supporting, as the soil was very fertile. No-one has lived there for some two or three generations since Haon drove the original inhabitants out or, more probably, wiped them out.

'In any case,' he concluded, 'if you decide to make the journey, that plateau could be your first objective. I cannot show you it from here because it is on the other side of a hill, but I believe the view from the original settlement towards the east stretches well beyond the far end of the plateau. You may therefore be able to plan the next part of your route when you reach the settlement, by careful observation of the distant terrain.

'That is all I can tell you about travelling on foot. Anything more would be pure conjecture on my part. I am sure the

Haonic city is a scientific and technological masterpiece but no doubt you will prove that for yourselves, if and when you get there.'

While Varac had been talking, Lekhar had been deep in thought, whilst listening with one ear to what was being said. 'The station,' she said. 'What about the station where we arrived after our journey from the power complex? There were at least two other platforms and some people, Varac, were there waiting for trains. I thought you said the townspeople are not allowed to travel.'

'As a general rule they are not,' replied Varac. 'The trains are only for workers and the lines only run to the factory sites on the outskirts of the town. I think I told you the town is forced to provide various commodities for the Haonites and that is where the workers have to go for that purpose.'

'But how are the things that they make transported to Haon's city?' asked Oj. 'Surely there must be a rail link for that purpose.'

'There is no rail or road link with the big city,' Varac insisted. 'All movement is by air to and from a small landing pad in the factory area. The town is completely isolated by land, presumably to deter any would-be adventurer from foolishly trying to reach the city. The only people allowed to travel are the soldiers or any other member of the Haonite race. Regular transport craft ply each night between the factories and the city and none is to be seen in daylight hours. Their motive power must be some clever adaptation of nuclear energy. In any case, the craft come and go noiselessly and without the aid of illumination of any sort. The uninitiated often speculate as to what process is being used and have sometimes gone so far as to think that the Haonic scientists have found a way of lifting and propelling material objects using extremely powerful radiation. If, on the other hand, they have discovered what causes gravitational attraction and have been able to counteract it, then silent and rapid flight over the face of the earth would be a distinct possibility.'

'If what you say has a grain of truth in it,' said Lekhar, 'then the Haonic scientists must have taken their research into the forces of the material world way beyond that yet achieved by our scientists of the plains. I suppose, if it is true, this has only been made possible by ruthless materialism, with no thought or energy being spent on the well-being of the individual person. Only the strong mentally and physically would be of any use in the Haonic system, and all those who needed help because of some degree of frailty would be ignored and would eventually perish.'

'That's strong stuff,' said Shimah. 'It's a philosophy which we just can't accept and if we are faced with such an attitude to life when we eventually confront Haon, it will take all the courage we can muster to defend our corner.'

Oj brought them from the philosophical argument to the practicality of their next move. 'All this doesn't solve our immediate problem,' he said. 'Are we to trek over the mountains, with all the risks that involves, or are we in some way to try to get Haon to come to us – with all that that involves?' he added with a touch of sarcasm.

'Well, I'm for making the journey on foot, at least as far as the plateau Varac has described,' said Lekhar. 'If we then decide to try to contact Haon from there, it would not involve the people of this town, who might otherwise suffer if we try to get him to come here.'

'That's a very sound argument,' agreed Aggorine, and it wasn't long before the other three had fallen in with the idea.

'It's agreed then?' said Aggorine, sensing that the moment for her to take charge of the arrangements had again arrived.

'Yes – agreed,' they choroused.

Varac held up a cautionary hand. 'Before you rush off to the plateau and to goodness knows what beyond, I have a proposition to put to you: will you please allow me to act as your guide? Since you have been here I have come to realise that, just by sitting here surrounded by my books, I am achieving nothing. You five young people have infected me with courage and enthusiasm, and above all you have given me at least a grain of hope that Haon may yet prove not to be invincible. Perhaps together we may be able to overcome his evil power. Please let me come with you. I may be of some use, even if it is only as an extra pair of eyes and hands.'

The five looked from one to the other and eventually Aggorine expressed their unspoken thoughts. 'You have done so much for us already, Varac,' she said, 'it would be wrong of us to expect you to risk your life on our behalf any more.'

'But I want to come, not only for your sakes, but for the

possible good which may result for my own people,' he pleaded. 'I expect I know the risks even better than you do and it is just possible I might be able to help you avoid them.' He paused and then looking away from them he added, 'But I shall quite understand if you decide you want to proceed without me.'

There was an awkward silence in the room after Varac's impassioned plea. Eventually Aggorine spoke again for them all. 'I know we should all be very happy to have you come with us but we feel we cannot make such a decision, involving, as it does, a very real risk to your life, without –' and here she faltered – 'without,' she repeated, looking from one to another of her friends with a deep questioning look on her face. For the third time she said, 'without,' but this time she had received agreement from the other four for what she now said and she continued, 'consulting Elcaro.'

Yma came to Aggorine's assistance. 'You see, Varac,' she said, 'Elcaro has done more than give a promise to help us in our journey. We have all been given a part of Elcaro himself and, on several occasions, by combining our individual gifts we have been able to hear Elcaro's warnings and advice. I am sure I am speaking for all of us when I say that we feel it is now right that you, our great friend, should share in our relationship with Elcaro, but we must warn you that whatever guidance we get we shall follow it to the letter.'

While she had been speaking, all five had encircled with their fingers the Elcaronic stones in their pockets. Now they brought them out and held them on the palms of their hands, their fingers touching as at the hub of a human wheel.

Varac gazed in astonishment as the five stones began to glow and eventually reach a brilliance which made him shade his eyes. Nothing was said. At least, no sound was heard, but mysteriously as before, Elcaro entered their very minds and the message came to all five very clearly: 'Take your friend Varac with you. He will help you and, what is more, because of his genuine desire to do good for his own people, I will help him too. Be guided by him as you move on from here to the plateau. When you reach there you will see more clearly what you should do.'

The five friends were overjoyed to receive such clear assurance from Elcaro that Varac should accompany them and, as the glow from the stones grew dim, they turned to Varac to see if he knew what had been decided. Imagine how thrilled they were to find his face bright with happiness and his eyes sparkling ecstatically.

'I know the decision already!' he almost shouted with delight. Then more calmly, though with no less of a thrill, 'I heard Elcaro myself as clearly as if he had been speaking aloud. He seemed to come right into my mind and I was instructed to go with you and to help you all I could. Elcaro will be with me too as we journey together. He has given me his promise.'

This most recent encounter with Elcaro, which had confirmed Varac's membership of the group and renewed and widened Elcaro's promise of help in the enterprise, had left them all in such a happy mood that the atmosphere in the room was charged with excitement and with confidence in the success of their mission. Each exchanged smiles and laughter with each other, shaking hands with Varac and embracing him as a brother – an extra brother in the common cause.

When eventually the state of euphoria subsided Varac spoke again. This time his voice was low and serious. 'Before we go any further,' he said, 'I have a confession to make.'

They all looked wide-eyed, silently questioning him.

'Until the startling events of a short while ago, I was impressed by your youthful enthusiasm and, though I felt that would carry you a long way towards your goal, I could not believe that it would be enough to overcome the powers of the evil Haon. Now that I have met Elcaro personally, so to speak, I know that, with Elcaronic guidance and power to help you, success is not only possible but highly probable – I might even say it is certain!'

'Not certain, by any means!' they chorused.

Aggorine went on to say, 'There is a lot which still depends on us personally and we must not become complacent and think that Elcaro will do it all for us. But our chance of success is increased by having you with us, Varac.' She cast her eyes around the group. 'Come now,' she said in her best leadership voice. 'We have work to do and plans to lay before we move out, and move out we must tonight. I feel in my very bones that tonight is the time.'

13

That afternoon was spent in a state of excited expectation, all of them knowing that they should get some rest before their proposed night march but no-one being able to settle. Aggorine's fingers were busy for an hour weaving a beta-wave screen net for Varac. It seemed sensible for him to be provided with the same simple device that had apparently protected the others from detection by Haon. Oj's ball of conducting string was certainly coming in useful, but when Varac's head gear was completed, there was not a great deal left. Nevertheless, Oj tucked what remained into his pack along with his precious knife and the few provisions Varac had shared out amongst them for the first part of the journey. Eventually all was ready. Everyone's pack had been checked and re-checked and yet there remained some little time before nightfall, when it would be safest to venture forth.

Varac's bookshelves proved interesting for all of them as they tried to relax, but they still remained on edge until Yma took her beloved flute and started to play. Varac had not heard her play before and he sat entranced by the mystical sounds she produced. The effect on the whole group was to calm their anxiety and raise their spirits once more. It was as if Yma's music had the power to cast out all doubts from their minds and fill them instead with joy and confidence. The sheer beauty of the music she produced seemed to overcome all fear and ugly thoughts, and soon everyone in that little room was at peace with the world, ready to face whatever might happen to them on the way to the Haonic city.

They decided to divide into pairs to avoid being too conspicuous as a group, should they encounter any soldiers on the way. Varac and Aggorine took the lead as they stepped out into the street from their refuge. A few moments later Shimah and Yma followed and Oj and Lekhar brought up the rear.

122

While they were still in the streets of the town, they reckoned they would not attract undue attention, dressed as they were in local costume which, in its drab uniformity afforded them a good measure of anonymity. The essential thing, Varac had said, was for them all to behave as normally as possible, giving the impression that they were three separate couples out for a walk in the evening air. Nevertheless, as Varac was the only one who knew which way to go, the others were to be certain not to lose sight of the leading couple.

It was growing increasingly dark as they neared the outskirts of the town but there was still enough light in the sky for them to make out the silhouette of the mountain range towards the east beyond which lay their objective. Progress through the town had been uneventful even though they had to pass the barracks where the soldiers were housed and which was always guarded by two armed sentries. Fortunately no interest had been shown in the three couples as they made their apparently aimless way past the guards and on through the maze of streets leading to the borders of the town.

Eventually the six friends found they had left the inhabited area behind them and, with no other people to give them the protection of being just members of the crowd, they began to feel more exposed and vulnerable. Varac and Aggorine made for the shelter of a group of trees and waited for the others to join them.

'The way leads along that line of rocks,' indicated Varac, pointing in the direction they had to go. 'I consider the next kilometre to be the riskiest part of our journey tonight. We shall have to pass within a stone's throw of the perimeter of the factory area which is always patrolled by guards, so we shall have to be particularly careful to avoid detection. It will be best for us now to stick close together and move silently from whatever shelter we can find, to the next.'

And so they moved on stealthily towards the line of rocks Varac had pointed out. They had made good progress for at least five hundred metres, making use of natural outcrops of rock and small plantations of shrubby trees for cover, but still they had not reached the perimeter fence of the factory area Varac had mentioned.

'We should be quite close now,' Varac whispered, and they all cowered beneath a particularly dangerous-looking overhanging rock. 'The next two or three hundred metres will be crucial.'

He seemed rather agitated and it was clear that the responsibility he had assumed as the group's guide was causing him to come under a good deal of strain.

Yma noticed how disturbed Varac was and placed her hand on his arm and whispered assuring words in his ear. 'It'll be all right,' she said, 'don't worry. We are all in this together. If we take care we shall reach the plateau safely.'

She tried to sound confident but she, as indeed they all were, was keyed up to a pitch of excitement in the face of the danger of their being discovered by the factory guards.

From their shelter they could see very little of the ground in front of them. Varac said he suspected the area would be clear of obstacles but equally there would be very little to afford them any protection from observation.

'The guards most certainly have infra-red equipment to enable them to observe without themselves being observed,' he said, 'and from what I know of them, they will always shoot first and ask questions afterwards. Somehow we must discover where the guards are, how many are on duty in the region and with what frequency they pass near enough to be able to see us. That's going to be very tricky in view of the fact that we can't see anything!'

'But we can,' interjected Lekhar, delving into her pack and bringing out her electronic binoculars. 'These little beauties may be small but they are very useful.'

Making sure the controls were set to 'receive' and to 'infra-red', she put the device to her eyes and scanned the area in front of her. 'I can see a small cabin type building,' she said, 'and it must be heated in some way, as it is giving off a degree of infra-red radiation. My guess is that it is some sort of guard house or observation post used by the soldiers and it is probably on a corner section of the fence. The trouble is I can't see anything but the cabin because that is the only object giving off enough radiation to activate my binoculars.'

She paused for a moment and then continued, 'I must use the infra-red transmitter to illuminate the surroundings. It means that I shall be risking it being detected but I guess the radiation from the source in the cabin will mask the narrow beam from my own binoculars.'

'Do you think that's a risk we should take?' asked Aggorine.

'Yes, I do,' retorted Lekhar, 'especially as there seems to be no alternative,' and with that she pointed the instrument towards where she suspected the fence to be and switched on the transmitter.

'I see the fence,' she whispered. 'The cabin is at the corner of two lines of fence, one which comes along towards our right and the other at right angles away from us, but I don't see any guards. They will probably be inside the cabin and let us hope they aren't being very active in their observation duty.'

'Perhaps there are no guards there at all,' suggested Oj. 'You did say the computer had reached a high degree of development, Varac. Maybe the post is simply manned by a robot system.'

'True,' replied Varac, 'but if that is the case, we must assume that there is constant surveillance of the surrounding area, which is going to make our further progress even more hazardous. If we activate the robot observation system, the area will soon be swarming with soldiers and, with the sophisticated equipment at their disposal, it wouldn't be long before they had us securely in their net.'

'Then we must put the thing out of action,' burst out Shimah. 'Give me the binoculars, Lekhar. Let me see what I can do.'

But before he could take the instrument from her she gave a startled gasp and whispered, 'I can see the whole of the area in front of the fence and some distance beyond as well. There must be an infra-red, broad-beamed transmitter in that cabin which comes on at full power and then switches off for an interval.' She continued to examine the ground they had to cover until the source from the cabin faded again. It had been on at full power for approximately half a minute and Lekhar now waited for it to come on again.

'We must time the interval as accurately as possible,' she said after explaining to the others what had happened. 'If the cabin transmitter is switched off for long enough we might have time to make a dash for a large rock I saw about fifty metres ahead of us, before it comes on again.'

There was general agreement to the plan and they set about timing the periods between the bursts of radiation from the cabin. After they had recorded five periods of the infra-red

125

illumination, Lekhar was satisfied that it was working to a regular pattern, twenty seconds on and forty seconds off – forty seconds, when it could be assumed that the recording instrument in the cabin would not be able to detect any moving object in its field of view. This should give them ample time to cross the danger zone to the cover of the rock.

Should they make a dash for it together or should they go singly or in pairs? On balance it was agreed they should stick together, especially as only one of them would be able to see the way by using the electronic binoculars. So it was that they arranged themselves in three pairs close behind each other in the shelter of the boulder which had protected them from observation, ready for the fifty metre dash when Lekhar gave the word. Lekhar and Shimah took the lead, Varac and Yma came second and Aggorine with Oj brought up the rear.

'Let's hope the period of switching on and off remains regular,' Lekhar whispered. 'If it suddenly changes, we might be in big trouble.'

They all stood poised and waiting to burst into action with hearts pounding and adrenalin running when Aggorine, who was just as keyed up as the rest put in a word of caution, realising that there was a risk of stumbling over each other in their anxiety to get to the other side as quickly as possible.

'Forty seconds,' she said, 'is enough time for us to walk fifty metres, let alone run, so let's take it at a steady trot when we get going.' With that she began quietly to beat time. 'One, two; one two,' she breathed and the others started to tap the ground with their feet in sympathy with her rhythm.

Meanwhile Lekhar was on the alert for the next burst of infra-red from the cabin – there it was at last. She started counting and as she neared what she estimated was twenty seconds she said, 'Get ready,' and then, when the cabin transmitter switched off, she waited a precious five seconds to be sure the illumination had faded sufficiently and then said, 'Go!'

Off they went two by two with Lekhar beaming in on the rock which they had chosen as their half-way haven in the dangerous crossing. The pace they had adopted in time with the beat Aggorine had set seemed pathetically slow, especially to the impetuous Shimah, but he kept in step and together all six reached their objective and were well under cover a good fifteen seconds before the infra-red 'flood-light' came on again.

'So far so good,' said Aggorine. 'What next, Lekhar?'

Lekhar was already spying out the land for the second half of the crossing and was soon able to report that another fifty metres or so would take them into the shelter of a small group of trees. And so, by repeating the procedure they all came safely past the dangerous observation post on the perimeter fence surrounding the factory area. The excitement of the last half an hour now behind them they settled down to collect their wits and to have a brief rest. It was Varac, worrying about their still being too close to the soldiers' guard post for comfort, who warned that they should be moving on.

By now it was quite dark, but their eyes had become accustomed enough to the lack of illumination for them to see the shapes of rocks and trees and sufficient of the ground in front of them to make reasonable speed. Varac now took the lead again, guiding them by a sort of sixth sense towards their immediate objective, the plateau behind the hill.

They had been travelling silently for about an hour, always upwards and in a general easterly direction and always on the alert for possible dangers, when Varac called a halt. In front of them and quite close at hand they saw what had brought them to a standstill. A rock face rose sheer to a considerable height and seemed to block their path completely.

'There must be a way through,' whispered Varac, still anxious not to be overhead by any unfriendly ear which might by chance be near at hand. 'The track which the people of old used to use coming to and from the town, must have had a passage-way of some sort through this barrier. We have obviously wandered off the track and must now scout around to find the opening.'

Aggorine immediately took charge. 'We must divide into two groups,' she said. 'Shimah, you take Lekhar and Yma to the left and Varac, Oj and I will go to the right. We can't risk a shout, so if and when the passage is found we must return here and go forward as a group again. I suggest we rendezvous here in any case, not later than in half an hour's time. Are we agreed?'

'Agreed,' they all muttered, accepting Aggorine's plan without question. And so they separated, Shimah and his party feeling their way cautiously to the left with Aggorine and the other two exploring to the right. Shimah, always rather more impetuous than his friends, was certain he would be the one to discover the passage, but the ground in their direction was strewn with boulders and every twenty or so metres a deep gully or dried-up water-course impeded their progress. After half the allotted time had elapsed and they had found no sign of the ancient way through the rock face, Shimah reluctantly had to turn his party round and make for the rendezvous.

Aggorine's group, meanwhile, had met more favourable conditions and they were able to cover more distance than Shimah, Lekhar and Yma. Even so, it was not until it was almost time to return, that keen-eyed Oj saw something which appeared to him to be interesting enough to warrant investigation. All the boulders along the way were irregular in shape, just as they had been when they had fallen centuries ago from the mountain side but the one which caught Oj's eye was much more regular in shape. In fact it was almost rectangular, which suggested to his skilled mind that it had been fashioned by the hand of some bygone craftsman. True the great stone was covered in lichen and was weathered by exposure to the storms of ages, but its general shape was still much too regular for it to be a natural formation.

Oj rushed towards the stone, Varac and Aggorine following closely, both catching some of his excitement at his find. But their initial optimism was soon blunted as they examined the boulder from all angles. No trace of a secret path could be found over, under or at the sides of the rock. Somewhat bewildered, but still fascinated, Oj and the others stood back to take a last look before returning to base to report failure. Then suddenly, Oj leapt forward again and attacked an area of ground just to the right of the great stone. He tore at the vegetation, throwing it behind him in his haste to uncover the rest of what he had glimpsed as they stood, apparently defeated, in front of the rock. The others joined him as he struggled to remove the soil and growth until at last a large circular stone lay bare, nestled closely against the edge of the rectangular one. What was more they had also revealed a channel hewn out of stone along which the stone had obviously been rolled years ago. Varac and Oj leapt to the task of moving the rock, convinced that behind it they would find the way through the cliff face. At first, though they strained their muscles to the uttermost, they could not move the great stone, but at last it shifted, and gradually gaining momentum it rolled quite sweetly about one metre away from the large rectangular stone which had been acting as a door post. Imagine the excitement they all felt when, sure enough, an entrance to a passageway appeared. It was as much as they could do to restrain themselves from plunging headlong into it, but it was Aggorine who wisely pointed out that they had overstayed their agreed time and should by now be well on the way back to the rendezvous with the others.

'Come,' she said, 'we must fetch the other three.'

'I'll stay here,' said Varac. 'While you are gone I can perhaps do a little exploration and find where the passage leads.'

But Aggorine would have none of it. 'No, we must stick together, Varac. We don't want to lose you now. Who knows what lies in wait for any intruder into the tunnel.' Her tone was firm but friendly and brooked no argument.

So they all three set off to meet up with Lekhar, Shimah and Yma. Meanwhile back at the place where they had parted company some little while ago, Lekhar's party had arrived on time after their disappointingly fruitless search. Now they paced around anxiously awaiting the arrival of the others. When about twenty minutes had passed they began to be really worried and were considering setting off in search of their friends, but suddenly they heard voices and out of the gloom appeared Oj with Aggorine and Varac in close attendance.

'Where've you been? We've been thinking you were lost or that something nasty had happened to you. You are nearly half an hour late,' Shimah burst out.

'We've found the way through,' replied Aggorine with obvious delight shining from her large dark eyes. 'Sorry we're late but we had quite a bit of clearing to do before we could open the entrance to the passageway. Come on, let's hurry back. I'm just longing to see where the path through the cliff leads.'

By now their eyes were quite accustomed to the dim light and they were able to make good time, travelling almost at a trot behind Oj who was leading the way. Soon the strange doorway lay in front of them once more and Oj was explaining to the others how they had first seen the upright rectangular rock, which they discovered was simply a gate post and then how some strangely circular shape to the side of the stone had turned out to be the actual gate itself. Then, rolled aside it had revealed the entrance to the passage they hoped would lead them directly to the plateau beyond.

It was Oj who took the initiative and bending low he stepped gingerly inside the opening. A draught of air met his face which suggested to him that this was a tunnel with an opening at the other end. It was quite dark inside but he moved forward confidently until he had penetrated some three or four metres. The others were not to be left behind and soon all six, with Shimah guarding the tail end, were following in line. Slowly they moved forward able now to stand erect, whereas previously they had had to stoop quite low to get through the opening. They could see nothing and had to feel their way along the right hand wall in order to make any progress. Suddenly Oj stopped and the others telescoped into him and each other.

'Hold hard,' he said, 'there doesn't seem to be any more wall!'

'What do you mean?' asked Lekhar who was next in line to Oj. 'There must be more wall.'

'Well, if there is, it's shot off to the right,' said Oj rather testily.

'Wait a bit, let's get my binoculars working,' continued Lekhar. 'It'll not give us a brilliant light but we should be able to see what's in front of us.'

With that she searched in her pack and extracted her precious instrument. Setting the beam transmitter to 'visible' she switched it on. In the faint light from the beam they were able to make out a blank wall in front of them. Had Oj not stopped when he did he would certainly have walked straight into it. The passageway had taken an acute turn to the right which is just what Oj had said. Now, with a little light to help, they set off again hoping that they would soon reach the other end. But it proved to be a very twisty path and it was very cold and getting colder with quite a powerful breeze blowing in their faces.

Imagine their delight when Oj gave a restrained shout. 'Light ahead!'

Sure enough they could all see it now and they pressed on, anxious to get out of the claustrophobic atmosphere of the tunnel.

As Oj came nearer to the source of light he broke into a run and the others had a job to keep up with him. Eventually they all burst out into early morning daylight, clear and beautiful, with the tips of the surrounding hills outlined in brilliant orange. They had indeed reached the plateau, and it now stretched before them towards the east and towards Haon's city in the high mountains.

14

Delighted to be out of the dark and forbidding passageway which had twisted and turned its way through the mountainside, apparently following the path excavated by the original dwellers on the plateau, who perhaps had used natural clefts or water courses in the rock, the five friends with their new-found companion and guide, Varac, just stood and drank in the fresh beauty of the early morning.

'How wonderful this place is!' breathed Yma as with arms outstretched she raised herself to her full height on tiptoe and embraced the beauty all around her, turning first one way and then the next, slowly at first then more rapidly until she was twirling round and round in an ecstasy of delight. The others soon caught her enthusiasm and joined in the dance and in no time a scene of sheer uninhibited joy was being enacted by the five young people who had come so far together and who had shared the same difficulties and dangers. It was a glorious expression of relief and relaxation which they were now enjoying with all their whirling, leaping and laughter.

At last, with much panting, they subsided in an exhausted heap on the grass, still laughing at and with each other, the nature and serious purpose of their quest momentarily forgotten. Sheer joy and delight in their mutual relationship reigned supreme. When eventually they recovered their composure they noticed that Varac had not joined in their mad capers, but had stood leaning against a boulder where he still remained with a bewildered look on his face.

' Come on, Varac!' shouted Shimah. 'What are you doing over there? – Come on and join the party.' He went over and, putting his hand on Varac's shoulder, urged him to come with him. But it was with considerable reluctance that Varac allowed himself to be brought into the group. Bewilderment was still written all over his face and as he and Shimah approached the others, they all realised that something was troubling him deeply. They stopped their quips and good-natured bantering and turned towards Varac.

Aggorine put the question into words; the question which each wanted to ask: 'What's the matter, Varac? What has happened?'

There was what appeared to be an interminable period of silence before Varac replied. Then with an intensifying of the frown on his forehead and a shaking of his bowed head from side to side he muttered: 'Never before,' – he paused as if he found it difficult to wrench the words out of his mouth – 'never before have I witnessed such a scene –' he raised his eyes to his young audience and continued, more firmly now – 'such a scene of abandonment of self control. You all seemed to have gone mad; to have lost command of your minds and I thought for a moment that it was all Haon's doing. I thought he had caught you off guard and had stolen from you your intellects and your understandings, leaving you as nothing more than imbeciles!'

Obviously concerned for their friend who had suffered such mental anguish, the five friends looked compassionately towards him until they could contain themselves no longer and once more peals of laughter rang out and they all jumped up and surrounded Varac, once more whirling round and round, but this time taking Varac with them.

As they danced, Shimah started chanting, 'Haon is a fool – Haon is a fool, Haon is a fool and a great big fool!'

At this Varac threw his arms in the air and with a tremendous effort, broke free from the cavorting young people. He ran towards the shelter of the cliff face, clapped his hands over his ears and collapsed in a terrified bundle. He lay there, clearly in great distress and would in no way allow any of the others to touch him.

'Go away,' he wailed, 'go away, you are mad – go away and leave me alone.'

'We are not mad,' said Yma eventually as they all stood around the distressed Varac. 'Have you never seen young people physically expressing the happiness they feel in each other's company and the joy they have in their hearts when they see beauty all around them?' She waited for a response but none came. So she continued gently, 'It isn't an abandon-

133

ment of our skills, our scholarship and our sense of values, but rather a fulfilment of them. We are not mad, Varac, dear friend. Do you not see that what you have witnessed is simply an outpouring of the happiness we each possess within our very selves which we cannot do other than share with other people?'

'We would share it with you,' added Aggorine, placing a gentle hand on Varac's arm. He did not pull away from her touch this time and his moaning ceased. Gradually he lifted his face towards them looking intently from one to the other.

'Share your happiness?' he murmured. 'I don't know what you mean. I have had no such experience before. Never in my whole life have I met people like you who show concern for the welfare of others, as you did for me when we first met, and who seem to have such a capacity for happiness, even in the face of danger, as you have just displayed so vividly. What is more, no-one has ever offered me a share of their own personal joy as you young people have this morning. Your attitude to life is so different from that of Haon under whose influence our people have been for so long. We have been made to believe that to survive is all that matters, and that there is nothing else to life beyond self-preservation and power over the other fellow and over the material world. Haon and his subjects have bent all their energies to master the mysteries of nature, not simply to use nature's power to improve their physical well-being, but also because they believe that power over nature will lead them ultimately to an understanding of the meaning of life itself. In the short time I have known you young people from beyond the most westerly wall, I have begun to realise that for all their knowledge, their technological skill and they physical prowess, the Haonites are totally incapable of experiencing the sort of happiness and joy in each other's company that you are able to do so readily and with such warmth.'

Varac, still visibly shaken though much more composed, slowly raised himself to his feet, helped by Shimah's strong arm. 'I still cannot understand how you can be so calm and apparently carefree, knowing that you are in mortal danger from the power of Haon,' he said, 'but' – and his face broke into an embarrassed smile – 'I believe I am learning a little about your peculiar ways. More and more I am coming to understand you and, whereas I was very interested, even intrigued by your attitude to life when we were talking together in my house, now I am beginning to experience some of that attitude myself. Previously I felt your quest was no more than a mad-cap scheme, doomed to certain failure, but now I begin to appreciate that, because you believe it can be a success, there is a distinct chance that it will be.'

As his words poured out, the tension eased and, gradually at first, then suddenly with all the enthusiasm they had displayed before, they once more began to laugh and shout and jig about. This time Varac was the prime mover. Grasping Yma's hands he whirled her round and round shouting at the top of his voice, 'Haon is a fool, Haon is a fool, Haon is a fool and a great big fool!'

They danced until, once more exhausted, they collapsed on the grass. For some time no words passed between them. The warmth of their friendship was enough. There was complete harmony that morning on the plateau beyond the dark and tortuous passageway through which the friends had passed the night before.

15

Not one of the six was enjoying the relaxed atmosphere more than Lekhar but it was she, with her logical, ordered mind who eventually roused them and brought them back to the reality of their situation.

Looking at Aggorine, she said, 'What now? – Don't you think we ought to be up and going?' Aggorine raised herself on one elbow, blinking in the morning light which was, by now, quite brilliant.

'I suppose we ought,' she replied with a definite degree of reluctance in her voice. And then, realising the implied urgency in Lekhar's question she added more positively, 'Yes, of course. Come on you lazy lot, we've got a job to do!' and with a gentle push and a none-too-gentle prod here and there she succeeded in marshalling her troops despite a deal of good-natured bantering.

Being now in a more serious frame of mind Lekhar suggested they should take stock of their new situation.

'When we decided to make for this plateau,' she reminded them, 'we said we would take an important decision when we reached it and I believe we should waste no more time now that we are here. The first thing to do is to explore the area and to base our future action on what we find.'

Not waiting to see if Lekhar had any further points to make, the headstrong Shimah leapt to his feet shouting, 'Come on then. The sooner we decide to search out Haon's headquarters, the better. I'm all for a direct approach – a frontal attack if you like. We all know Ecila is out there somewhere and we can guess what danger she is in, danger which must be increasing as each day passes. She must be rescued!'

Looking admiringly at her brother, with his fine physique, Aggorine momentarily believed that Shimah could, in fact, confront and overcome the greatest of evils, storm Haon's citadel and rescue Ecila single-handed. But she brought him gently back to earth by suggesting that it would be prudent to spend a little time scouting around as Lekhar had suggested, and then to act together.

'Well, if we must! But let's get on with it!' Shimah acquiesced reluctantly.

The plateau stretched before them for several kilometres towards the east and varied in width from about two to four kilometres at a rough estimation. To examine it entirely would demand considerable time and energy so it was decided that they should make their way along the northern edge where they would get more advantage from the warmth of the sun. In fact the general atmosphere of the whole place was one of comparative warmth and peace. Surrounded as it was by high and almost vertical cliffs it was protected on all sides from long-term extremes of weather conditions. For the original inhabitants, all those years ago, it must have been a most sheltered and agreeable place in which to live, and it was easy to imagine how they must have struggled to defend their homes against the power of the Haonic forces, and what a devastating change must have taken place in their way of life as they were forced away from their beloved plateau to live in abject slavery under the heel of their evil oppressors.

The six friends, rested after their night-time trek and refreshed by the sheer beauty of the plateau, made good time towards a landmark pointed out by Varac. He had spied what he thought were the remains of the original settlement, nestling under one of the taller of the sheer cliffs to the north. As they approached they could indeed make out the shapes of what had been buildings, now overgrown and in ruins. It was a sizeable town which they eventually entered and they could still make out most of the street pattern. There were no major buildings except one which was sited in what was clearly the main square and was probably the administrative centre. Apart from that, the houses were obviously quite modest in size and structure, catering for what must have been a contented and homely people.

A great feeling of sadness overtook the friends as they stood in what was once the centre of the town, now just a ghostly skeleton, with no vestige of life. No words were exchanged but they each knew how the others felt standing where those feet of years gone by had trod while the inhabitants went about their daily business. No doubt their way of life had been serene, living close to the soil in this beautiful place; their only possible enemy, the climate, which at this altitude must vary considerably from season to season, even though the massive ring of mountains would have sheltered them from the worst extremes. In their imagination the friends who now stood amongst the ruins, conjured up a picture of a happy, peaceful community, quite self-contained and with no desire to quarrel with anyone, nor yet to impose their ideas and way of life on others – a haven of peace protected from hostile surroundings by the mountains. Suddenly their lives had been shattered, as Varac had reported to the friends, by the forces of Haon. Their town had been pillaged and the people either exterminated or taken for slave labour to work for the power-crazy invaders.

Tears welled up in Yma's eyes as these thoughts went through her mind and, as if to offer some comfort to those who had suffered so long ago and also to express her own feelings, she put her beloved flute to her lips and played a beautiful, sensitive lament for those long gone from this place which had been their home.

The music stirred the emotions of all the group, first to a deep sympathy and sadness and then to anger. Shimah, feeling near to tears himself and, perhaps, not wanting to display the fact, suddenly jumped up and banged his fist violently against what had possibly once been the doorpost of a house, now covered with moss and lichen. Ignoring his self-inflicted pain he burst out with an intense denunciation of the one who had caused such suffering.

'Haon did this! Haon killed these people! – What can we do to him which would punish him enough!'

He turned away from the others, not wanting them to see the anguish on his face and that he was not only thinking of the long-gone villagers but of little Ecila, even now in Haon's power. His mood broke the reverie and the tenor of Yma's music changed subtly but then dramatically. Anger and resentment were in every note she now played and she rose to her full height, moving first this way and then that, now striking a defensive pose and now one of attack, matching her music to the attitude she adopted. The others watched as her expressive music and her lithe figure played out for them their own hatred of the evil forces which had wreaked such havoc on what had been a haven of peace all those years ago. Yma's eyes were flashing and her face flushed as she sank to rest after her emotional outpouring. Her performance had stimulated the others into action and together, when Yma was rested, they quit the place which had stirred them so.

They made their way towards the eastern end of the northern cliffs, hoping to find a pass which would take them on what Varac told them should be the final stage of their journey, to Haon's headquarters. But after searching and surveying the whole length of the eastern ridge until it was almost too dark to see, they had to admit defeat. No pass through or over the mountains could be found.

'Perhaps the morning will bring the solution,' said Aggorine, though not with much conviction in her voice. Somewhat disheartened, the others grunted their obvious doubts. 'We've come this far,' she went on, 'and we're jolly well not going to fall at this, nor any other hurdle,' – trying to rally their flagging spirits. 'We'll get to Haon even if it means sprouting wings and flying over the mountain!'

Her words of encouragement certainly made them all feel a bit more confident and, it being a balmy night, they went back some half a kilometre to a sheltered, grassy area they had noticed a while ago, and settled down to sleep and wait for the dawn. What seemed to be an insurmountable hurdle at the end of a long day, could, perhaps, be cleared in the morning in some way not yet apparent.

Aggorine however found she couldn't sleep, her mind actively searching for a practical solution to their problem. But none came and she tried to switch her mind off and get to sleep. For the comfort of it, as she lay on her back, she thrust her hands deep into the pockets of the Haonic style uniform they had all acquired from the baggage compartment of the train. In her right pocket her hand found and clasped the stone which had been the gift of Elcaro. It was warm to the touch and gave Aggorine a good deal of pleasure, and before she fell asleep, a smile lit up her face as if she had realised that perhaps their problem would be solved by calling on the resources of Elcaronic power. Elcaro had indeed promised to sustain and help the young people on their journey, especially when they found that even their outstanding skills and intelligences were not equal to the task before them.

They were all awake early to a beautiful dawn. The supply of 'magic' food which had so mysteriously been provided throughout their journey, once more appeared on a nearby flat green area between two large boulders. Apart from being most satisfying, what they found so surprising was that, in spite of its unchanging appearance it never became boring. It was as if the nature and even the taste of the silver balls always matched their appetites, and with a little imagination they could have been eating one or other of their favourite conventional meals as they consumed their silver packets of energy.

As they breakfasted, sitting around in a circle Lekhar first broached the subject of the mountain wall which had failed to throw up a suitable pass or pathway the day before. It appeared that she, like Aggorine, before she fell asleep, had been comforted by the thought that Elcaro might help solve the problem. Lekhar, the logical thinker, had to accept that many of the happenings along the way had been beyond her understanding and she had fully accepted that, what she could only describe as 'supernatural forces' had been shown to exist. So she was the one that morning to propose that they should try to communicate with Elcaro and ask for guidance.

Aggorine was not a little surprised to hear Lekhar's suggestion, but equally she was delighted to find that she had not been the only one of the group whose thoughts had turned to Elcaro in the night. She brought out from her pocket her own Elcaronic stone and stretched out her hand towards the centre of the circle. The others followed her example, the five stones lying on their five hands at the axis of the human wheel. Imagine their dismay when they realised that no glow nor warmth were appearing in the stones, even after waiting some time. It was then that they became aware of the fact that Varac had quietly removed himself from the circle of friends and was standing apart, looking disconsolately at the others. Having no token from Elcaro as the others had, he felt very much an outsider, and had crept away to leave them on their own as they tried to listen to Elcaro's advice. Realising that Varac's withdrawal had temporarily severed the friendly relationship between them, Aggorine was quick to try to put things right. She rose and went to fetch him.

'Come,' she said, 'Elcaro wants you to know all that we are

to learn from him. Do not break away from us. Have we not proved that we are firm friends and are walking along this route together?'

She took his hand and brought him to the others who welcomed him back with warmth and made a place for him in their group. Now as they sat in silence and contemplation, no vestige of sorrow remained on Varac's face. Instead his face shone and tears of happiness welled up in his eyes. These young people cared so much for him that they were prepared to share with him their precious relationship with the benevolent Elcaro.

Again, as before, no words were spoken but their common problem was presented to Elcaro through their thoughts. This time into their minds came the disturbing message that they should go no further. The physical dangers of the journey would become greater and greater and the influence of Haon would increase to such an extent that there was a possibility of their being forced to succumb, particularly as Haon would almost certainly threaten to destroy Ecila, should the others not surrender.

'You must stay here and wait,' seemed to be what Elcaro was advising.

They broke up in silence and each wandered away aimlessly, quite bewildered by the strange advice which had come to them from Elcaro. They had expected to hear of a way to surmount the remaining obstacles which lay between them and Haon, but instead they were to remain inactive and wait here on the plateau. But wait for what? Elcaro had given no hint as to why they should wait or for what, except that it would be too dangerous to move on further.

But had they not faced up to dangers already? Were they now, at the last fence, to be denied the chance of clearing it and reaching their goal? They all found it very puzzling and not a little frustrating. They had been prepared to accept the risks involved in their quest, especially after their first contact with Elcaro at the beginning, when they had been promised help from him. And now it seemed Elcaro was not prepared to help them any more. Were they being left to fend for themselves? Had Elcaro really deserted them?

They, all five, were falling deeper into the depths of despondency, not knowing what to do and hating the prospect of inactivity and waiting for the unknown. All of them were downcast, but Shimah especially so. Shimah, the athlete, the headstrong, capable young man who still felt within himself that he was able to meet and overcome all physical barriers and dangers, particularly in order to rescue Ecila, he it was who eventually turned from despondency to anger. Kicking the stones in his path and picking them up to hurl at some imagined target, he eventually gave vent to his feelings, shouting vengeance on Haon and all his works. Stopped now in his tracks he faced the impenetrable eastern wall which rose sheer from the ground about half a kilometre from their overnight resting place. He spread his arms wide and high and yelled to Haon to do his worst, he was ready to do battle!

The other four ran to Shimah, knowing his patience had snapped. Strangely they were not able to get close to him but stopped short some metres from him. He turned sharply towards his friends, some fire having now gone out of his anger, and with renewed tears of anguish running down his cheeks, he looked at each one of them and, as if it was tearing his very being apart to utter the words, he said quite deliberately, 'Elcaro has failed us but I am not finished with this journey yet. You can stay here if you like, but I am going on. Somehow, with or without Elcaro I will scale those cliffs, rescue Ecila, or die in the attempt.'

Both Aggorine and Oj made as if to move towards Shimah but he took a defensive step backwards, holding both his hands in front of him to stop them coming further.

'Don't try to stop me,' he said quietly. 'My mind is made up,' and without another word he turned from them and strode away towards the cliffs.

'We must stop him, he will destroy himself,' wept Aggorine. 'What can we do?' She looked from one to the other for help but she knew that once Shimah had decided on a course of action, whatever the consequences, only he himself could alter his decision by careful thought and analysis of the situation. Right now he was in no condition to take a rational view of his actions. She broke down and sank to the ground while the others, equally distressed tried to comfort her.

'O Elcaro, what have you done to us?' she wailed. 'Why is it that you seem to have deserted us? Please, please if you are still concerned for us, bring Shimah back.'

142

Oj put his strong arm around her and held her close. He tried hard to find words of comfort and, when eventually he gave expression to them he was surprised to hear himself saying, 'Elcaro has not deserted us. It must be we who have not understood the message. Shimah will be safe, I am sure – we must recover our trust in Elcaro.'

The others had heard his words and found comfort themselves in them. But what was the meaning of Elcaro's insistence that they should go no further? The question was now buzzing in each of their minds but it was razor-sharp Lekhar who suggested a simple answer.

'We are not to approach Haon any more closely because Elcaro must know that Haon will approach us! It's really quite straightforward,' she said excitedly and with as much satisfaction as if she had just solved one of her most complicated mathematical problems. 'I am sure I'm right,' she added, to give further strength to her argument.

At first the others were reluctant to accept such an obvious statement but they all had a great respect for Lekhar's reasoning powers and, though at first without much conviction, but soon quite readily, they found themselves agreeing with her, and furthermore their mood changed dramatically from despair to confidence once more.

'But when and how will Haon come?' Yma said, expressing the query in all their minds.

'Who knows?' replied Lekhar. 'I expect Elcaro has left us to work out that problem for ourselves. We shall have to prepare for the unexpected and be quite clear how we are to act if and when he appears. We should waste no time as we have no idea how much time we have. I suggest we have a council, Aggorine, and you are the best one to set it going and to keep us in order!' – she smiled at her little teasing remark and Aggorine, now almost herself again, managed a smile in return.

'But what about Shimah?' she asked.

'Shimah? I am sure he will be back with us before long,' retorted Oj, who had been watching the departing figure of Shimah in the distance. He saw that his friend had almost reached the foot of the sheer cliff and could just make out that he had begun to hesitate, casting first this way and then that for a pathway forward. Oj could imagine the frustration which Shimah was experiencing and he expected that eventually frustration would burst into anger again, but anger with himself this time, not with Elcaro. Then the anger would give way to a calmer appreciation of the difficulties facing him if he continued to try to go it alone – and Shimah would then remember his friends and, when he was ready to swallow his pride, he would return to them. He would find them in a much more confident frame of mind than when he left them, and would himself be able and anxious to add his ideas to their plans for the reception they would provide for Haon.

While all this was happening, Varac had not been with the five friends. Where was he now? They searched for him but to no avail. He had disappeared! They called his name but the only response they got was the echo from the distant cliffs.

'Well, Lekhar,' said Aggorine, 'you warned us to be prepared for the unexpected as far as Haon was concerned, but here we are, already faced with another sort of unpleasant surprise. Where *can* Varac have gone, and how was it that not one of us saw him go? I can't believe that he has decided to desert us. We had become such close friends so why should he leave us without a word?'

'Perhaps he thought it was his presence with us that caused Elcaro to leave us apparently to our own devices,' said Yma. 'If you remember, we were so downhearted ourselves for a long time, thinking that we had indeed been denied Elcaro's help, that Varac could have come to the conclusion that he was the problem and have decided to break away from us in the hope that Elcaro would then help us again. It was some time before we realised that we were not interpreting Elcaro's advice correctly, and by that time Varac would have gone.'

'You may be right,' said Lekhar, 'but that still doesn't explain how and where he has gone. If he has indeed decided to sacrifice himself for our benefit, and sacrifice it would be, for he would stand little chance of returning to safety to his own town on his own, the sooner we find him, the better.'

'But we have searched and called for ages already,' said Aggorine. 'What else can we do?'

'Well,' replied Lekhar, 'put yourself in his position. If you had convinced yourself that it was you preventing the group's progress, and that the only answer was for you to leave, would you reply to the shouts, having found somewhere to hide until the coast was clear and you could make good your final escape?

Of course you wouldn't!' She paused and looked in all directions over the plateau. 'We may have searched already,' she continued, 'but there must be hundreds of places we have missed. Come on Aggorine, what do you say to a further search before it gets dark? Yma? Oj, what do you say?'

'But what about Shimah?' said Aggorine. 'If he returns and finds us gone, what then? He will feel deserted himself.'

'Then one of us must stay here while the others search,' said Lekhar. 'I will stay and I suggest we fix a time for us all to reassemble here. It will have to be here, because Shimah may not have returned by the time we arrange and I couldn't then leave, to meet up with you at some other location.'

So it was agreed. There were only four hours of daylight left and therefore the rendezvous time was set half an hour before dark, which gave just three and a half hours for the search.

Oj was not at all happy at the prospect of Lekhar being left on her own, but she was determined, and reassured them that she would be quite safe. 'I can find plenty with which to occupy myself,' she said brightly. 'It will give me an opportunity to examine the rock formation around here and I haven't yet had a chance to use my little laser analyser. So don't worry about me, I shall be quite happy pottering around!'

Oj was still not very pleased at the arrangement and he couldn't get it out of his head that Elcaro had warned them to keep together as much as possible. Already Shimah had gone off somewhere on his own, Varac had disappeared, and now they were going to leave Lekhar isolated. What if Aggorine, Yma and he himself became separated while seeking for Varac? If that should happen, they would indeed be in trouble and very vulnerable.

16

As if they were all of one mind Yma, Aggorine and Oj made off
in the direction of the ruins of the old town which had so
affected them earlier and yet had intrigued them by its
atmosphere of peace. Years before there must have been
tragedy and violence in its buildings and its streets, but all was
peaceful know. They reached the centre after some half hour's
walking. They could have made it sooner but they had, on the
way, made several diversions into a variety of rock formations
thinking perhaps to find Varac hiding in one of them. On
reaching the town centre, still without sight or sound of Varac,
and standing there in the midst of the ancient ruins, the three
friends did not experience the sadness which had oppressed
them all when they had first stood in the place. Instead they
were each struck by a strange fear, as if they had unwittingly
been caught in a trap set and operated by an evil power.
Instinctively and cautiously they backed against the remains of
what had been some sort of monument or idol marking the
centre of the square. Their eyes flashed around them trying to
see the source of the fear which had come so suddenly upon
them. But nothing was to be seen and no sound could be heard.
  'What is it?' whispered Yma. 'I'm scared – but I don't
know why.'
  'So am I,' replied Aggorine and Oj together.
  Oj, standing between the girls, spread his arms across them
as if to protect them. 'There's something here which wasn't
here when we came before,' he said in a whisper which was
barely audible. 'We had better beat a retreat as fast as we can.'
  'Wait,' said Aggorine. 'Remember that Elcaro's advice was
to wait on the plateau, and we all agreed that meant we might
expect a confrontation with Haon, or, if not Haon himself, then
someone sent by him. – Perhaps it's about to happen!'
  'At least let us find a less exposed place where we can observe

146

whatever might happen and yet at the same time feel a little more secure. Into that ruined building – quick about it.' Oj moved rapidly, matching his actions to his words. The girls were quick to follow him and in next to no time they found themselves inside what had once been a spacious building. With what remained of the walls surrounding them, they each felt more secure and gradually the fear which had gripped them moments before subsided and after about ten minutes had elapsed with nothing untoward happening, they began to wonder if it wasn't just the tragic atmosphere of the old town which had caused them to react as they had. Much more relaxed now, Aggorine was just about to suggest that perhaps after all they should not wait here but beat a retreat as Oj had advised, when they became aware of some movement in the far corner of the square. Immediately they were on the alert once more and, peering through cracks in the wall they each waited with bated breath to discover what it was which was moving about in the otherwise town of the dead.

Gradually five figures emerged from the mouth of one of the alleyways leading onto the square, and as they came out into the open it became clear that four were Haonite soldiers in uniforms precisely like those worn by the soldiers who had given Varac such a roughing-up just before the five friends had made contact with him. The soldiers were walking on either side of the fifth person who seemed to need their support. He was limping and the soldiers had to half carry him as they moved together towards the open square where they came more clearly into view.

Oj realised it first and hissed, 'It's Varac! – They've got Varac and he's hurt!' He turned to the girls and, with flashing eyes and clenched fists, he repeated in a long-drawn out whisper, 'They've captured him – they've got Varac!' and it was as much as Aggorine and Yma could do to stop him rushing out to try to rescue their friend.

'The odds are too great,' Aggorine interjected. 'We'd do neither Varac nor ourselves any good by trying anything now.'

'At least he's still alive,' interjected Yma. 'Let's see what happens now.' And although Oj was still seething with rage and wanting to take positive action, the girls' advice prevailed and they returned to their observation of the strange events taking place in the square.

The soldiers had put Varac on a flat boulder near the centre of the square and two of them had taken up positions close by him, presumably to guard against any attempt he might make to escape; a completely unnecessary precaution judging from the fact that Varac had obviously received injuries which made him incapable of moving without assistance. The other two settled down some way away and became engrossed in a quite animated conversation, from time to time glancing in Varac's direction and indicating him with outstretched arms. Were they discussing what they should do to him? – Were the three friends about to witness a gruesome act of execution? That thought made Oj quite determined to rush to the defence of his friend, should the soldiers make any belligerent moves towards Varac. Whatever they were discussing and whatever plans they were making, they were certainly in no hurry.

It seemed like an age, but in reality only ten or fifteen minutes had elapsed since the Haonite soldiers had arrived with Varac, when the next scene in the drama unfolded. Suddenly, overhead, something strange approached – a spherical capsule, similar to that which the friends had seen previously, as they hid in the mouth of the tunnel leading to the power complex. It came to rest on the far side of the square. Immediately Varac was lifted bodily by the soldiers and carried towards the strange craft which seemed to absorb its extra five passengers without any apparent hatchway being opened. No sooner had the embarkation been completed than the transport capsule rose and disappeared from view faster than eye could follow towards the mountains at the eastern end of the plateau.

Oj could not be restrained now and he rushed out into the square, peering into the sky in the direction the strange craft had taken.

'They've got him!' he yelled. 'They've taken him away to their headquarters and now we shan't see him again!'

He was quite devastated, sinking to his knees and burying his head in his hands. He had come to like and admire Varac, and to think of him now being a captive in the hands of the Haonites, and probably destined to be tortured by them was more than he could stand.

'Why did you stop me trying to rescue him?' he burst out at Yma and Aggorine. 'At least I could have shared whatever fate

148

has in store for him.'

'Calm down, Oj,' murmured Aggorine. 'We too have lost a friend, remember. The odds were too overwhelming and you know it,' she added more forcefully. 'Come now, we must face this new situation and live in the hope that wherever they have taken Varac we shall eventually find him and maybe by some miracle he will survive any interrogation and torture to which his captors may subject him.'

Reluctantly Oj rose to his feet his face still registering his deep sense of grief for the loss of his friend. Gradually he turned towards the east and drawing himself up to his full height he flung his clenched fists into the air, his head went back and his eyes flashed as he shouted defiantly, 'Hold on Varac! Haon or no Haon, we are coming for you. – Hold on!'

With that he whirled round, taking a last look at the spot from which his friend had been spirited away, and made for the path which had brought them to the square. 'We must get back to the others,' he shouted. 'Come on you two!'

Yma and Aggorine, surprised at Oj's sudden change of mood, had difficulty in keeping up with him as he sped away in front of them. Fortunately both Aggorine and Yma could produce a fair turn of speed when absolutely necessary, and they managed to keep in touch with Oj without actually catching up with him. Soon they were within hailing distance of the place where they had left Lekhar, and the girls could hear Oj calling her name. He had slowed to a walk, presumably to be able to hear Lekhar's response and this allowed first Yma and then Aggorine to reach him. Now he stopped completely.

'Listen,' he said. 'We must listen for Lekhar.'

He called her name again but there was still no answering sound. Again he called, but still no reaction from Lekhar.

'Where can she be? Perhaps she's wandered off in search of rock specimens and is now too far away. Let's press on,' said Aggorine, and taking the lead again, suited her actions to her words. They all took off at a trot and within five minutes came to the area where they had agreed to rendezvous with Lekhar, and hopefully with Shimah, if he had returned from what they considered to have been a headstrong and fruitless journey to find a way out of the plateau over the eastern mountain wall. But there was no sign of either of them.

'Now what?' exclaimed Oj. 'First Shimah goes off, then Varac is captured and now Lekhar has taken it into her head to disappear! When do you two intend to vaporise?' he said rather flippantly, though in his heart he had a feeling of dread that their whole expedition was being torn apart by some influence beyond their present understanding.

His relief was unconfined when Yma exclaimed, 'There they are, over there towards the east! Look, there are two of them and they are coming this way. It *must* be Lekhar and Shimah.'

Oj leapt into the air as if to get a better view, but actually to give vent to his feelings. He let out a great roar and rushed off in the direction of the distant figures. The girls followed and it wasn't long before all five friends were reunited. Unashamedly they clasped each other by the hand and embraced, all talking at once, happy to be safely together again.

When the initial enthusiasm had passed, Shimah raised his voice to gain their attention and poured out his apologies for the trouble he had caused. 'How can you forgive me for being so angry and acting so foolishly in going off on my own?' he cried. 'I know now it was a wild goose chase and I could well have put you all in danger and have been the cause of our journey coming to a sticky end. What on earth possessed me I cannot tell.' His voice tailed off into nothing more than a whisper, and the others could only just hear him repeating Ecila's name over and over again. He seemed to have forgotten the others for a moment, as his deep sense of loss, and the frustration in not being able to spirit Ecila out of the hands of her captors got the better of him. There were tears in his eyes when Aggorine tried to comfort him with her arm around his shoulder.

Shimah looked at her and in a voice trembling with emotion he whispered, 'I have failed her, haven't I? – failed her – and I don't know what else to do.'

'Of course you haven't failed her,' replied Aggorine. 'We've all suffered a set-back, but we are together again and together we must go forward. Our goals remain the same: to be reunited with our dear Ecila and to confront Haon. At the moment we seem to be thwarted in both of those aims but we've had difficulties before and have been able to overcome them. I am sure our journey is not destined to end here. Don't forget that Elcaro advised us to await events and his advice has always helped us solve our problems up to now, so there is every reason to believe that we shall be shown how to extricate ourselves from the situation in which we now find ourselves. Take heart, old fellow, I am sure you will see Ecila again and perhaps sooner than any of us expects.'

Shimah rallied to Aggorine's encouraging words and with a simple, 'Sorry – yes, you're right,' he forced a smile.

'Tell us what you found when you went in search of a way over the eastern mountain,' said Oj, more to get Shimah back on the beam than to satisfy his curiosity.

Reluctantly at first, then with more of his old enthusiasm creeping into his voice, Shimah told them how the plateau ended most abruptly, to be replaced by near-vertical black cliffs which rose sheer from the ground to some thousand metres into the sky.

'I could see from the beginning, that in no way was I going to be able to climb that lot,' he said. 'My frustration and anger boiled over again and I literally beat my fists against the smooth rock and shouted my defiance of Haon and all his works until I was quite exhausted. I must have sunk down on the ground, completely whacked, and probably passed out, because the next thing I remember was hearing my name being called from a long way off. At first I couldn't remember where I was, but then, seeing the cliff wall, it all came back to me and I began to realise how foolish it had been to go off on my own and leave my friends behind. – But there was my name again! – was it coming from the mountain itself? I sprang to my feet facing the east and shouted a reply.

'Again the voice came "Shimah – Shimah!" Could it be Ecila calling me in some miraculous way? It was certainly a female's voice but I couldn't be sure from where it was coming. The echoes from the cliffs confused me and I spun round and round searching for a sight of the one who was calling. It was then that I saw Lekhar, a tiny figure in the distance. It was her voice coming quite strongly over the plateau. I have to admit that momentarily I was disappointed, but reason soon prevailed, and I realised it couldn't have been Ecila. No doubt Haon has by now made it impossible for her to communicate with us.

'My disappointment soon evaporated and was replaced by a sense of relief. Seeing Lekhar coming towards me – and I could see that she had heard my shout and located me for she was now running and waving her arms – I went to meet her. The frustration remained, – and still does, come to that – but I wasn't angry any more. When eventually we reached each other Lekhar fell into my arms – or I into hers – both of us puffing and panting. All I remember her saying between puffs was, "Thank goodness I've found you." I couldn't find any words to express my feelings except that I remember calling her by name several times and saying, "Thank you – thank you."

'On the way back here Lekhar told me how you had discovered that Varac had disappeared and how you had decided to make a search for him leaving Lekhar at the rendezvous spot in case I returned. How grateful I am for that! – She told me too that she had become convinced that she should come to look for me, knowing that she had to be back alone or with me before you other three returned from your search. And how grateful I am for that decision too. She came just as my foolish pride might have got the better of me and made it very difficult indeed – possibly impossible for me to crawl back to you again. But here I am and, as Aggorine says, we are all together again, and I promise to try very hard not to go off on foolish and self-motivated goose-chases any more!'

Shimah's return and his pouring out of his story had done a great deal to restore the group to its normal deep sense of comradeship and friendship, and Oj, who had asked Shimah what he had found, felt it appropriate to bring the situation right up to date and recount their strange adventure in the old ruined town. Lekhar and Shimah listened attentively and with no little degree of amazement as first Oj, then Yma and Aggorine related details of their search for Varac and how they had seen the Haonite soldiers spirit him away in one of their strange crafts.

'So Varac is still alive,' observed Lekhar, 'but you say he was injured and the soldiers had literally to carry him.' She paused in thought. 'It seems odd,' she mused. 'Why should they bother about taking him alive back to the city of Haon? After all, to them he was only one of the subservient people from the satellite town. – Quite expendable to Haon I would have thought. – Strange, very strange' – and her voice tailed off as her mind became deeply involved in trying to find a logical reason for the soldiers' behaviour.

'Perhaps Haon was looking for us and gave instructions that Varac should be brought back for questioning,' said Oj. 'It seems a reasonable explanation to me.'

'You may be right,' conceded Lekhar, 'but I have a feeling that there is a deeper significance in Varac's disappearance and subsequent journey with the soldiers, but at the moment I cannot for the life of me think what it can be.'

'Well, whatever the answer might be, I for one am feeling quite exhausted,' said Aggorine. 'It will soon be dark and I suggest we find a sheltered spot to rest for the night. Tomorrow things might become clearer.'

Yma had already made her way towards an outcrop of rocks where a huge overhang offered a cave-like refuge which would give them all the shelter they needed. The dramatic events of the day had taken their toll of the energy and verve of all of them, and soon they lay sprawled out on the soft ground ready for sleep to renew their strength. But sleep wouldn't come. Their bodies were tired but their minds were still active, each pursuing his or her own train of thought. Eventually Yma raised her flute to her pursed lips and poured soothing music into the night air. As she played, anxiety drained away from their minds to be replaced with a warm feeling of comradeship. It was as if Yma's music spread protecting and comforting arms around them until one by one they fell asleep, once more completely at peace and sure in their heart of hearts that all would eventually come right.

17

They slept soundly, blissfully unaware of what was in store for them when they woke. The morning light was just painting the peaks of the mountains to the west of them when Oj roused himself from sleep and suddenly became aware of the fact that they were not alone. Quickly he woke the others and together they gazed in amazement and considerable apprehension at the scene confronting them. There were at least ten Haonite soldiers standing in two lines between the five friends and one of the strange craft which they had seen before, one of which had spirited Varac away.

Though no words were spoken, it was clear that the intention was that they were to board the craft. At first both Shimah and Oj were for making a fight of it but Aggorine laid a restraining hand on each of their shoulders.

'There are too many of them' she whispered. 'Let's see what happens.'

The soldiers stood impassively, hardly moving a muscle, not seeming to be concerned in the slightest that the five were now fully awake and actively discussing the situation confronting them. But their very presence in such strength made any attempt at escape out of the question.

Eventually Aggorine took the initiative once more. 'We have no option,' she declared. 'It is clear we are required to go with them and as they could so easily have dealt with us while we slept it also seems clear that for the moment they mean us no harm. Let us go quietly and with dignity.'

Turning to face the two lines of soldiers she drew herself up to her full and imposing height, tossed her beautiful brown curly head and with the suggestion of a smile in her large, dark eyes she addressed them with all the confidence she could muster. 'Whether you understand me or not, I would like to thank you very much for finding us in this plateau from which

154

there seemed to be no escape. We will gladly come with you and we look forward to meeting the leaders of your people of the mountains.' With that she went towards the transport craft, followed immediately by the other four.

As the little procession moved forward the soldiers, as one man raised their right hands in what could only be understood as a salute. Encouraged by their gesture, the spirits of the five young people rose considerably. The polite behaviour of their captors meant that whoever had given them their orders had insisted on the group being treated with respect. Nevertheless the escorting soldiers closed in around the sides and rear of the little procession as it came closer to the awaiting craft, like sheepdogs enfolding a flock.

There didn't appear to be any specific doorway through which they passed, but one minute they were outside and the next they were all enclosed and seated most comfortably. The soldiers had all come aboard with them and they too took seats around the group, presumably to keep an eye on them, though there was not one vestige of emotion to be seen on any of their faces.

The eyes of the five friends were everywhere, trying to take stock of the interior of the strange craft. It was not like anything they had experienced before. There seemed to be no formal shape or structure. The walls, if they could be called walls, were more or less spherical and appeared to be made of a pink soft material which glowed warmly and gave illumination to the whole of the interior. Everything they touched was made of a spongy yet resilient material, and the whole atmosphere created by the interior of the craft was almost one of ethereal well-being. All five friends felt happy and contented, despite the fact that they were now prisoners of the Haonite soldiers who were surely escorting them into the presence of the one they dreaded most, their arch enemy Haon himself.

As they sat, quite relaxed, one sharp command was uttered by the person they took to be the captain of the ship, and they all expected it to be a signal to start the engines and get airborne. But no engine noise could be detected. Instead an even greater calm and silence fell on all of them, and each experienced a feeling of tremendously close affinity with the others in the body of this most remarkable form of transport. It was as if they had lost their own individuality and integrated with all the others into a common body. There was no sense of panic, no desire to fight what was happening, just a gentle sense of floating, with a complete inability to do anything about it! The whole pleasurable experience seemed to last only a very short while before a second sharp command restored them all to something akin to normality. Bemused, the five friends looked at each other as if to assure themselves that, despite their inexplicable experience, they were still alive and back in full possession of their individual faculties.

Aggorine made as if to rise to her feet, intending to demand an explanation from the soldier nearest to her but she was silenced by the sudden raising of his hand. Nothing was said but she knew she had to wait to ask her questions. First they would presumably move to disembark, and they all waited for the soldiers to escort them back to the outside world, wondering all the while what it would be like and who would be there to meet them. But while they waited for some hidden door to open in the pink sphere which enclosed them, suddenly their whole surroundings changed. The craft in which they had travelled so mysteriously, equally mysteriously disappeared, leaving its whole pay-load of passengers standing on solid ground once more!

The shock of their disembarkation was such as to make it virtually impossible for them immediately to take stock of their surroundings, but when they had come to themselves they saw that they were in a large courtyard almost surrounded by grey stone-built walls towering high on three sides but with one side completely open. The soldiers had by now formed up into a line between them and the open side of the square and the impression each of the five friends had was that this was indeed the soldiers' barracks, and that at any moment they would be ushered into the presence of their commanding officer, or whoever it was who had ordered their capture.

The moments passed without any apparent activity and they were able to form a clearer picture of their surroundings. Beyond the line of soldiers could be seen great mountains outlined by even more magnificent snow-capped peaks in the distance. The five friends could not but be awe-struck by the view. The rugged beauty of the scene before them was quite breath-taking. Though they couldn't see the terrain beyond the walls of the buildings on the other three sides of the square, they had no doubt that it was similar and probably just as impressive. What was certain, however, was the fact that they had been transported miraculously from the comparatively low-lying plateau to which Varac had led them and where they had been advised by Elcaro to await events, over the mountainous peaks into the very heart of the realm of Haon. What awaited the five friends here was as yet a complete mystery. Their early encounters with Haonic forces led all of them to suspect the worst but they were not finished yet. Even as they stood waiting for the next move, confidence and courage began to return to them and turning to each other with gestures of comradeship, and smiles of friendship coming back to their faces, they knew that together they would face up to any ordeal with high hopes that, against all odds, their mission would be accomplished.

18

Despite their efforts to put a brave face on their predicament, the five friends, standing in the centre of the courtyard, guarded on the one open side by the phalanx of soldiers, and overshadowed by the high stone walls on the other three, made a pathetic little group. Still dressed in the clothes they had taken as disguise from the transport module when they left the power complex, and still wearing the caps to hide the conducting string hair nets, they looked and felt quite bedraggled. This pathetic group of young people who had had the temerity to invade the territory of the powerful and tyrannical leader of the eastern mountains region, now stood on the threshold of the encounter with Haon which they had all been seeking and yet dreading at the same time. They had no weapons, no power, no influence, and yet they still hoped for the success of their mission to free Ecila and to overcome Haon's power and scientific superiority in the control of the natural forces.

They gathered close to each other for comfort and support, waiting for the next move. Shimah, of the five, was the most agitated. His deep concern for Ecila stirred his mind into activity. Could she be a prisoner in these very buildings? How had she stood up to the treatment of her captors? Had her confinement affected her attitude to life – and to him in particular? These disturbing questions kept running through his head.

'Why do they keep us waiting here?' he eventually burst out, and turning to the soldiers he shouted, 'Come on, get on with whatever it is you have to do with us!' and he punched the air in his frustration. The soldiers remained unmoved but, as if in answer to Shimah's demand, a door was flung open in the centre of the building remote from the open end of the courtyard and an imposing figure of a man emerged, flanked by a soldier on either side. He must have stood all of two metres tall and was dressed in military uniform of a cut and design quite different from that of the rank and file soldiers. His uniform and bearing marked him out as an officer, and one of considerable rank. He approached the five friends without displaying emotion of any sort on his face, neither indicating any of his own feelings towards them nor what he intended to do to them.

Expecting the worst, the young people were surprised and not a little relieved when the officer halted in front of them and held out both his hands as if to encompass them all and said slowly but clearly in their own language, 'I have been sent to welcome you to the city of Haon, our great ruler. Follow me.'

With that he turned on his heel and made once more for the open door through which he had emerged. Absolutely astonished, the five friends looked at each other in disbelief. The welcome had been the last thing they had expected but it had done their spirits a deal of good. With much lighter steps than they had thought they would ever tread again they followed Aggorine's lead and trailed after their new-found host.

Aggorine caught up with the officer and managed to catch his eye and say, 'Thank you for your kind welcome.'

He retorted, 'Do not thank me, I am under orders to receive you.'

'Thank you all the same,' she replied. 'It is very kind of you to receive us and welcome us.'

'Kind?' he queried. 'What is "kind"? – I am only carrying out orders. You will follow me.'

The officer spoke very deliberately, obviously having difficulty in finding the right words in the language of the plains. But he had made himself understood, and continued into the inner recesses of the building with the group of five tagging on behind.

After six flights of stairs and several corridors, the little procession reached its destination. Rapping on the door the officer waited the invitation to enter before ushering his charges into the room. He did not follow but closed the door behind them leaving them to discover that, despite the voice which invited them to enter, they were quite alone in a large room. It was furnished only with a long table to which twelve chairs were drawn and on which was a most appetising spread, food such as the travellers had not seen since their brief stay with Varac in the satellite town. There were windows along the side opposite the door through which they had come and all five, despite the temptation to sample the food, made straight for these to try to get an idea of where they were and what the Haonic city was like. All around as far as they could see were mountain peaks soaring into the clouds with no sign of habitation in the distance. Closer in however they could see a geometrically regular pattern of streets and houses, most of which were built to the same design. The inhabitants of the city could be seen moving about, mostly on foot, but a number of buses could be seen threading their way along the network of roads. The friends were surprised to notice that there were comparatively few smaller vehicles. The people of the city were obviously dependent on their own two feet or on the buses to get about the place.

'It all looks well organised,' observed Lekhar.

'Too well, if you ask me,' added Oj. 'I should have thought there was scope for variety, especially in the designs of the buildings. It all looks far too regimented for my liking.' He turned from the window remarking – 'Well, I suppose if that's how they like it, who are we to criticise? – Their food looks good to eat, in any case, and am I hungry!'

The other four clearly felt the same way and it wasn't long before they were tucking into the variety of dishes which had been prepared for them. When eventually even Oj had eaten enough they turned their attention to an examination of the room itself. There was little of comfort in the furnishings, and the walls were decorated with a matt paint of a pinkish tinge, while the ceiling was quite unadorned except for its white paint. Four simple pendant lights hung from the ceiling and the whole atmosphere of the room was one of workmanlike efficiency without any provision for relaxation. Everything was superbly clean and fresh, and the food they had eaten had been beautifully prepared.

They spent some time looking out of the windows again and, judging from what they could see, it was clear they were in a city of considerable size surrounded by massive mountain ranges which formed an almost impenetrable barrier between it and the outside world. The building they were in com-manded a view of the rooftops and streets below and they came to the conclusion that this was probably the dominant administration building of the city. The question in all their minds was, 'Did Haon live here, or had they been brought here en route to his headquarters?' Whatever the answer, it was certain that their destiny no longer lay in their own hands but in those of their captors. They could do nothing but await events.

They had been in the room approximately half an hour, and having fed well and taken stock of their surroundings, a mood of contemplation came upon them. Sitting around the table they each became bound up in their own thoughts, trying in their own individual ways to answer the questions, 'Why had Haon, once he had discovered them, allowed them to remain alive? He could so easily have rid himself of them as they slept on the plateau. And why were they being treated more as guests than as prisoners?'

They remembered their first violent encounter with the old man of the mountains, and the confrontation between him and Elcaro when they had been protected from his wrath by Elcaro's declaration that they held the secret of life, the secret which Haon would never possess unless the six friends decided to reveal it to him; then the journey through the mountains which they had been impelled to take, first by some mysterious power and then by the desire to rescue Ecila who had been so strangely spirited away from them.

There was no doubt that Haon had caught Ecila off guard in an intensely emotional and artistic mood. Then he had, by one of his technological tricks, separated her from her friends and since then had used her capture as a lure to ensure the remaining five would make their way into the heart of his domain. The ploy had certainly been successful. Here they all were, presumably within a short distance of the nerve-centre of Haon's world, and presumably also within a short time they would have another and perhaps final confrontation with Haon himself.

They were heartened by the certainty that, between them they possessed some knowledge which Haon intended to extract from them. Their lives would not be in danger until he had taken possession of that secret of life as he called it. Nevertheless all five of them knew that their powers of resistance were not unlimited and that some time or other they might be forced to give in.

But what was it that they had? – 'The secret of life?'

Aggorine didn't know. Yma didn't know. – Lekhar had tried to work it out but she didn't know, and Oj and Shimah, though so full of life, they didn't know either! So what was it? – Wherein lay the answer? As they all sat there in that bleak room thinking back over the past and speculating about their future, they each individually wished they knew, so that they could more easily deny Haon the knowledge he sought from them and which Elcaro had so clearly said they possessed!

It was Lekhar who broke the silence and found she was expressing the thoughts uppermost in all their minds when she burst out, 'Well what is life all about? – and why do we know the answer and old Haon doesn't?'

The other four were not a bit surprised to hear Lekhar pose the question they each had been thinking about, because the close friendship and affinity between them had developed to such a degree that often they had found recently that their very thoughts were moving along the same lines.

'I wish I knew,' chorused Oj and Shimah together and Aggorine indicated that she felt the same. Yma alone said nothing but rose from her chair, moved across to one of the windows and peered out across the city roof tops to the magnificent mountains beyond.

'How wonderful it is to be alive!' came eventually to her lips from deep down inside her. 'So much beauty in everything. Look at those mountain peaks, rising and falling like a massive musical score. Life is beautiful and to be able to appreciate and enjoy beauty is to begin to know what life is all about. – Perhaps that is part, at least, of what we possess which Haon does not.'

The others looked towards her and then came to group themselves around Yma to share the view of the mountains which had prompted her observation.

'It may not be logical, but it must be accepted as a distinct possibility,' said Lekhar. 'I don't see music written in the mountains but I admit to being moved by their grandeur. As I look at them I find pleasure in trying to work out how they were formed and what terrific forces must have been involved. To me their beauty lies in their structure and in the possibility of working out the mathematical explanation of those forces.'

Oj smiled and said, 'Yes, they are magnificent, aren't they? How wonderful it would be if one could find a way of conquering them by building bridges between them or boring tunnels through them. What enjoyment that would provide me! For me the mountains' beauty lies in the sheer practical problems involved in getting over or through them in the most efficient way. I suppose you all think that's a funny way to talk about beauty, but that's how I see it. For me there's great satisfaction and enjoyment in the actual doing of a job – and what a job the mountains would provide!'

'I don't think that's a funny aspect of beauty at all,' said Shimah, warming to the discussion. 'I think beauty also lies in action, with the satisfaction of a job well done.' He paused and half closed his eyes as he looked to the distant peaks and then continued, 'I see them as a wonderful challenge too, but I would get my happiness from scaling the highest of the peaks. The achievement would be beauty enough for me, but if Ecila could scale the heights with me she would show me the beauty of the natural world which always comes to life in her eyes and we would share our different concepts of beauty together, to our mutual ecstasy of enjoyment.' He turned away from the window. The mention of Ecila's name had brought Shimah down to earth and the immediate problem of her rescue. There was a suspicion of tears in his eyes when he added, 'If only we knew where she was!'

Aggorine, as always tried to comfort her brother. 'Soon, soon we shall know,' she whispered. 'Try to be patient a little longer.'

'You haven't heard what I see in the mountains yet,' she continued, turning herself once more to the view. 'I can understand how it is that we all see some different aspect of beauty out there, but it isn't just that exquisite view which prompts our emotions. Wherever we go and whoever we meet, our emotions are stimulated one way or another and I'm sure we can all recognise some beauty and some ugliness wherever we look. The mountains make me think of trips with friends into the valleys and lower slopes, of the warmth of the sun and of the smell of the flowers, the splashing of the streams over the rocks. That is a beautiful thought for me. But even more beautiful would be the satisfaction and joy it would give me to lead a party of young or old people into those valleys so that I could share their happiness in the beauty I would show them. That would be beauty for me in the mountains – a rather intangible thing, but to me quite wonderful.'

There was a silence between them as they each continued to savour what had come out of their little bit of self analysis, and a real sense of joy spread over them until they could contain themselves no longer and peals of happy laughter filled the room and must have echoed throughout the entire building. What a relief it was to realise that their spirits were proof against all misfortune! Though differing in interpretation, they all possessed the ability to discern beauty and to appreciate the close bond between them which this love of beauty nurtured. The joy which each experienced in his or her own perception of beauty was shared with the others and this sharing and caring for others cemented their friendship and enhanced the happiness they found in each other's company.

Was this, then, what life was all about? Could it be that the mountains themselves had begun to reveal to them the answer to the riddle?

When their laughter had subsided, Yma, somewhat breathlessly came out with a remark meant at first to be light-hearted but, once uttered, made them all raise a quizzical eyebrow and wonder if she hadn't in fact unwittingly hit upon a most important subject which might well affect their attitude to Haon when they eventually came face to face.

All she said was, 'I wonder if poor old Haon can see anything beautiful in the mountains?'

'Or in anything else at all?' added Lekhar, giving weight to the question. 'Perhaps that's what's wrong with him!'

'Maybe we shall soon have the chance to find out,' said Aggorine. 'They surely don't mean to leave us in this room for evermore, do they?'

As if in answer to her question, a voice, coming from beyond the door, broke into their discussion. In their own language, but rather stiffly, it said, 'You are to come out now and the guard on the door will show you to your quarters. You will find fresh clothes there, as it is assumed you require a change after your journey.'

The voice ended as abruptly as it had begun but the door now stood open and there, sure enough, was a soldier who had presumably been standing guard ever since they arrived. Without a word he gestured that they should follow him and turned on his heel and led them to the end of a long corridor.

The first door he opened was for the girls, as he clearly indicated. The boys were to occupy the room next door. Little as they liked being separated, there seemed no alternative but to go along with their guide's instructions.

Once inside their respective rooms, a quick survey showed them to be much more comfortably appointed than the room from which they had just come. Though retaining a somewhat austere overall appearance, there was a warmer feeling altogether, to which well-sprung armchairs, soft carpet and two or three occasional tables contributed. Furthermore each room was one of a suite. Each had a shower room, wash basins and toilet and there was a clean and comfortable bed provided for each occupant. Just as the voice had promised, the wardrobes were stocked with a variety of clothes not dissimilar to those they used to wear at home on the plains, and in a choice of sizes too.

It wasn't long before both the girls and the boys were revelling in the quite unexpected luxury of hot showers and clean clothes, and within an hour all traces of the old uniforms and remnants of their own clothes, including the anti-beta-ray headnets, for which there now seemed to be no further use, had been removed and all five were sporting the outfits of their choice.

Oj and Shimah, as may be expected had chosen trousers, shirts and pullovers, topped by soft leather jerkins. Oj's rig was in a medium brown colour which complemented his flaming red hair, while Shimah had chosen dark blue with flashes of red at the lapels and pocket which seemed to go well with his more effervescent nature. The transformation from the drabness of the uniform was quite dramatic and with a smile Shimah said, 'I don't think the girls will recognise us now!'

The three girls had understandably taken longer in choosing their outfits. For one thing, they had had more choice than Oj and Shimah, but they had also enjoyed the experience of trying on the variety of clothes available.

Eventually Aggorine settled for a smart mid-green combination of trousers, blouse and jacket which suited her admirably and gave her the effect she had wanted. The stand-up collar of the jacket framed her lovely face and showed off her immaculately symmetrical features to perfection. Her eyes, like dark amber pools, always beautiful, became even more the focus of any observer's attention, radiating to them her care and concern for their welfare, and at the same time, conveying to them a confidence in her ability to take charge of any problem with which they may be faced, and to lead them wisely and safely towards its solution. The whole outfit suggested beauty combined harmoniously with efficiency.

Lekhar had brushed her copper-coloured hair from her forehead and secured it with a green ribbon. She had chosen no frills, but now wore a severely-cut suit over a white shirt-type blouse. The jacket of the tan-coloured suit had three-quarter length sleeves which allowed the blouse sleeves to protrude. There she stood, waiting for the comments of her friends – complimentary or otherwise – and seeming to be saying, 'Well, where is the problem which needs solving?' She knew she looked attractive in quite a different way from that of the other two girls, and she felt very comfortable in the clothes she had chosen.

Yma was much longer in fitting herself out. She had brushed out her long dark brown hair which now reached below her shoulders and in which the reddish tinges had been highlighted by the luxurious shower she had had. She felt clean, warm and comfortable and quite feminine once again after the rigours of the journey. Trousers were not her choice, nor yet the well-cut suit which Lekhar was wearing. Her mood was for something soft and flowing. There was a long skirt which took her fancy, but in the end she chose a full-skirted dress of palest pink with long, tightly fitting sleeves to her wrists. 'Quite impractical,' she told herself, but nevertheless she kept it on and looked quite superb in it.

19

They had been given plenty of time to rid themselves of their drab gear and now they were all clean, fresh and clothed in much more attractive garments, the boys in their room and the girls in theirs began to get impatient in anticipation of the next move.

Eventually, without warning the boys were summoned with a peremptory order from the guard outside their door, and immediately afterwards the same command was issued to the three girls. Almost simultaneously, therefore, the five were reunited in the corridor, and there were exclamations of surprise and not a little admiration, as they each surveyed the transformations which their wash and brush-up had brought about. Smiles of pleasure and unreserved compliments were exchanged until the guard in his stilted and limited language of the plains brought them back to earth with an order to follow him. He had not reacted in anyway since he had first taken charge of them. There had been no smile nor yet a snarl, simply the indifferent demeanour of a man under orders to carry out a task and not to reason why. As his tall frame and broad shoulders moved away from them there was nothing to do but follow.

Aggorine led the way and found herself becoming more and more preoccupied in rehearsing the few words and phrases of Haonic language she had learned from Varac. Being a natural linguist, she was pleased to find that she as able to recall and even build on what Varac had taught her, and felt it was certain to be of some use now they had been brought into the heart of Haon's domain.

Shimah had brought little with him from his home beyond the mountains. His fine physique and the regular exercises he always imposed on himself were his stock-in-trade, though he always found satisfaction in sharing conversation with Lekhar and discussing scientific and mathematical phenomena with her.

Lekhar and Oj had both been careful not to discard their little treasures when they had thrown away their old clothes. Lekhar had chosen her new outfit, not only for its style and colour, but because it had pockets just capacious enough in which she could store her small electronic binoculars, her pocket computer and her little laser analyser-synthesizer. She was determined not to be parted from them. They might yet come in extremely useful.

Oj's ball of conducting string had been much reduced in size but he stuffed it in one of his pockets together with his pocket knife which always served as his first-line tool kit. He would have felt at a considerable disadvantage without it.

Yma brought up the rear of the procession, her fingers caressing her beloved flute. She could not imagine being able to tolerate life without the means of making music. Denied all other instruments at the moment, her flute was of paramount importance to her and she was determined not to part with it under any circumstances. She had no pockets in her dress, but there had been a small vanity bag provided to match the clothes of her choice, and this she now carried over her arm. In it, together with a fresh white handkerchief lay her Elcaronic stone, the gift from the glowing mountain after their first encounter with Haon. The stones, the symbols of Elcaro's promise, had become part of them all and of course they had all been careful to transfer them from the old uniforms to a safe pocket in their new clothes. There could be little doubt that they would need the wise counselling and maybe the direct intervention of Elcaro as they now, as they assumed, approached the 'lion's den'.

Their way led along corridors and up several flights of stairs. Eventually they reached what was apparently the top storey of the huge building. They were led through a series of double doors, each guarded by two soldiers, until at last they entered a large room in the centre of which there was a long table, big enough to seat some twenty people. The ceiling was high but, like the smooth walls, completely undecorated. There was no apparent source of lighting or heating but, despite the absence of windows the air was fresh and pleasantly warm, and the illumination bright without being glaring. The soldier left them alone in the room, his escort duties now completed. The doors were closed behind them by the two guards on duty outside. Even if they had contemplated it, there was no escape. They now must face whoever or whatever they had been brought here to meet.

They hadn't long to wait. There had been only a few moments for them to take stock of their new surroundings before a door opened in the far wall, and what was clearly an escort party of four soldiers entered the room and formed up in pairs on either side of the door. Eventually a fifth figure appeared in the doorway, paused a moment and then moved slowly to the seat at the head of the long table.

As a complete contrast to the severity of the room itself, this person was dressed in a multicoloured robe which enveloped him or her – it was impossible to tell which – from the shoulders to the floor. This was topped off by a garish head-dress, secured with a shining metallic circlet, which gave the impression of a halo hovering over the head of the wearer. The face had either been heavily made up or was secreted behind a mask. From the other end of the room it was not possible to discern which was the case, but whether make-up or mask, the richness of the robe and headcovering were matched by the lavish colouring of the face.

The wearer of this fantastic array was tall and broad and, whatever his or her age might be, the bearing was that of a leader.

The apparition sat down, spoke and the voice betrayed the sex to be masculine. The deep tones rolled towards the five friends and commanded them to be seated. With incredulous eyes fixed on their host they took seats at the end of the table remote from him.

The voice continued in firm and authoritative tones, picking its way precisely and carefully through the language of the plains: 'So you have arrived at last!' it said.

No-one could answer. They were all awestruck and not able to concentrate on what was said. The question uppermost in each of their minds was, 'Who is this? Can it be Haon himself?'

Without waiting for any comment from them, the voice spoke again in precise and accurate plains language.

'We have been expecting you for some time, and would have collected you earlier had we not found some difficulty in

169

tracking you down before you arrived on the plateau.'

'So the "hair nets" had worked!' thought Lekhar with not a little satisfaction, and her logical brain went on to realise that here was further proof of the highly-developed technology of the mountain people. They were clearly able to detect the beta-ray 'transmission' from active brains at some distance, and hence determine the position of the possessor of that brain. The simple screening property of the conductive hair nets had thwarted that process and made it necessary for Haon to search for them in some other way – But what other way? – The answer to that question would be a most interesting one.

'But you are here now, and I trust the reception arranged for you was to your satisfaction,' continued the voice at the other end of the table.

Aggorine began to realise some sort of response was called for, and as the group's accepted leader, she was undoubtedly the one to make it. With an involuntary movement, her hand sought out the pocket containing her Elcaronic stone and confidence began to creep back into her as her fingers encircled it and she felt its warmth seeping into her very being.

Rising to her feet, squaring her shoulders and, adopting a defiant look to her face with her brown eyes flashing straight at the colourful mask, she said, 'Yes, we are here and would have arrived undetected if that had been possible. Our reception was totally unexpected but I have to admit that it was most acceptable. We have travelled a long way and we have but two aims. One of our number was removed from our group in the early part of our journey. We assume she was taken by command of the ruler of this mountainous domain in order that she would become the bait to lure us onwards and to prevent us giving up our quest. If she is here, we wish to see her and demand that she is released from custody. The other aim is to meet face to face with Haon to tell him of the suffering he has caused amongst the people of the plains, and if possible to find a way of removing the constant threat of the devastation which our people have suffered from time to time.'

'Do you think you are in a position to demand anything?' interrupted the voice. 'You seem to forget that you are uninvited guests in this place, that your lives lie in the palm of Haon's hand and that he could crush you all if he so wished.'

'Yes, we know all that,' shouted the impetuous Shimah,

leaping to his feet. 'Why doesn't he get on with it and wipe us all out? – I'll tell you why! He's afraid of us and the power we have which lies in our secret. He needs us alive until he has extracted the answer from us – and that he will never do – never!'

'Bravo, bravo, young man!' cried the voice, 'I admire your spirit but your argument is very shaky. You must know that we have ways of controlling the mind, and if necessary we shall employ them on you and your friends. But I hope it will not come to that. Since your first meeting with Haon, when you foolishly embarked on your journey, I am sure, being the intelligent people you are, you will have observed on many occasions the control over the forces of the material world which Haon possesses. His scientists are second to none in the universe, and this I hope you will appreciate more and more as you stay with us.

'Your first encounter with Haon should have been your last. You were intended to be so frightened by the grotesque apparition, the flailing arms, the mad old man bent on your destruction, that you would turn tail and run for home. But no, with the support of Elcaro you did not run, but pressed on, unarmed, deeper and deeper into our domain. Haon became most impressed by your foolish courage and took the notion to engineer a meeting with you. He is intrigued to find out what enables you to ignore the overwhelming odds against you and to press on towards your goal. Hence your presence here now. We thought for a while that we had lost you. It was when you had reached the great lake and, thinking our equipment had developed a fault, it was some time before we realised that you had discovered a way of blocking the sources of our information. By that time we guessed you would have discovered the entrance to the power plant and we hoped you would find the exit which led by the tubular transport to the satellite town. This you must have done, because you surfaced again in that town, only for us to lose contact with you again very soon afterwards.

'The area from the town towards the east is very barren, as you well know, and we could get no information on your position. We guessed, however, that you would find the way to the plateau, and there eventually we found you. You know the rest.'

Looking – or rather directing his mask-like face towards Aggorine he continued, 'I presume you are the one known as "Aggorine" and that you are in command of the group. Haon has been impressed by your cool leadership even though you must have realised that you had no chance of success. We in these mountains have always had to fight against the terrain itself, but most of all against the extremes of climate. Years ago we had to subdue the inhabitants of what are now called the satellite towns. They could not offer much resistance to our Haonic forces and they now live only to serve our great nation.'

Aggorine made as if to interrupt but was waved into silence by the being at the other end of the table who went on to add, 'As I have indicated, we respect courage and leadership above all else, not only in the physical sense but equally in the field of intelligence and the conquest of the forces of the natural world. We admit that we have little time for weaklings of any sort. Over several generations, from small numbers, we have built up a nation of first class citizens, some of whom excel physically, as you will have seen in our soldiers, and some who excel intellectually. You have already been given glimpses of the resulting technological achievements of our scientists which far outstrip those of other communities outside our borders, and in view of the undoubted excellent brains which each of your group possesses, it has been decided that you should be shown some of the other controls we have managed to achieve over our environment.'

This time Aggorine would not be put off and in as steady a voice as she could muster she commented, 'I see that arrogance is also one of your main characteristics. You and your predecessors most certainly have made some astounding discoveries, but at what cost! – There must have been many, not only of those in the surrounding towns but even from among your own people who, because they did not or could not make any contribution to progress as you see it, simply went to the wall and perished.' And with emphasis on every word she ended, 'Have Haonites no heart? Are they never concerned with the welfare of others? What quality of life is there if based only on the survival of the fittest and to blazes with the hindmost?'

With eyes flashing she remained standing and the others rose from their chairs and grouped themselves around her in a gesture of complete agreement and support. They waited for the expected explosion from the other end of the table but surprisingly none came. There was however a long pause during which the soldiers shifted uneasily. They could never have heard such outspoken criticism of the regime before and they too expected something dramatic to happen.

But there was no outburst. Instead in a calm and deliberate voice these words came from behind the mask. 'Our predecessors knew nothing beyond the need to survive; hence our way of life to this day is as it is. It has given us power beyond imagining; power perhaps one day to rule not only the whole world but to conquer the universe.'

As the five friends continued to stare at him the strange being rose from his seat and stretched himself to his full height. Completely enclosed by his highly coloured robes, he was an imposing figure, flanked as he was by his bodyguard of soldiers. Perhaps now would come the outburst of rage, the devastating blow which would seal their fate. The thought passed through all their minds. But instead, in imperious tones, he addressed them thus: 'You do not recognise me. How could you be expected to? But you have seen me before in different guise and mood. For I am none other than Haon himself, ruler of this mountain domain, as I have been for more years that I can remember. Yes, it was my image you saw on the first mountain slopes and it is I who have been following your progress since then. It is I who took your sixth member from you. She was so engrossed in the colourful hologram my scientists created for her that I was able to catch her off guard and transport her to my city by a device you yourselves experienced when you were brought here from the plateau.

'You lesser beings believe you can control and even overcome certain physical problems by the power of thought. You call it "mind over matter". We have gone much further than you can imagine with the power of thought. Our scientists have concentrated much effort into researching the human brain and have been particularly interested in the radiation given off by the brain when activated by particular thought processes. We have now reached a point where we can amplify the beta radiation from an active brain and receive those signals over considerable distances. This enabled us to keep track of you as you journeyed through the lower slopes. The process is similar

173

to the system used to amplify the weak signals coming in from outer space. – I believe your people use a device called a maser for this purpose. It is one thing that we seem to have in common. But we have applied this system, which stimulates the emission of radiation by excited atoms, to control the force of gravity itself.'

Here Haon paused for the implications of his statement to sink in and before he could continue, Lekhar, whose scientific brain had been racing ahead of the others, interjected, 'But you would need an independent power source to augment the weakness of the beta radiation.'

Haon turned towards her. 'You are clearly a young scientist of note. I must arrange for you to share your thoughts with others in the research laboratories. You are quite correct. We have developed a nuclear-powered amplifier which converts the smallest electromagnetic wave into a concentrated source of power without changing the characteristics of the original. Hence our ability to lift and transfer any object we choose silently and rapidly from one place to another, simply by feeding the appropriate thoughts into the amplifier.'

'Very impressive!' remarked Lekhar. 'I look forward to seeing your research laboratories and talking to your scientists.'

For the moment her inquisitive brain had clouded her vision of the situation they were all in. Here was Haon, their erstwhile enemy and present captor, treating them to an insight into the very real achievements of his people. Why should a person such as he, the evil ruler of the mountains, be prepared, even anxious, to reveal to them, five young people from the plains, some of the secrets which gave him such awe-inspiring power over the material world and the lives of people?

Lekhar and indeed all the others, were duly impressed by what he had had to say to them but suddenly, warning bells sounded in their minds. The question uppermost for them now was, "What ulterior motive did Haon, whom they knew as a dangerous leader of a powerful nation, have in treating them to such an unexpected welcome?". And flooding back into their awareness came the memory of the warnings given to them by Elcaro to be wary of Haon in all his guises. 'He will only be interested in capturing your minds in the hope of discovering the intangible answer to the secret, "the meaning of life"!'

By now, not only Aggorine but the other four were clutching their own Elcaronic stones and, by the second, were gaining courage and confidence to face this latest ploy of their rival. Suddenly Shimah, who could contain his rising anger no longer, took two or three steps forward, which prompted the soldiers to move to prevent his further progress. Undeterred by their restraining grip he simply flung his voice towards Haon, making no effort to free himself, though every muscle was tense and ready for action.

Jutting out his jaw he shouted, 'Do not try to fool us any more. Your boasting will get you nowhere with us because we know you as you really are. We have experienced your wrath at first hand and we have seen with our own eyes the ruthless destruction you caused to descend onto the people who lived a peaceful life on the plateau. You have subdued the folk who live in what are now your satellite towns, and all because you have the technology and the power to crush everything which stands in your path; the path you think will lead you to world domination.'

Aggorine came to try to restrain him but he would have none of it. He shrugged his sister's hand from off his shoulders, saying, 'I will not be stopped. Haon must hear it all now.'

And turning once more towards the colourful figure at the end of the table, who had stood quite impassively throughout Shimah's outburst he went on: 'Well, we five young people and our sixth member, whom you took from us, – we now stand in your path. Exterminate us if you will, but it will not advance your cause one iota. We know what life is all about and you want to know what we know. But you will never know – nor *can* ever know, because you are so bound up in yourself and your own aggrandisement that you are blind to the beauty of nature and beauty of human relationships. Even if we wanted to, we could not teach you these things, old man. Your whole way of life, your whole attitude towards everything would have to change. – So you see, it is you yourself who stands in your path – get out of your own way!'

With these last few words shooting like arrows from his lips, Shimah, with a dexterous twist of his powerful arms released himself from the soldiers and, standing defiantly with head high, shoulders braced and arms folded across his chest, he waited for the vitriolic response, which must surely now come

175

from Haon.

They stood facing each other. Shimah tall, erect and coura-geous in the face of imminent danger, stared straight at the mask which hid the face of the one who wielded so much power in this land. There was no way of telling what effect Shimah's words had had on Haon. He just stood as if stunned into immobility. Surely he must react! – But no – he stood facing Shimah; whether in admiration of the young man's courage or in contemplation of some terrible retribution, there was no indication whatsoever.

The spell was eventually broken by Shimah's four friends who simultaneously began, tentatively at first then more boldly to applaud. 'Well done! We agree!' came repeatedly from all of them and they clapped their hands in synchronisation until the rhythm of their words and their clapping broke into unres-trained laughter. Their situation was certainly nothing to laugh about but the five young people felt a tremendous joy and release from tension in their laughter. At last the mood changed and the gaiety subsided into silence once more. But still Haon did not react.

'I'm beginning to feel sorry for him,' said Yma under her breath.

'So am I,' agreed Aggorine.

'I don't think he knows what laughter is all about,' said Lekhar.

As for Oj, he just exchanged glances with Shimah which seemed to say, 'What now?'

It was Yma who answered the unspoken question by direct-ing her words towards the old man. 'We are sorry,' she said, and at last they detected a movement as he turned towards her. 'Yes, we are sorry to have been so rude as to laugh at you, but we are even more sorry that you obviously could not appre-ciate why we were laughing. What a life you must lead, not able to understand anything but outright power. Oh! poor Haon! – We are truly sorry for you. You have everything under your control except the spirits of joy and beauty, comradeship and love. The whole essence of life itself eludes you and we are unable to teach you about it. As Shimah so boldly told you just now, your whole attitude would have to change if you were to ˈve the slightest chance of learning what life is really meant to

At last the outburst came: 'Sorry? Sorry for me? How dare you, you puny creatures! You have no power over me. You will discover that I have ways of making you do as I wish.'

'Hurrah! – now we see the true old man once more, all threats and bombast!' Shimah, still in a very defiant mood actually smiled as, once more, he threw his words at Haon.

But Haon did not look back. He had turned on his heel and was already disappearing through the door as Shimah spoke. He barked a command to the soldiers who came to active life once more, making it quite plain that the five young folk were to move through the door at the other end of the room. Their confrontation with Haon was at an end.

With two soldiers before and two behind, the procession passed from the room, along several corridors, down a number of flights of stairs before reaching the room where they had been received first of all. The door slammed shut behind them. The starkness of the room compared with the comfort of the rooms where they had washed and changed their clothes, indicated that Haon had, for the moment, abandoned the kid-glove welcome. It also meant that they had withstood the wiles of the evil old man in this first encounter. But what was now in store for them? What other ploys would Haon produce to try to break them down?

20

Left alone and now behind locked doors again with the guard undoubtedly posted outside, the group was in danger of disregarding their minor triumph over Haon and becoming sorry for themselves. They moped about the room, only exchanging the odd word or two, each of them standing for minutes on end silently gazing out of the windows towards the mountains which had so inspired each one of them. Now their thoughts turned wistfully to the plains beyond the mountains and a great longing for home and their parents and friends took hold of them.

Yma and Lekhar looked at each other as they stood hand in hand for mutual comfort and Yma sighed, 'Shall we ever go sailing together again? Shall we ever sleep in our own bed-rooms again?'

Lekhar gave a wry smile, 'Well,' she said, 'we are still alive and, though I can't think of any logical reason why we can ever hope to return home, so many strange things have happened since we left that I am quite prepared to believe that the unexpected, illogical thing will happen to take us safely out of this god-forsaken place.'

To hear these sentiments from Lekhar caused Yma's spirits to rise and she smiled back at her sister and squeezed her hand saying, 'Let's hope so.'

As if to add meaning to her hope, Yma turned to the mountain range once more and in her mind converted the rise and fall of the peaks into a powerful musical score. The drums rolled, the trumpets blared and the strings floated majestically from one great chord to the next. She could hear it all and her eyes regained their sparkle as her flute almost found its own way to her lips. Her deft fingers moved over the instrument and ʼught it to life as the melody streamed out of it. No flute had ʋroduced such music before, haunting yet powerful, exciting yet soothing. The whole room was filled with the most wonderful sounds which caused all their hearts to leap with joy once more. With her eyes still on the mountain 'score' and her music moving amongst the rugged 'chords', sometimes as a gentle breeze caressing the rocks and sometimes flashing like lightning between the peaks, Yma gradually became aware of what she could only interpret as a response to her playing. There was a distinct message coming into her mind, a message of appreciation and of encouragement. As she looked more intently she saw in the far distance one of the highest of the mountain tops start to glow with a brilliant white light.

She stopped playing and exclaimed, 'It is Elcaro! – Look, Elcaro is shining as brightly as he has ever shone before, and I'm sure he is shining for us, – to let us know that we are not abandoned, we are not alone.'

The others rushed to Yma's side and gazed in the direction she indicated. Sure enough, there was the bright light, like a star on the horizon, and into their very beings came the message, unspoken but as clear as crystal: 'Take heart. Watch and wait and all obstacles will be overcome!'

Silently they stood together, looking towards what they all knew to be the highest peak of the Tarara range, until the light from Elcaro eventually faded and went out. Then, hardly able to contain their excitement any longer they turned to each other with happy faces and sparkling eyes. For no reason other than the desire to share the confidence in their future which Elcaro had restored, they shook hands and embraced without the slightest embarrassment, dancing around the room and singing at the tops of their voices any old tune which happened to come into their heads. It was a scene of uninhibited elation. Their newly-restored confidence in the eventual success of their mission, in the face of all the evidence to the contrary, had brought them back onto the beam and it was now time for them to take stock once more of their situation.

Though she didn't want to curtail the festivities, Aggorine felt it her duty to calm things down and get them all round the table for a Council of War. Shimah was the last to sit down and as he did so he banged his fist on the table. 'We're always having to wait and watch,' he exclaimed. 'What I want is some real action. It did me good to give Haon a piece of my mind in that other room, but I was longing to rush him and tear off his

179

silly mask and demand to be taken to Ecila. I don't know what stopped me; not those zombies of soldiers, I can assure you. I suppose it was Ecila's safety which held me back. It would have been typical of the evil old man to vent his anger on her, if I had attacked him.'

'I think we are all glad you managed to control yourself, Shimah,' said Aggorine. 'He holds all the powerful weapons at the moment and you could so easily have destroyed the very small chance of success we felt we had at that time. But now that Elcaro has been in touch once more, we can allow ourselves considerably more confidence.'

'But I still say that Ecila is our first priority,' pressed Shimah. 'If we can be reunited with her we shall be able to concentrate more fully on Haon himself. I don't think for one minute that he will ever be made to change his way of life, with its devastating control over the lives of others, so I propose we consider how we can remove him altogether. – Yes I mean destroy him and all his evil with him! – But Ecila's release must come first.'

'Strong words,' said Oj. 'I tend to agree, but how on earth can we, with no forces at our disposal, bring about Haon's downfall?'

Indeed, how on earth can this be done?' interjected Lekhar. 'Perhaps not "on earth" but out in space! Do you remember when we were talking to Varac in his room, how he told us that there was a myth surrounding Haon's origin and that he had been marooned on earth by the retreating army from another planet? I wonder if we could send him after them, or even get them to come to collect him!'

'Now you really are deserting your logic, Lekhar,' teased Yma. 'I'm afraid your idea is too far into the realms of fantasy for me to begin to believe in its possibility.'

'Maybe so, maybe so,' mused Lekhar. 'We shall just have to wait and see, shan't we?'

'I should imagine we stand as much chance of getting rid of Haon as we do of converting him to our way of life,' said Oj. 'He is so fully in command of all his scientific and military forces and so committed to the philosophy of the survival of the fittest, that neither course seems remotely possible.'

The five friends seemed to be arguing their way into an ssible situation when their attention was suddenly switched from future possibilities, or impossibilities, as the case may be, back to the present once more. The door of their prison unceremoniously swung open and the soldier standing guard stepped inside the room.

'What now?' was the question they all asked themselves but it was not long before they were able to find the answer. Food was brought in and placed on the table by two other soldiers who withdrew without a word.

The guard then indicated that they should eat and in halting plains language added, 'You are to be moved from here.'

'Moved?' queried Aggorine. 'To where and for what reason?' But the guard just stood inside the door and said nothing. There was much speculation amongst the friends as to the answers to these questions but there seemed nothing they could do but obey instructions. The food was plain but satisfyingly tasty and soon they had all eaten and drunk as much as they needed. Their impassive guard, seeing they had finished, opened the door and recalled the two who had brought the food, in order that the table might be cleared. When all was as it was before their meal, they expected the guard to resume his vigil outside. To their mild surprise he remained in the room, closed the door and moved across to the far wall. Here he opened a cupboard door which had not been immediately apparent before and took out a number of long cloaks with hoods, all made of the same drab material from which the peasant clothes had been made and which they had discarded earlier.

'You will choose a suitable cloak and put it on,' instructed the guard. 'You are to enclose your heads with the hoods and wait for a guide who will take you where you are to go.'

At least they were not to be left forgotten in this stark room, so it was with a mixture of anticipation, excitement and not a little trepidation that they complied with the guard's instructions. Hardly had they all disappeared beneath the voluminous cloaks, than a knock came on the door which made the guard spring into action. He swung open the door and stood erect and motionless to allow entrance to a figure equally engulfed by a cloak and hood similar to their own. The visitor spoke more fluently and clearly in their native tongue and told them it had been arranged for them to be taken on a tour. 'We shall go on foot and it is necessary that we all remain incognito – hence the

181

cloaks. Come with me and keep close. I do not want to lose you!'

The fluency of the language and the more friendly intonation in the voice dispelled any doubts in the minds of the five friends about their safety in following the unknown guide, so they all filed out into the corridor which was dimly lit but sufficiently bright to allow them to see where they were going.

Yma was the last out of the room and she couldn't resist looking straight at the guard, smiling her most winning smile and saying, 'Thank you for looking after us!'

He did not react.

21

The caterpillar procession of hooded figures moved silently behind the guide who had warned them to be as quiet as possible. All five friends were wondering who this mysterious person could be who had the authority, even the audacity to take them so easily from their prison room and was now leading them further and further into the depths of the building. Down and down they were led until, having reached a wide hall or landing which Oj estimated was at least five storeys below ground level, their leader held up his hand to bring them to a halt.

'Wait here,' he whispered. 'I will return shortly,' and he disappeared through a small door in the far wall of the hall. While the door was open a noise like that of a well-oiled engine reached their ears and prompted the speculation that they were close to the power centre of the building, perhaps even to the nerve centre of Haon's city. They were silent while they waited, each straining to hear any noise which might give them a clue as to what was behind the door through which their hooded guide had passed. Only the faintest hum could be discerned but certainly there was some machinery working not too far away.

It wasn't long before their guide rejoined them. 'All is ready. Come with me,' he said, and led the way into a completely darkened room, shutting and locking the door behind them.

They could see nothing but felt they were not alone. At a word from the one who had been their guide, lights were switched on to reveal other people seated around a large round table. When the lights had ceased to dazzle the five friends, they saw four men and two women, all of whom were dressed in white overalls, save one. That one was cloaked as they themselves were, except that he had thrown back the hood to reveal his face. He stood up and came towards them with outstretched arms.

'Welcome, my friends,' he said, 'I have been longing for this moment when we would be reunited.'

'It's not possible,' breathed Aggorine stepping back a pace while peering intently at the man. 'Varac, is it really you!? We saw you captured and taken away by the Haonite soldiers from the ruined city. You were injured. How can you now be here safe and well? We were convinced that you would either be dead by now or at least imprisoned in one of Haon's dungeons.'

'Dear Aggorine,' he said, 'yes it is indeed I, Varac, the one you befriended and in whom you put your trust,' and with that he embraced her and then each of the others in turn.

Their questions poured out seeking answers to how Varac was able to survive and how in fact he was now here amongst people who were obviously his friends.

'Come now,' he said, 'I promise a full explanation, but for the time being I want you to accept me as your friend and to meet these other six people who have all been anxiously waiting to make your acquaintance.'

The one who had fetched them from their prison had now removed his cloak and was seated with the others at the table. At Varac's invitation they joined the others, having themselves removed their cloaks. Varac lost no time in individual introductions but straightway assured the five friends that they were perfectly safe in this room.

'These men and women are the leading scientists in this complex,' he said, 'and this room is totally screened so that no radiation of any sort can enter or leave it. These people have known about your expedition from the outset and, like me, are sincerely anxious that it should be a success. For the moment you will have to take my word for that, but we hope to prove our sincerity by giving you as much information and support as we possibly can.'

He paused as if not knowing where to start and then continued: 'Many questions must be in your minds. Please have patience and we will try to answer them. First, as you may by now have deduced, we are all of the Haonite race but we certainly do not share the Haonite philosophy. As scientists, we have been responsible for much of the research into the control of the human mind. This we have done by Haon's explicit command. We have been given all the facilities we needed and there is no doubt that great strides have been made. But there is one command Haon was unable to impose on us, namely the command over our minds. In order to do our work, even Haon realised we had to be free from any such control. However, such was and still is, his awesome power, that it has been too dangerous for us to step out of line. Consequently we have provided him with the means to control nuclear power safely and to use it to probe the inner recesses of the human brain. You yourselves were tracked by the beta ray amplifier we designed, until you cleverly thwarted that at source by the simple headgear you made out of Oj's conductive string!'

Oj smiled wryly and caught Lekhar's eye who knowingly returned his smile.

'Many other advances in technology have been achieved; for example the nuclear/thought process transportation system which you also have experienced. Developments in the field of laser beams have enabled us to produce holograms on a very large scale. Sadly also we have had to provide Haon with the most sophisticated weapons of war, to bolster his control over his domain and to fuel his mad desire one day to control the whole world.'

Lekhar took advantage of another pause and asked, 'Have there been any discoveries which have had no bearing on military might?'

'Certainly,' replied Varac. 'My friend here on my right,' indicating the man closest to him, 'my friend, whose name is Pector, will, I am sure, be pleased to tell you about his work.'

Pector stood up. 'Please,' said Varac, 'let's keep this as informal as we can. Do sit down.'

So Pector sat, but still looked a little embarrassed. Nevertheless he said, 'Please excuse me. My understanding of your language is not as detailed as Varac's.' And he continued slowly and deliberately, 'My work has been on the human brain and was originally an offshoot of that being done to control the thoughts and actions of the person. The direction in which I and my assistants went was towards the control of sickness. We found we could irradiate certain areas of the brain so as to stimulate the body's natural defences against sickness. It has proved rewarding and the people who have had the treatment have certainly lived comparatively illness-free lives. But here again Haon decided that only those for whom he had any use in the defence of his leadership should be so privileged.' Pector turned to one of his female colleagues and said, 'Rionee has done some equally interesting work. You may have noticed that very few people here wear spectacles. This is a direct result of her work.'

'Not only mine,' said Rionee. 'Many people have contributed.' Turning to the five friends she went on. 'It really is based on the very simple fact that the focal length of the eye depends to a large extent on the refractive index of the material, and particularly of the cornea and the lens, of which it is formed. We simply discovered drugs which, when injected directly into the eye, would either reduce the refractive index to cure short sight or increase it to cure long sight, the strength of the drug depending on the degree of malfunction of the particular eye. At the moment we have to repeat the treatment about every six months, but we hope one day to produce a drug which would have a permanent effect.'

Varac came back into the conversation at this point. 'There has been considerable research done over the years and the results which we have produced are the culmination of those years of work. What my colleagues and I have done and still are doing is to continue research in the direction laid down in the distant past. That direction is what we have come more and more to detest. By the rules dictated by Haon, only work on projects designed to give him power and control can be carried out. He has no time for what he considers to be weakness, no time for those who become ill – they get well again if they are fortunate. His attitude to the human body is that it is a vehicle to provide him with an efficient power structure and to be able to carry out his every instruction to the letter. He cannot accept that he has any responsibility towards people as persons in their own right. His soldiers never question his authority because they quite simply cannot do so. One of the very first weapons which some of our scientific predecessors gave him was a device which used the phenomenon of telepathy, amplified it and controlled it. Ever since then Haon keeps the secret of the device to himself and, at will, can direct the actions and thoughts of his military forces. Even when the soldiers are not being instructed by Haon directly, they have become so used to relying on the telepathic power of Haon's brain, that their own brains seem to have become numb and incapable of even contemplating any sort of rebellion.'

'Oh, what a state to be in,' breathed Aggorine with a sigh which came from the very depths of her being.

'But what about you and your colleagues?' queried Shimah. 'Surely you could do something to change the course of events. Surely you care about other folk sufficiently to try to improve their lot.'

'Precisely,' replied Varac, 'and that is the very reason why we are all sitting around this table tonight! Secretly for some years we have been seeking ways of limiting Haon's power, but sadly we have met with little success. But then two things happened almost simultaneously which gave us more hope. First, Haon himself called me into his presence and demanded that his scientists should initiate research into the very nature of life itself. He said he wished to be in informed of the meaning of life on this planet and we were to come up with the answers.'

'Some task!' interjected Lekhar.

'How true,' replied Varac. 'But when I reported to my scientific friends we began to wonder why Haon had issued this order. Could it be that there was a glimmer of hope that he was realising there was more to life than dictatorial power? We had no way of telling.

'But then the second thing happened and that was your appearance on the slopes of Mount Tarara. Never before had anyone from the plains dared to come into Haon's territory with the explicit intention of meeting with Haon himself and trying to parley with him. Oh yes, he knew why you had come right from the start, but he thought your expedition would be short-lived, especially if he gave you the scare of your young lives! He was, as you know, sadly mistaken. Not only was your resolve strong, but the timely intervention of the magnificent Elcaro ensured that Haon had to retreat, temporarily at least, and that your mission would go ahead more purposefully than before.'

'We remember that well,' said Aggorine, 'and we remember how it was Yma's love of music and her skill in that field which kept us safe and helped us to find our way through that first mountain wall.'

Varac continued, 'That encounter with you and your

obvious courage and concern for each other, together with Elcaro's declaration that you know the secret of life, had a profound effect on Haon. He decided that he must lure you to his headquarters where he planned to extract the secret from you. He made us arrange for Ecila to be transported here to act as your bait. He had learned enough from that first encounter with you to realise you would never give up your search for her. He didn't appreciate why you would do so, because the welfare of any other individual was and never has been of any concern to him, but he was clever enough to see you had a totally different attitude to living from that of his own.

'Our spirits rose when I was again called into his presence and he recounted what had happened. He told me he wished you to be brought here, but that you were to be allowed to make your own way. However, to ensure you didn't lose your way or even perish he instructed me to act as your guide!'

An expression of enlightenment spread over the faces of the five friends.

'So you engineered the encounter with the soldiers in the queue at the town hall and deliberately stumbled in our direction,' said Aggorine with more than a tinge of sharpness in her voice.

'For which I beg to be forgiven,' replied Varac. 'It was essential for me to remain incognito and, though I know it was an underhanded thing to do, I wanted, above all, for you to accept me as a friend. In this I believe I succeeded.'

'You certainly did and we too were delighted to have found someone with whom we could communicate and from whom we could find out more about Haon and his domain,' conceded Aggorine in a more friendly voice.

'When Haon gave me the job of meeting you and guiding you here, he insisted that I play the part of a peasant, find out all I could about you and report every detail to him on my return,' continued Varac. 'You cannot begin to imagine the thrill which his words unwittingly gave me. We scientists had also become aware of your presence on the outskirts of our country and had been wondering if there would be any chance of meeting you. But in Haon's presence I had to be wary of showing any enthusiasm for the task he had given me though I could hardly wait to be released so that I could get back to my friends here with the exciting news.

'I lost no time in getting together the things I would need and took the earliest transport available to the town where we met. My rooms had to be as authentic as possible with the trappings of an intellectual recluse. There was little enough time, but at last all was ready just before you arrived by the tube train from the power station. Most of the rest you know, but what I would like to emphasise and get you to accept is the fact that besides collecting information for Haon, which was of secondary importance to me, I myself wanted desperately to learn all I could about you and your attitude to life. Not one of us here had ever met anyone from the plains face to face, though, through clandestine study we had become increasingly aware of the major differences between our two systems. Caring for the welfare of others, particularly the less fortunate was alien to all we had had instilled into us from birth. Your perception of the beauty and harmony of nature, art, music, personal relationships and so many other aspects of life was something we just did not understand. However, we scientists, as I have already indicated, had to have our freedom of thought left unimpaired, and it was through our research into the structure of matter that we became increasingly aware of two fundamental things. First, we could only discover and use what already existed, and secondly that, however deeply we probed the factual secrets of nature, there was always much which remained beyond our understanding.

'Our predecessors had always maintained that they would eventually find the answers to every problem and that science would control everything, but our generation of scientists has come to recognise more and more that it is possible that a power and an intellect far greater than ours exists and probably controls all natural phenomena. We have, in short, developed a' humility unknown before amongst our race. Through that humility we have experienced a friendly warmth in our relationships and a readiness to help each other overcome our weaknesses. Previously we would never have accepted that we had any weaknesses!'

As Varac was speaking all of his colleagues around the table were nodding their heads in agreement.

'So you see,' he concluded, 'how thrilled we all were when out of the blue the opportunity came for us to discover at first hand more about your ways and your attitudes. Again, I beg

189

you to forgive me for the gross deception I played upon you. Perhaps it will be some compensation for you to know that, right from our first encounter you all had a profound effect on me. Your love for one another, and the care and friendship you afforded me, kindled in me feelings towards you I had not even imagined possible previously. It was the spontaneous laughter and obvious joy you expressed on the plateau which affected me most. At first it reduced me to a defensive imbecile and then lifted me up to heights of happiness I have never before experienced.'

'But why did you leave us?' queried Yma. 'By chance, when we were searching for you, we saw you at the ancient ruined town, apparently injured and carried off by some of Haon's soldiers. We all presumed you had been captured and beaten up again.'

'My instructions from Haon were to escort you to the plateau and then leave you to be captured yourselves. Even though I had learned a great deal about your concern for others, I never thought you would split up and come back to look for me and I didn't know that you had, in fact, seen me collected by the soldiers until you revealed it when you saw me again in this room. The injury I sustained by tripping over a boulder in my haste to get secretly away from you. I twisted my knee, which made it difficult to walk, though I did manage to struggle to the old town where the transport was to pick me up. I'm glad to say I have now recovered.'

By now the five friends were bursting with excitement. Only a short while ago they had been alone, but now they had allies, and very powerful ones at that. Confidence in the success of their quest had increased enormously and though Varac and his colleagues had opened so many secrets to them, more questions still remained to be asked. However, before they could formulate them, Varac forestalled them by warning that time was running short and that they should be thinking of getting back to their prison room.

'Everything must appear as it was a while ago,' he said. 'Tomorrow we will meet again, when we hope to prepare a plan of action. We scientists are resolved that Haon's power must be curtailed, if not destroyed, and I know you, who come from the plains, have the same burning desire for change, so that our two peoples can live in peace.'

Varac looked a fine figure of a man standing at the head of the table as he delivered what was tantamount to a declaration of war against their tyrannical leader. His eyes shone with the excitement which the meeting had generated and his words instilled courage and confidence into his listeners.

A general murmur of assent came from all present, each equally resolved to bring about their common objective or perish in the attempt. How they would proceed was still to be worked out. Perhaps at tomorrow's meeting they would decide on their plan of action.

Into the momenetary silence following Varac's historic declaration, not able to contain himself any longer, Shimah burst out, 'What about Ecila? We seem to have forgotten her, and the fact that Haon still holds her as hostage. She still is our highest priority and we can't proceed until she is safe.'

He looked around the table and then directly at Varac. 'You know how much she means to us, Varac. Tell me where she is, if you know, and somehow I will pluck her out of Haon's grasp.'

'I'm sure you would if it were at all possible,' Varac replied, 'but your knight-in-shining-armour act won't be necessary.' A broad smile had spread over his face. 'As exciting as our meeting has been,' he continued, looking at Shimah, 'I have kept what I knew to be the most precious piece of information until last – at least, most precious to one of our friends in particular.'

Shimah leaped to his feet as the implication of Varac's words struck him. 'Where is she?' he demanded. 'Don't tease me any more – where is our Ecila?'

Varac's smile softened with his concern for his headstrong young friend. 'She is quite safe and well,' he said softly.

'But where is she?' repeated Shimah.

'Not far from where we are now,' replied Varac.

'Can we see her? Can we?' Shimah went on, full of excitement and without waiting for an answer he turned to the others and said, 'We all want to see her, don't we? It's been so long, and we were afraid she may not have survived.'

His four friends, hearing Varac's incredible news, were hardly able to believe their ears and Aggorine spoke for them all and said, 'Is it *really* true? *Is* Ecila safe and here in your care?'

'Yes, it is and she is!' replied Varac, beaming at them all.

Shimah was bubbling over by now and, in his impatience, grasped Varac by the shoulders as if to shake him until he produced Ecila, but Yma came to him and said, 'Let Varac explain. Be patient if you can.'

Reluctantly Shimah dropped his hands and said, 'Very well, go on Varac. I'll try to be patient,' and gave him a wry smile.

Putting a comradely arm around Shimah's shoulder Varac said, 'When Haon instructed us to try to discover the meaning of life itself, I asked if we could observe Ecila at work, saying it would be a great help in our research. To my amazement he agreed, and what is more, he allowed me to arrange for her to be moved into our laboratory complex for that very purpose. Consequently we have been able to provide her with all she needs and, what is more important, to protect her from the wiles of Haon.'

The wonderful news affected them all, but Shimah, with eyes glistening with tears of joy almost shouted, 'How wonderful! Take me to her, I must see her and let her know we have come to take her home!'

'Patience, patience my dear young friend,' said Varac, 'we must still be cautious. We are not yet free agents and an ill-considered move could ruin our whole enterprise. I cannot yet take you to Ecila, but to further allay your fears I can show her to you.'

As he spoke he moved over to one corner of the room where he slid back a panel to reveal a monitor screen. 'We were able to install this observation panel as part of our research into Ecila's behaviour.' He switched on the device and immediately all five friends pressed forward.

'There she is, there she is!' breathed Shimah. 'Can she see or hear us?'

'No, I fear not,' replied Varac, 'but, as you see, she seems to be quite at home. She has recently started to paint again. At first she refused to look at an easel, much to Haon's annoyance, but she was quite determined not to bend to any of his wishes, let alone his instructions. Her resistance led to him agreeing to her move into our custody and since then she has become increasingly content. Needless to say we have done all we can, secretly, to convince her of our concern for her. She knows how worried we have become over the state of our country's way of life and that we are working, despite the danger of discovery by Haon, towards a nationwide change of attitude.

'When we told Ecila about the progress of your journey and how we hoped to enlist your help in our own undertaking, she was thrilled. The moment she knew you were still seeking for her she became very excited. That moment was the turning point in her attitude to her captivity and she asked for canvas and paint and all the other artist's requirements so that she could begin again to express her feelings through her art. The pictures she produced were such as we had never seen before. The beauty and the love which shone out from them affected us deeply, just as your uninhibited gaiety and laughter affected me when we were together on the plateau. By observing Ecila's work and talking with her, we scientists are gaining an insight into the culture of your people which, up to now, had been impossible for us to obtain. Strangely, however, she herself has not been totally satisfied with her work. Nevertheless Ecila has been an inspiration to us. As I have said, to us her pictures are beautiful, but she explained that to her they are incomplete. She feels that, despite our friendship and the knowledge that we share a common cause, the threat of Haon and the fact that she is still his prisoner, is inhibiting her in her work. But she says she is convinced she has a part to play in our attempts to defeat the evil of the Haonic regime. What that part will be she does not yet know, but she says she will know what to do when the time is ripe.

'In our own ways we all share a similar objective and now we are all together we must plan our united effort carefully and execute it smoothly and successfully. Haon has built up his power by and through the technological control over people and the environment which we and our scientific predecessors have provided for him. Now he must fall by a combination of our scientific ability and the power which lies in your love of beauty in all its forms and in your deep concern for the welfare of other folk.'

All those assembled in that screened room were inspired by Varac's words and they would have stayed there and then to discuss ways and means of achieving their aims but Varac broke the spell by switching off the monitor and saying that tomorrow he would arrange another meeting. Meanwhile the five friends should now return to their room.

'But what of the soldiers who guard us?' enquired Aggorine. 'Surely they will betray us to Haon?'

Varac smiled. 'Don't worry about them,' he said, 'we have been able for some time to break into Haon's thought-stimulated control computer and ensure for ourselves a measure of direction over the minds and actions of the soldiers. They will not harm you, nor are they able to betray you. My colleagues and I detest the way in which Haon has turned so many fine people into near robots, and we long for the day when we can release them to live their lives as individuals rather than as mere extensions of Haon's wicked will. Meanwhile we have to use our technological know-how, as I have already said, in our quest for a radical change in our society, and this control of the soldiery is just one temporary use of that know-how.'

'And a very useful one at that,' said Oj.

'Come now,' said the one who had brought them, 'it helps to wear our all-concealing cloaks as we move about the complex. They are recognised as the general-purpose clothing of the scientific fraternity and therefore it ensures our freedom of movement if we wear them at all times when not in our laboratories.'

Following his instructions, they were soon safely back in their secure room with the guard posted outside. They were delighted to find that not only had food been provided but some rather more comfortable furniture had been moved in, during their absence.

The momentous meeting with the scientists and, most of all, their sight of Ecila, had brought them all to a peak of excitement. The reunion with Varac and the explanation of the part he had had to play in the course of their journey, coupled with the obvious esteem in which his fellow scientists held him, raised their hopes of success far higher than they had believed possible earlier. Tired as they were, it was some time before they were able to rest. Their thoughts were occupied with the question, 'What will tomorrow bring? Success or failure?' But eventually all except the impetuous Shimah were asleep. He couldn't get the vision of Ecila out of his mind. He had seen her, and for that he was grateful, but he would not be happy until they were actually together again. Perhaps that was one thing which tomorrow would bring! At last, with that wonderful possibility in his mind, he, too, fell into a peaceful sleep.

22

They were all awake early in anticipation of what the day ahead might bring. By the time they had all freshened up, two soldiers had laid out breakfast for them. It was not of outstanding quality but palatable, and enough to satisfy even Oj's seemingly insatiable appetite.

There was nothing then to do but await events. Surely Varac would not leave them too long before calling them to the 'council chamber'. However it was an hour before their guide of yesterday came for them and led them, cloaked as on the previous day, to the same screened room where their fortunes had changed so dramatically. Only Varac was there when they entered, but the expression on his face told them that he had some further exciting news for them.

'I can't credit it,' he began. 'Haon seems to be playing into our hands!'

'What has happened?' they all asked together, bubbling over with anticipation.

'He sent for me early this morning,' Varac continued. 'I went with mixed feelings, as you may imagine, wondering whether he had discovered our plot, or if I was going to be punished. My surprise could not have been more complete when he turned his masked face towards me and said that I was to arrange your removal to the laboratories where we scientists were to observe you, and if necessary experiment on you. He required me to complete my report on you and your way of life in not more than three days.

'My heart was pounding as I listened to him but, for obvious reasons, I had to hold myself in check so as not to give the old man any inkling that I welcomed the new instructions. Mumbling something about "doing my best", I left him and made haste to call my colleagues together in this very room. They, too, welcomed the turn of events and have since then been

196

preparing a suite of rooms ostensibly to act as an observatory where we can watch your every move. Come, I will show you to your new accommodation. I think you will find it more comfortable than the prison room you occupied last night. Furthermore, as Ecila has now served Haon's original intention for her, by acting as bait to lure you on, we have decided she can now join the family once more!'

They were all thrilled at this wonderful news but it was Shimah who leapt so high into the air that he almost touched the ceiling. He was beside himself with happiness and was close behind Varac as he led the way from the room.

A relatively short journey took them to their new quarters. As Varac had promised, they were very comfortably appointed with a bedroom and bathroom for the girls and a smaller suite for the boys at either end of a warm, airy room which was to serve as a common room for them all. From the windows they could view right across the mountains to the west. Yma was certain she could pick out the top of Mount Tarara in the far distance and, as she looked, she curled her fingers around her Elcaronic stone and the memories of Elcaro and the help and advice he had given them throughout their journey came flooding back to her.

She wondered, 'Will he help us now, or are we beyond his effective range?' and immediately was ashamed of the very thought, because Elcaro had promised to be available to them always. She knew, however, that the inevitable confrontation with Haon was something they would have to face themselves. Elcaro could advise and encourage but whatever action had to be taken it would have to be put into effect by the five of them.

'No! the six of us,' she blurted out, much to the surprise of the others who had not known the meditation which had gone on in her mind before her outburst.

But it didn't matter, for at that very moment Ecila herself came through the door. Now they were six once more.

Ecila did not hesitate. With tears of joy running down her cheeks she fell into her sisters' arms. Yma and Lekhar hugged her tightly, and they too were in tears. Oj, her brother, came next. He put his arms around her waist and lifted her high above his head with a shout of triumph. Aggorine with laughter and tears combined, welcomed her next with hugs and kisses while Shimah, strangely shy, waited patiently until

197

she turned to him.

Ecila held out her arms to him and uttered the first comprehensible words since she had come into the room. 'Forgive me?' she said.

Taken aback, Shimah asked, 'For what?'

'For the harsh words I threw at you just before I was spirited away. I must, even then have been under some evil influence, or how could I have spoken like that to you of all people?'

'Forgotten, forgotten, forgotten,' emphasised Shimah. 'We are all together again now,' and he took her outstretched hands in his and pulled her close to him and held her tightly. 'Welcome back,' he whispered into her ear, 'welcome back.'

Gradually the electric atmosphere following the great reunion lost its charge and it was obviously time to look to the immediate future. Haon had given Varac only three days to come up with his report, so no time must be lost in making plans. But Varac had written a warning note and placed it on the table for them all to read.

'Be careful. These rooms are not screened,' it said. 'All secret discussion must take place in the council chamber.'

When they had all read the note, Varac took it, placed it in his pocket for safety and for eventual destruction.

So it was that when Varac had left them to themselves they sat around in the comfortable chairs and in turn the five travellers recounted all they could remember of their journey. Ecila was eager to hear it all and then it was her turn.

She could remember nothing from the last words she blurted out to Shimah until she came to at Haon's headquarters. Haon himself, hideous mask, colourful clothes and all had visited her once or twice in the room which had been fitted out as a studio for her. Strangely, she had not been frightened by him but rather had felt sorry for him, decked out in such a dreadful combination of colours with no form or beauty to them.

He had tried persuasion at first to get her to paint for him and to explain her paintings to him, so that he too could do the same. When this failed he turned once more to threats and ranting. Finding Ecila immune to this approach also he had eventually turned her over to the scientists who, it can be guessed, treated her much more kindly and, in the more friendly atmosphere, she had been able to start several canvases of varying abstract subjects, but up to now had not been able to complete any of them. She herself couldn't understand why this had not been possible, except that she assumed that just one completed masterpiece from her brushes, might have given Haon the chance of reading her mind and probing her very soul. This she would never allow to happen and so subconsciously she became more and more inhibited as a painting progressed until she lost all inspiration and was forced to leave it unfinished.

'I have seven such pictures in the studio,' she said. 'I am not at all satisfied with them, but would you like to see them? These rooms are right next door to the studio and I'm sure we are free enough to go there.'

Aggorine and Shimah had never seen one of Ecila's paintings and eagerly agreed to her suggestion. Yma, Lekhar and Oj, knowing what talent she had, were intrigued to find out what was missing from the unfinished canvases. So, unhindered, they trooped into Ecila's room which had all the trappings of an artist's studio. One outside wall was a huge window and through it could be seen a large section of the city with its severe buildings, large geometrical square and mathematically arranged streets. Beyond this the mountains ranged in complete contrast. Soaring peaks, great divides and rugged outlines stretched as far as the eye could see. The houses and streets were drab beyond imagining. There was no colour, not even in the mountains at the moment.

However, Ecila told them how, each morning, she rose early to catch the colours of the day's beginning, which for her made the distant landscape dance and sing as the sun from the east washed them in a golden yellow glow, and how in the evening a different mood took hold of the mountains as the reds and deep purples of the setting sun put them into sharp silhouette and seemed to push them so close to her that their power and magnificence almost overpowered her.

One canvas was still on her easel but was covered from view by a cloth. Six others stood facing the wall behind where Ecila had worked on them. She went to these first and brought them out one by one, without comment, and placed them on a display rack for all to see. Their effect on Aggorine and Shimah was one of amazement. They both expressed their admiration at the obvious skill of the painter and the wonder of the colour combinations, but even they had to admit that they could not feel what Ecila had been trying to convey to the observer. Yma, Lekhar and Oj all recognised her style from previous works of hers they had seen, but even more readily they realised that a vital spark of inspiration was missing from each one.

There was a sadness in Ecila's face as she herself looked along the line of paintings. 'They will have to be destroyed,' she said. 'Despite Varac's kindness and concern for my welfare, I was not able to express myself fully and freely and, as you see, what I produced were just meaningless daubs.'

'I think they are wonderful,' said Shimah, trying to console her.

'Maybe they display some skill,' Ecila replied, 'but there is no beauty in them. So they must be destroyed.'

Then she turned to the easel and her mood changed dramatically. Her face lit up and her eyes twinkled as she said, 'I am not going to show you this one yet. It isn't ready and I don't want anyone to see it until I have finished it. This one I started on as soon as I heard of your arrival and have been working on it feverishly since then.' Pausing for a moment she added modestly, 'I hope it will prove to be something rather special.'

'We shall all look forward to the unveiling,' said Aggorine.

'You bet we shall,' added Shimah who was still running high on a cloud of happiness at being with Ecila once more.

'But you must leave me to get on with it,' insisted Ecila.

'Can't I stay?' pleaded Shimah.

'No, not even you,' laughed Ecila. 'Go on now, back to your rooms all of you and leave me to my paints.'

So reluctantly they turned away and left her alone in her studio. The first thing Aggorine saw when they entered their own room was a note in Varac's hand placed prominently on the table. It simply read, 'Continue to take care. We meet tonight. I will fetch you.'

When they all had read it, without comment Aggorine screwed it up and concealed it in her pocket. They wondered what the meeting would be about. Could it be that Varac already had a plan of campaign to suggest to them, or were they just going to swop ideas? They would just have to be patient. Varac's cryptic note had sparked off various trains of thought in each one's mind, and it was difficult for them not to share them verbally, but the warning had been clear that, because the room was not screened, they should not risk Haon listening in to their conversation. Instead, therefore, they settled down to a period of quiet contemplation and rest, though both came with great difficulty to Oj and Shimah. Eventually the two boys started exchanging stories of their childhood and were surprised to learn from each other that they shared a number of interests.

Shimah's physical prowess had already been displayed on the journey, while Oj's practical proficiency had also been put to good use. But Oj too was quite an outdoor fellow himself with no mean skill at athletics, and Shimah also shared Oj's interest in practical activities. Both were of a scientific and mathematical turn of mind, though they had to admit to Lekhar's superiority in these matters.

Lekhar herself sat at one of the windows gazing into the distance and Aggorine came to keep her company.

'Shall we ever travel back over those mountains?' she said.

To which Lekhar replied, 'Logically speaking, no. I cannot see how our situation would allow any such return journey. But you never know,' she added as she smiled wryly.

Aggorine left her to her reverie and went across to Yma who was busy taking her precious flute apart and cleaning it carefully.

'Will you play for us?' she asked.

'In a while, perhaps,' replied Yma.

So Aggorine sat down apart from the others, thinking how much she cared for them all and hoping against hope that she would be able to lead them back to safety once more.

Lekhar suddenly remembered the bits of electronic equipment she had brought with her. She delved into one pocket and brought out the little laser analyser/synthesizer and wondered if it was undamaged. Maybe it would prove useful yet in their encounter with Haon. She must check it over. Setting to work with nimble fingers she soon proved that the device was indeed still functioning perfectly and then she began to wonder if, by modifying the design, all the power available could not perhaps be concentrated into one potentially lethal beam. She had no desire whatever to possess a weapon capable of killing, but a laser beam of sufficient power might be put to other uses and could be instrumental in getting them out of a tight corner.

Her clear, scientific mind was soon grappling with the problem she had posed herself and in a short while she came up with a possible solution. Seeing Lekhar doing something practical, Oj couldn't resist going over to her to see if she needed any help. Oj himself was certainly no fool when it came to scientific matters and he soon cottoned on to what Lekhar was doing. He produced his famous multi-purpose knife, and together they set about the re-wiring of the circuit. Eventually it was ready for testing, but before that was possible they were all interrupted by the main door of their common room opening to reveal the figure of one of the scientists whom they had met the previous evening. It was Rionee. She held her finger to her lips and beckoned them to follow her.

Silently all five followed her the short distance to the council room where they found Ecila and all their other new allies already seated. Varac himself greeted them and invited them to take their place around the table. He began to speak slowly and deliberately, and it was clear that he was labouring under a great weight of responsibility.

'Haon is impatient,' he began. 'Though he gave me three days in which to report to him and reveal what we had discovered of your secret, he now demands the result by tomorrow morning. All of us here are to present ourselves before him; we scientists to present our report and you young people from the plains to be questioned further by Haon himself. What the outcome will be, no-one can predict.'

'What will you say to him in your report?' asked Aggorine.

'I have thought long and hard,' he replied, 'and I have come to the conclusion that I have no alternative but to tell Haon that the secret of life, as you understand it, is not a biological one which can be discovered through scientific experimentation, but that it lies in your attitude to living itself. Your caring for other people's well-being, even at the expense of your own, your love of beauty in all its forms, your rejection of the philosophy of power and greed and perhaps, above all, the joy and happiness you get out of all aspects of your life; these are the things I have to tell Haon tomorrow morning. I shall also reveal to him that, unlike previous generations of scientists, I and all my colleagues are now convinced that we can only discover what exists already and that there are many things beyond mankind's understanding. We are not all-powerful beings, nor can we make Haon into the ultimate power he wishes to be.

'None of the remarks are likely to be accepted, let alone understood by Haon, because he has no other philosophy except the survival of the fittest and the most physically powerful. There is no doubt in my mind that he will explode with rage and there will end our hopes for a radical change in Haonic society. There also will end your fateful journey in search of peace between our two great peoples.'

Varac's last words were emitted with a deep sigh and he slumped into his chair, the picture of despair.

Aggorine immediately went to him and encircled him with her arms. 'Do not give way,' she said. 'All is not lost until the final whistle. We are still alive and we must go on hoping. It will be brave of you to present such a report to the old man and no doubt he will react as you say. My friends and I are overjoyed that you and your colleagues have come to understand some at least of our approach to life but perhaps even you do not yet appreciate its power. Even Haon may be affected by it when he comes face to face, or should I say, "mask-to-face" with it!' and she forced a laugh.

She looked around the table where all sat in silence at the gravity of Varac's words. 'Let us not despair,' she encouraged them. 'We have a good deal on our side.' She lifted Varac's face and looked deeply into his eyes. 'Do you still believe Haon's rule of this domain to be evil and in dire need of radical change?'

A dark frown came over his face. 'Yes, above all things, I and my scientific colleagues believe that,' he declared.

'Then it is up to us to try our level best to bring about that change. We must not falter now.' Aggorine's words acted as a clarion call to all those round the table.

Varac himself stood up again and placed his hand on Aggorine's shoulder. 'She is right,' he announced. 'Forgive me for being so despondent, but the weight of responsibility and the realisation of the enormity of the task facing us, overcame me while I was alone writing the report and contemplating the consequences. Now we are gathered together again, things look different and a new surge of courage is giving me hope. I am experiencing some of that power which Aggorine mentioned just now, the power which comes from a complete conviction

203

that your cause is right when it is directed to the welfare of other people and not to your own selfish desires.' He laughed a joyful laugh and turning to her he shouted, 'Am I not learning fast Aggorine?'

'You certainly are,' she replied, 'and the best of it all is that you have learned it by yourself by your observations and your innermost thoughts. No-one has told you that you *must* believe. Your conviction is all the stronger because of that.'

There was a great murmur of approval from the others and, from the light in their eyes, it was clear that Varac's friends also felt much as he did. Aggorine took her seat again next to Varac and waited for his lead. They were all calmer now. There was no more despair, nor yet was there any emotional fervour. The time had come for planning the confrontation with Haon as far as it could be planned.

'We have to accept that Haon will have the ascendency over us right from the beginning,' began Varac. 'He has already fixed the time for us to be ushered into his presence and no doubt he will be surrounded by a sizeable bodyguard. Our secret use of the thought-stimulated control computer does not yet extend fully to Haon's close bodyguard. With the ordinary soldiery we can command their thought patterns completely, but we have, as yet, only succeeded in achieving a partial control of the élite bodyguard. Tomorrow, during the confrontation, we can only rely on the reactions of these soldiers being somewhat slowed down. Let us hope that will prove to be sufficient for us to grasp whatever initiative may present itself to us. At the moment, I cannot see any alternative to our simply trying to take Haon prisoner. It would seem to be unrealistic for us to be able so to turn the tables on him as to destroy him utterly.'

Aggorine pursed her lips and nodded in partial agreement. 'There may be another possibility,' she said. 'Varac, when you were telling your story in the first of our meetings in this room, you said that Haon's encounter with us and with Elcaro had a profound effect on him. Could it be that there is a chink in his armour and that even he got a glimpse of the happiness which we share through our mutual relationships? There is no doubt that he believes we have something which he has not, and, even if he only wants to possess it for himself in order to become more powerful, there is the possibility he will give us the opportunity to find that chink in his defences again. If we do, who knows what might happen!'

It was clear that amongst the scientists, Aggorine's suggestion was considered, at best, as a very outside chance.

'Whatever happens,' said Varac, 'let us hope we are all alive at this time tomorrow. Let us now return to our various quarters and prepare ourselves individually as best we can for the great enterprise which we are to embark on in the morning.'

So solemnly the conspirators went their several ways. Very little conversation took place in the six friends' common-room that evening. Oj concerned himself with trying to work out the best way to tackle Haon, should he become belligerent. Shimah's approach to that problem would be much more direct and aggressive than Oj's method, but they exchanged a few words on the subject and it was clear they were prepared to enter the fray, should it become necessary.

Ecila repaired to her studio. Her seventh picture was almost completed and she wanted it to be ready for tomorrow. There was no question in her mind but that she must take it with her. She felt in her bones that it had an important part to play, and it had to be as perfect as she could make it.

Lekhar and Aggorine chatted for a while but then settled into comfortable chairs, each contemplating the morrow. Lekhar's thoughts turned to the sequence of events which had brought them from their home on the plain to their present situation, and to how her logical mind had tried to grapple with the strange happenings on the way. She realised she would never again see just black and white in any argument, but that she would always have to take account of the unexpected, and even the inexplicable, affecting the outcome of any problem. Would the unexpected happen tomorrow?

Yma had seated herself at one of the windows. As she peered out over the grey roofs to the grandeur of the mountains beyond, her fingers moved automatically over the smooth body of her flute and snatches of melody flitted through her mind. Eventually she put the instrument to her lips and gave sound to those melodies. She played quietly so as not to disturb the others, and as she played, tears filled her eyes as the music reminded her of home. Then the mood changed. The mountains, powerful and forbidding yet beautifully magnificent,

205

determined the tune she played, and that in turn made her defiant in the face of what was to happen the next day.

So they all in their own way prepared themselves for the ordeal to come and finally went to their beds to sleep peacefully until morning.

23

The mountains to the west were tinged with the golden glow of morning sunshine from the east when they awoke but it did little to lift their spirits on this particular day. Try as they may, they could not but be affected by the great cloud which metaphorically hung over them, menacing and filling them with foreboding. When looked at through Lekhar's cold, hard logic, there seemed once more no way in which they could expect to overcome the evil power of Haon. But as they sat, fully cloaked around the table, waiting for the summons to come, they almost unwittingly slid their hands into the pocket containing their own Elcaronic stone, and gained comfort from the warmth of its touch. There were no words to share but each one felt sure that Elcaro would give them courage to face their ordeal and perhaps guide them to a happy solution.

At last the knock came and Varac led his six colleagues into the room. They too were fully cloaked. No greeting was necessary. Varac simply said, 'It is time,' and led them into the corridor and then along a passage to a moving stairway which took them up and up to the very top of the building.

The inevitable guard who had accompanied them opened a door leading off the top landing and ushered them into a room some thirty metres square. There was no furniture save for a platform at the far end on which was mounted a large highly-coloured chair, which presumably Haon occupied when he gave audience to any of his subjects. The room was brilliant in the morning sunshine which flooded in through the great plastic dome which formed the roof and the walls, and through which the whole panorama of the mountain domain could be seen. It was as if they were inside a huge bubble which might burst at any moment and scatter the occupants over the countryside.

Still fully covered by their cloaks the six young people and the seven Haonic scientists stood alone, just inside the door through which they had come, and waited.

After what seemed an eternity the masked and gaudy figure of Haon entered through a door behind his throne. They had expected at least a fanfare of trumpets to announce his arrival, but all was strangely silent. Flanked by a bodyguard of a dozen of his élite soldiers, Haon took his seat. The room was now brilliantly lit and every bit of Haon's hideous mask and robes shone in the light, making him look, in the eyes of the young people, quite ridiculous. If Haon had assumed his appearance would cause them to tremble before such a mighty man, he was sadly mistaken. In fact the opposite was the case. Despite the serious situation in which they were placed both Yma and Aggorine could hardly suppress a giggle at the ludicrous sight of this great ruler decked out in the most hideous combination of colour imaginable. Ecila's artistic nature was revolted by Haon's appearance, but at the same time she began to feel just a little sorry for him.

At a signal from Haon, two of the soldiers came and pulled back the friends' hoods onto their shoulders and thrust them all forward until they were within five metres of the throne. Turning his masked face first to one and then the next, Haon gazed along the line, the more to intimidate them before speaking.

In a slow and emphatic voice he addressed them: 'So, we are assembled at last. Six foolish young people from the plains who thought they could overcome the power of Haon and who think they alone know the secret of life. You are here as my prisoners, to do with as I choose.'

'Not as you choose, Haon,' interrupted Aggorine firmly.

'Silence!' roared the old man. 'You will not speak unless you are given permission.'

But Aggorine, having determined that attack was the best means of defence, was not to be intimidated and with her head held high she flung her words at Haon. 'Our journey here was of our own choosing. We came to bring peace to you and to our own people so that we could live in harmony. We have a great gift to present to you!'

Haon was struck speechless with rage, but it was clear that Aggorine's words had had their effect. When he had forced himself to calm down a little he said in a slightly more

208

conciliatory tone, 'A great gift? What can you have to give to me? I have all the power in the world.'

Pressing her minimal advantage Aggorine continued: 'Do you not know, O Mighty Haon? Do you not even now realise that the secret of life does not lie in power, in greed, in self-centredness? Have not even your own scientists yet convinced you? They have been watching us for long enough. They have been reporting our progress and our behaviour ever since we encountered you on the slopes of your domain, when Elcaro set you back on your heels by revealing to you that we "six young plainsfolk", to use your own words, – we held the secret of life, which you in your most belligerent manner demanded he give to you. Why do you not listen to your scientists and learn from them? Or is it that you are frightened to accept what they have to tell you?'

Varac and his colleagues were obviously agitated at Aggorine's boldness. In their experience, no-one had ever spoken so daringly to Haon and they expected that, at any moment, he would react violently, as was his custom. But no such reaction came. Instead Haon rose slowly from his seat and came down until he was close enough to Aggorine for her to see his eyes glinting through the slits in his mask. The other five friends grouped themselves around her in a gesture of support and agreement with what she had said.

Haon, peering straight into Aggorine's eyes said, 'You are a stranger in this land and therefore cannot know that I, the mighty Haon, can never be frightened by anything or anyone. But I am nevertheless interested in you young people of the plains. You have shown much courage in the journey you have made and that is why I wish to find out more about you.'

'Then listen to your scientists,' repeated Aggorine, returning Haon's gaze without flickering. 'If you would learn about us and our way of life, hear first what they have to say.'

Haon shivered visibly as if he were making a great effort to control his rage but he turned from Aggorine and made his way back to his chair. As he mounted the platform he stumbled and would have fallen had not Shimah leapt forward and caught him in his powerful arms.

'Leave me,' the old man shouted. 'I do not need your help.'

'Everyone needs help,' replied Shimah. 'I don't care to see even you hurt yourself while I am near enough to prevent it.'

'Humbug,' growled Haon. 'Humbug!' and waved Shimah away. When at last he was seated he called Varac forward. 'What more have you to report? You have had these inter-lopers under surveillance for a sufficient period and now is the time when I demand you reveal everything you have disco-vered about them, and most particularly this secret of life they are supposed to possess. Tell me how I can possess it too.'

Varac moved slowly to the front of the group, showing obvious reluctance to begin his report.

Haon waited, showing uncharacteristic patience until at last he burst out, 'Well, come on. Out with it, whatever it is you have to say. You have never been slow to speak of your achievements in the past. Can it be that in this most important piece of research you and your team of scientists have failed?'

The words stung Varac into action and, matching Aggor-ine's boldness, he spoke firmly and precisely, looking always directly at his interrogator. 'No, O mighty Haon, we have not failed. On the contrary we have discovered truths beyond our imagining, truths which have had a profound effect on our attitudes and on our very lives. If you will hear me out, I hope so to impress you, that you too will be able to benefit as, indeed, we have.'

'Get on with it, get on with it!' barked Haon.

Varac turned his gaze momentarily from Haon's mask and cast his eyes over his six young friends before continuing. 'Before these plainsfolk entered your domain, O Haon, our research had always been directed towards gaining control over the forces of the material world. You, yourself have often admitted the success of our efforts and the power which our results have given you to rule your domain and its inhabitants. But the deeper we probed the mysteries of the structure of matter, the more we realised what vast areas there were which lay beyond our understanding. "No doubt," we told ourselves, "one day we, or our successors will master all the secrets," but, in telling ourselves this, it gradually became clear to us that we were only able to discover and use what is there already. The logical sequence to such a thought was to ask the question, "What power, what super-human power lies behind the design and production of such a vastly complicated system which we call the material world and into which we scientists have been probing?" When we began to look at our research with this question in mind it seemed to take on a meaning quite different from anything we had experienced before. We became aware of the perfect regularity and even harmony which exists in the way in which material things are constructed. Against all our traditional upbringing and attitudes, we began to respect whatever this super-human power was, which must have brought our world into existence. What is more, we began to respect and help each other to the point where we were often just as concerned about our colleagues' work as we were about our own.'

'Weakness, weakness!' shouted Haon. 'Only the fittest can survive. To be strong and powerful is everything.'

'How right you are,' continued Varac, his words gaining in authority as he spoke. 'It is good to be strong. These six young people are strong but not necessarily in the way we have always understood strength. They are strong in character and can laugh in the face of adversity and so overcome it. They have a strong sense of comradeship and so enjoy each other's company to the full. They have a strong sense of responsibility and so, having undertaken a task for the good of other people they will continue against all odds until they are successful in their mission. They have a strong sense of fun and enjoy life to the full. Perhaps one of their most powerful attributes is their ability to perceive and enjoy beauty in everything; beauty of form, beauty of human relationships, beauty in art, in music, in mathematics, in science and maybe above all, beauty in the way in which the material world is constructed and in the way living plants and creatures fit so harmoniously into the pattern of that material world.'

Varac paused before his concluding words, expecting Haon to launch a withering attack on him for daring to imply that such characteristics constituted strength and power greater than his own. But no attack came. Instead, as they all watched him, Haon appeared to shrink back into his throne, pulling his legs up to his body and crossing his arms across his chest until he was lying there in the foetal position, his head sunk upon his hands.

When his voice came it was no more than a whisper. 'What are you doing to me? These alien thoughts are striking at my mind like daggers. I cannot stand it. I cannot stand it. . . .' His voice trailed off into nothing. But then he roused himself by a great effort and, turning his gaze onto the soldiers, demanded that they take everyone away. 'Clear the room,' came from behind the mask. But the soldiers made no move. Haon no longer controlled their thoughts or their actions.

Varac and all with him could not believe their eyes. Haon the mighty one, now reduced to a pitiful, cringing individual. Where now was his power, his greed, his hatred of all but himself?

Varac had intended to end his report by a condemnation of the Haonic power structure in the belief that his words would have precipitated Haon to violent action, during which, with the bodyguards' minds partially under the control of his scientist colleagues, they would have stood a chance of seizing Haon and forcing him into submission. It had seemed the only course open to them which held even the slightest chance of success.

He had never dreamed of the dramatic effect which his description of the young people's life style would have on the old man. He was so taken aback by the totally unexpected turn of events that he was quite speechless and could only stare in amazement at the figure of the all-powerful leader now hunched in such a dejected way on his throne. It flashed into his mind that he, himself, had suffered in the same way that first day on the plateau when the young people's laughter and gaiety, which he had never experienced before, had sent him cringing behind a rock to try to escape from what appeared to him to be an alien force. He had come through the experience and had greatly benefited from it. It had helped him enter more fully into the caring and sharing ways of the group. It had shown him the beauty of their way of life more clearly than anything he had observed before. Would it affect Haon in the same way?

As they watched the now pitiful figure, wondering what the next move would be, Yma put her flute to her lips and her fingers conjured up the most enchanting music imaginable. Quietly at first and then more fully her melodies filled the great domed room, and she began to move forward, closer and closer to Haon. She was doing what he had so rudely demanded that day by the lake. She was playing just for him. Her loathing of the old man had been quite replaced by compassion. Could she, through her exquisite music, strike a chord of understanding and appreciation in his ice-cold heart?

With the soldiers now standing in numbed silence, the group of friends followed Yma's lead and began to move rhythmically towards and around the throne. Haon put his hands weakly to the sides of his mask, apparently in a vain attempt to stop his ears, but Aggorine boldly took his hands into her own and attempted to lift the old man onto his feet. She could see his eyes through the slits in the mask. They were not now full of fire but looked tired and had an air of desperation about them.

'Come,' said Aggorine gently. 'Come and dance. Come and see the mountains and for the first time see how beautiful they are.'

Gradually, with Yma's music creating a magical atmosphere in the great room, Haon stirred himself and, with a tremendous effort, put his feet to the ground and, still holding Aggorine's hands, stood up. Oj and Shimah came to support him on either side and together they moved towards the western wall, swaying gently in time with the melody.

'Beautiful?' breathed Haon, 'the mountains, my powerful mountains, beautiful?'

'Look at them through new eyes,' replied Aggorine. 'See how they rise and fall majestically and see how colourful they are and imagine what wonder there is in the way they are constructed. See in your mind's eye the glorious, breathtaking views as you stand on the summit!'

A shudder suddenly went through Haon's old body and he tried in vain to break away from those who supported him.

But Aggorine continued. 'That is part of the secret of life,' she said. 'Life is nothing without the ability to appreciate the beauty of nature. But above all, the richness of life lies in the joy and the happiness we get through sharing everything with others, – our talents, our understandings, our insights, our very substance. Listen to Yma's music. It is essentially beautiful and is for all of us to share and enjoy. She doesn't keep it to herself but gives her talent freely to us all.'

There was clearly a great struggle taking place in Haon's old frame. These concepts of life were completely alien to what he had always known. He shook violently within the grasp of Oj and Shimah, as if he were physically trying to overcome the effect Aggorine's words were having on him. Even though she knew he was a tyrant and had perpetrated immense suffering on those under his control, Aggorine could not help but pity him at this moment. But, realising that the main purpose of their whole expedition was to eradicate the evils of Haonism, and that Haon himself seemed unbelievably unable to withstand the truths which she was pouring into his ears, she determined to continue his education.

'There is more to come, old man,' she whispered. 'Look at Oj and Shimah who are supporting you. Oj sees beauty in all the practical things in life while Shimah revels in the beauties of physical achievement. Neither of them glories in the fact that they can beat all comers with their respective skills. For them the joy of being able to do the things they can, is all they ask for. And what of Lekhar? You know her to be a brilliant mathematician and scientist, but she sees the intrinsic beauty in her studies, and is only concerned with how her work can further the well-being of her fellow human beings. She does not seek power for power's sake.'

By now Haon was in such a torment that even Shimah and Oj had difficulty in holding him. Suddenly, with a tremendous effort he broke loose but immediately fell on his knees. Shimah and Oj made as if to help him up but he would have none of it. He cast a glance in the direction of his soldiers but they continued as completely disinterested spectators, so strong now had Varac's control over their minds become.

Haon's struggle was clearly not simply a physical one. Mentally he was tormented by what was happening within his very consciousness. Never before had he even considered that his way of life could in any way be improved. Power to him, held in his own hands, had always been all-important. But now these alien thoughts of loving and sharing, of beauty and joy were striking blows which threatened him in a way he could never have conceived before these six puny young people from the plains had entered his life. He remained on his knees, a poor shrunken figure but he looked up as Varac came close to him. His arm rose slowly and a bony finger, on which his huge emerald ring of office glinted in the sunlight, pointed at Varac.

'You – you – traitor!' The words burst from behind the mask. 'You have done this to me. Your predecessors gave me the power – you have taken it away! Guards, seize him – seize him I say!'

But the guards made no move. Varac's control was complete.

'Traitor – traitor!' Haon repeated and with a superhuman effort he leapt from the floor to fasten his hands around Varac's throat shouting obscenities at him. Immediately Shimah and Oj pulled him off and held him firmly in their powerful grip.

Varac, rapidly recovering his composure looked deep into the eyes behind the mask. 'Traitor to you, maybe, O evil one, but loyal to the people of this great nation whom yóu have tormented for two thousand years. At last we scientists have been given a vision of what life should really be like, and we now intend to share that vision with your erstwhile subjects. They will henceforth live in freedom and learn the joys of living once more.'

'You cannot get rid of me,' snarled Haon. 'I came from immortal stock to this planet two thousand years ago and have survived while generations of your human weaklings have come and gone.'

'You were rejected by your own because you were too evil even for them. They left you marooned here after your rebellion and their unsuccessful invasion of our planet,' interjected Varac, 'and now, at last the values held dear by our "weak human race" have reached even your cold heart and you will die.'

His voice was strong and full of authority as he added with all the power at his command, 'Your evil life will end, O mighty one. You know it will. At last you, even you, have tried to absorb the truths about life which these six young people have taught us and your vile nature cannot live side by side with these truths; those truths which encompass freedom, joy, loving and sharing and an appreciation of the beauty in all things.'

Haon cringed to hear those words again but this time he made no reply.

During these extraordinary scenes, Ecila had stood silent on the fringe of the group clutching the rolled canvas of the picture she would not show to the others when they had visited her studio, because it was unfinished. She had promised it would rank with the best of her work. This she knew because it had almost painted itself. As she had taken up her brushes she had been inspired in so powerful a way that the composition

215

had seemed to take shape with little or no conscious thought on her part. She was sure it was Elcaro who was directing her work because she had been conscious of an unusual warmth emanating from her pocket in which she had secreted her Elcaronic stone, and permeating her whole body, even to her finger tips.

Now she held the completed masterpiece and she knew this was the time to display it. She now knew for whom it had been painted, none other than Haon himself. He had wanted to witness her art. He had demanded she paint for him. Well she had now done so and he would be the first to see the finished product.

She came forward until she stood about a metre away from Haon and turning to the light she unfurled the canvas without a word and without any ceremony.

Haon alone with Ecila could see the picture and for a long moment he stared at it. The effect was dramatic. He let out a blood-curdling scream, lunged at the picture to tear it in pieces, but Ecila was too quick for him and Oj and Shimah were there to bar his way. The scream continued for what seemed an eternity while the others stared horror-struck to see the old man in such agony. While they stood watching, rooted to the spot, waiting for they knew not what, the room became filled with a light, so intense that all eyes were blinded. A great roaring accompanied the light and the huge plastic dome above their heads shattered into a million pieces and fell as confetti around their feet.

Throughout it all the scream could be heard, but gradually becoming weaker and weaker until it faded away completely. Then there was silence.

Varac and Aggorine were first to regain mobility followed quickly by the others. The light had faded and they were able to see again.

Haon was nowhere to be seen. Where he had stood lay a pile of hideously-coloured garments, mask and all. But that was not all. At the western edge of the room, facing the mountains stood a youth, in stature very similar to Shimah. His broad and powerful shoulders, narrow waist, straight back and muscular hips and legs were those of an athlete. He was completely unclothed save for the rays of the morning sun on his back, which appeared as a cloak of gold, matching his fair hair which

216

fell to his shoulders.

All in the room stood thunderstruck by the vision of the young man. Who was he? Where had he come from? Where was Haon now? All these and many other questions flooded through their minds but no-one dared move or utter a word. A great gasp of astonishment had come from each one as their sight had been recovered and they saw the youth standing where, a few dramatic moments ago, Haon had stood, screaming in mental torture as Ecila unfolded her picture before his eyes. Now all was peaceful. The noise and chaos were over and still the young man stood facing the western mountains.

As they watched, he raised his arms, slowly outstretching them to encompass all that he saw. In the silence two words came from him which made the hearts of his observers beat with excitement.

'How beautiful!' he said, and though they could not see his face, they knew he was smiling.

Suddenly Varac became most agitated for he had seen something quite incredible. On the index finger of the young man's right hand was a ring. Could it be an emerald? – Could it be the very same emerald which had last been seen on the old man's bony finger? Such a thing surely was impossible.

Varac moved closer to the youth who still stood gazing at the mountains with outstretched arms. He had removed his own cloak and now placed it on the shoulders of the young man who, at the touch of the cloth on his skin seemed, for the first time to be aware of the presence of others in the room. He gathered the cloak around him and turned so that his face was visible to them all. He was smiling, his deep blue eyes sparkling and darting from one to the other as if he wanted them all to share in the happiness which he was clearly experiencing at the moment.

Varac was nearest to him and saw to his horror that the ring on the right hand was indeed the very same one that Haon had always worn. He gazed at it aghast and then peered into the eyes of the youth, asking an unuttered question.

The answer came. 'Have no fear, with the removal of his devilish mask the evil and tyranny of Haon have gone for ever. The ring is the only legacy he left. It will serve as a reminder of the cruelty and repression which the people of this domain suffered under him, so that we may appreciate all the more the

217

new freedoms we shall enjoy henceforth. If you will have me, with your guidance and help, I will be your new figurehead and together we will live in peace and happiness.'

Varac, seeking more evidence, in a true scientific manner, asked, 'Who are you and where did you come from?'

'I cannot in all honesty answer questions like that, simply because I do not know the answers. What I do know however is that, in some miraculous way, I know who you are. You are Varac, scientist extraordinary, these some of your colleagues, and these six young people are from the plains beyond the western mountains. I know too that you have together been working to rid this country of evil and corruption. So in a most remarkable way, I suppose you are all responsible for my being here. You have created me by destroying all the loathsome features of Haon's character and now, together, we will set about creating an age of peace and prosperity in which no individual shall be reckoned more worthy than another. There will be no oppression and all the power produced by scientific research will be directed towards improving the lot of all the inhabitants of this realm.'

The young man spoke with the authority of a born leader and one who clearly had the welfare of others at heart. Varac was so impressed by his words and by his sheer personal magnetism, that he put all doubts out of his mind, offered his hand to him, which was grasped firmly and warmly. Immediately Varac's colleagues crowded round the youth, confirming their allegiance by a shake of the hand.

In the excitement of the phenomenal turn of events the six friends from beyond the western mountains seemed momentarily forgotten. They stood together to one side and watched with great joy as the scientists celebrated with uninhibited enthusiasm the unbelievable victory over evil and their discovery of a leader pledged to care for all his people.

At last Varac turned to them. He led the young man towards them and said, 'These are our friends from the plains. They have shown us the way to live life to the full. To them the credit of this wonderful transformation belongs.'

They all, with one voice, contradicted him, declaring that it had been he and his fellow scientists who had been the spearhead and who had protected them throughout, at which they all burst out laughing and exchanged compliments in a truly friendly way.

Coming to each one in turn, the new young leader of the mountain race embraced them.

'Aggorine, you have shown us the beauty of personal relationships, the joy of caring for others, and the essence of true leadership. Yma, your love of music and your exceptional skill have brought us all to recognise the beauty of harmony and the comfort of providing enjoyment for others. Lekhar, your understanding of scientific problems and your command of mathematics, coupled with your logical mind, combining, not for personal gain or power, but for the benefit of all, have shown how knowledge should truly be employed.'

He came next to Oj. 'You are the practical one of the group, are you not? Your skill and understanding of material things are outstanding, and furthermore your keen brain is able to encompass so many more aspects of life than most people can. You have been an inspiration to us all in your ability easily, and often simply, to find solutions to the more practical hurdles which often defeat others less skilful in these matters.'

When he stood in front of Shimah who matched him in stature and the glow of youth, he put his hands on his shoulders and with a twinkle in his eye said, 'I think you and I would wrestle until eternity with neither of us prevailing. What do you say?'

Shimah returned the young man's light-hearted quip, saying, 'Maybe you're right – perhaps we might try one day!'

'Perhaps we might,' the young leader laughed, 'but if we do, I know it will be simply for the enjoyment of the game and not for the winning. You have shown us that the beauty of strength lies not in imposing it on others but in its use for the enjoyment and benefit of others.

At last he turned to Ecila.

'You were Haon's captive, were you not? In fact you were his stubborn captive who would not fully display her artistic skill to him, for fear that he might score a victory and capture it himself.'

'I could not, even if I had wished to do so,' she replied. 'Inspiration and vision are needed to create a picture of quality, and the evil atmosphere of this place was so strong that it was impossible for me to find either, until . . .' and here she hesitated – 'until the moment I knew my friends were with me again. It was then that I picked up my brushes and found myself impelled to paint. I knew immediately I started the picture that it was not only going to be inspired, but prophetic as well. My brushes moved over the canvas guided by some benign force and all the while, in the distance through my west window I could see a brilliant glow from Mount Tarara. Elcaro was my inspiration. I was simply the instrument through which the forces of evil and the forces of good were finally to be torn apart. – How? – I did not know until a short while ago when I unfurled the picture in front of Haon. Elcaro had chosen my picture to be the fatal blow to his evil character. You all know what happened.' Ecila bowed her head in humility. 'I was simply the instrument,' she whispered.

Aggorine came to her and folded her in her arms. 'You have contributed more than all of us,' she said. 'You suffered captivity and withstood the wiles of Haon, and then Elcaro chose you to deliver the final strike which rid this domain of tyranny.' After a while she said, 'Show us the picture and let us all share your supreme artistic talent.'

'The young man took Ecila's hand saying, 'Please – we too would be part of this great achievement.'

There were tears of emotion in Ecila's eyes as she took the rolled canvas and, in front of them all, allowed it to open. Bathed in sunlight, the picture was seen in all its wonderful detail.

What was revealed made them all gaze in incredulous amazement, not only because of the masterly way in which Ecila had treated the subject but largely because of the subject itself.

A tall, beautifully proportioned young man with shoulder length fair hair and deep blue, penetrating eyes, stood in the foreground, right on the edge of the picture with his feet planted firmly on a threshold. Dressed in a shimmering golden gown he looked every inch a leader. His arms were held forward with the palms of his hands open, welcoming all who looked at him. He held his head erect and his gaze was to distant horizons. The whole figure seemed to glow with the confidence of one who knows that the new future holds so much promise for all who would come with him.

Behind the youth across the bare stone slabs and towards the left hand edge of the picture, giving the impression that it was receding back and back, away from the young man, was a hideous, gaudily coloured figure of what had once been a man. Now huddled on its haunches with one scrawny arm outstretched towards the youth it looked the essence of evil and ugliness. Behind the creature was chaos, confusion and destruction, which itself appeared to be dragging the creature with it towards the back of the scene and, one could imagine, eventually right out of sight.

As they all stood gazing at Ecila's masterpiece no-one said a word until Varac whispered, – 'The ring, he hasn't got the ring on his finger.'

Ecila looked up and said simply, 'Look on the ground by his right foot. He hasn't yet presumed to take it up and with it his leadership.' And there the emerald lay.

'What magnificent artistry! What prophetic vision!' breathed Varac. 'No wonder Haon screamed when he saw his destiny so clearly illustrated!'

Ecila smiled her appreciation and all the others crowded round her to add their congratulations, but the young man stood apart. His serious demeanour showed how deeply affected he too was by the significance of the picture. Eventually, when she could move, Ecila rolled up the canvas, walked towards the young man and gave it into his hands.

'It is for you,' she said. 'Perhaps when you look at it it will remind you of your friends from the plains. Perhaps also it will help you to come to terms with the fact that by the power, the brilliance and the sheer goodness of Elcaro, working through your wonderful scientists and your friends, you were wrenched apart from the evil nature of Haon in order to rule your people with care and consideration and to work for peace.'

'I shall treasure it always,' he said and raising his voice for all to hear he declared, 'I dedicate my life to the service of the people of this country. My name shall be "Haonson" and, under me, I trust we shall together establish a people as renowned for their friendliness, helpfulness and consideration for others as in the past we have been hated and reviled for our worship of greed and selfish power.'

A great shout of acclamation from all in the room, including, to their own surprise, the soldiers themselves who had until now been subdued under the powerful thought control of Varac and the other scientists.

The newly named Haonson held up his hand on which the emerald glinted. 'Come,' he said, 'there is much to do. Let us make a start,' and he led the way to the council chamber.

24

Two days had passed since those remarkable events in the great domed room. Already workmen had cleared up the litter of shattered plastic and carried it away. A few coloured rags were found in one corner, covered with broken pieces of the roof. The last vestiges of Haon's presence went ignominiously and almost unnoticed to be burned along with the other rubbish.

In the new-found freedom the six young people were royally entertained by their hosts. Haonson himself was hardly ever out of their company, and together with Varac they were taken on tours of all the major installations which hitherto had been completely under the control of the evil one. Now all the expertise of the new generation of scientists would be directed towards the well-being of the whole population.

Many problems lay ahead; of that they were all aware. Of paramount importance was the freeing of the minds of the military personnel in such a way as not to risk an insurrection, and also the presentation to them and to the whole population of their new leader. After generations of suppression, it was going to prove a major task to give freedom to those who had never known the meaning of it.

'It will all take time,' Haonson declared, 'but together I know we can achieve the benign revolution we all desire.'

Gradually all the staff in the headquarters building realised that things were going to be very different from now on. Wherever he went, Haonson's magnetic personality won the respect and support of those he met. On the second day of the new regime he addressed a group of some hundred or so military leaders. Introduced by Varac, who related the historic changes which had taken place, Haonson explained his policy for the relaxation of central control. He saw the military as being crucial to the success of the policy and asked for their complete co-operation.

It took some time for the realisation to sink in that the evil of Haon had been destroyed and that this new young leader was offering them the chance to come fully alive for the first time. Eventually the unmistakable sincerity of this fine young man infected the whole gathering. To a man they stood and, with no inhibitions whatsoever, cheered him to the rooftops. The first major hurdle had been overcome.

Haonson explained how each commander would be made responsible for the rehabilitation of his own body of troops and how Varac would help by gradually reducing the power of the central thought controller over a period of two or three weeks. By that time new attitudes and codes of behaviour would have had a chance to be assimilated by the rank and file. At the end of the meeting, he reaffirmed his dedication to lead the country towards freedom and again they gave him a great shout of support.

Yma and Aggorine, Lekhar and Ecila, Shimah and Oj were all fêted as they accompanied Haonson and Varac wherever they went. But thoughts of home began to fill their minds. Their mission had met with outstanding success and now it was time to return. So in the evening of the second day Aggorine approached Varac and told him of their wishes.

With a sad look on his face he said, 'I knew this moment had to come, my dear friends, but I have been dreading it. We have become very close and you have done so much for us. How can we ever repay you?'

'Repay?' she replied. 'It is sufficient in itself that we have found friendship here and that friendship will undoubtedly flourish in the days and years to come. After all, with your superb nuclear powered, thought-controlled transport system, you will always be only a wish away from us.'

'There is one thing we would like to do. If it is possible, we would like to revisit the slopes of Mount Tarara on the way. It was there where we first encountered Haon and where Elcaro came dramatically into our lives and to our immediate rescue.'

'I was hoping you would suggest that,' replied Varac. 'If you agree, I should very much like to come with you on your return journey, which I hope will be considerably more comfortable than your previous travels! Perhaps Elcaro will speak to me again.'

The decision having been taken, the rest of the evening was devoted to animated chatter amongst themselves. There were few preparations to be made. Oj and Lekhar spent some time together converting Lekhar's laser machine to its original design.

'I didn't have a chance to prove how lethal it could be,' she said, 'but it was good to feel that I could have stopped Haon in his tracks if it had become necessary!'

'Now that's fighting talk,' said Oj smiling.

'Yes, I know,' she replied laughingly. 'I'm sure I wouldn't ever have had the courage to fire it! But it was a nice little problem redesigning the circuit, wasn't it?'

Oj agreed, and soon their clever brains and nimble fingers had restored the device to its more peaceful form.

They slept fitfully that night. Excitement at the prospect of seeing their homes and their parents once more was not conducive to sleep. The early morning sun rising over the eastern mountains saw them all up and ready to go.

Varac was an early visitor and he assured them that all arrangements had been made for their departure. He suggested they leave at mid morning which would give enough time for them to say farewell to Haonson and the many friends they had made. Haonson himself was not far behind Varac in coming to visit them. He was a magnificent figure standing erect and clothed in a golden cloak which hung loosely from his shoulders to the ground. A simple garment but worn with dignity, it gave him the appearance of a chieftain among men. His handsome face glowed with vitality, and the six friends knew that his reforms would succeed, and that their journey had been crowned with success. He did not leave them, but accompanied them on their rounds of goodbyes until it was time.

A great crowd had gathered in the courtyard and a triumphant shout greeted the young leader as he escorted his six friends from beyond the western mountains, towards their transport.

'Come back and bring more of your people whenever you can,' he said as he embraced them each in turn. Finally he turned to Varac. 'Don't forget to return will you? I need you,' and they laughed together as they shook hands.

As before, the travellers found themselves absorbed by the transport vehicle and without realising it they were on their way. It took only moments for them to reach the very spot where Haon had all but destroyed them, and as they stood looking up to the peak of Mount Tarara, memories came flooding back. As if to welcome them, the tip of the mountain became brilliantly white once more. Elcaro was waiting for them to speak.

'We are back, Elcaro,' they each called out in turn. Then Yma, as the eldest, voiced their gratitude. 'Thank you for all your help and guidance. Without your protection and assistance we should undoubtedly have failed in our quest.' Pulling Varac forward she continued, 'This is Varac, our dear friend from the mountain kingdom. He and his scientific colleagues were beginning to appreciate the magnificence and beauty of the natural world before we came. Together we have rooted out the evil influence of Haon, and an era of caring and sharing has begun under their new youthful leader Haonson. But again, we could not have achieved anything if we had not had your power and wisdom to guide our actions and our thoughts. We owe all to you.'

'We do, we do,' the other shouted.

Elcaro replied with words which entered directly into each of their minds. 'I know Varac and welcome him and shall always be ready to help him, his young leader and his people in their road back to fruitful and joyful living.'

As they stood gazing at the brilliance of Elcaro and absorbing his words, their attention was suddenly directed towards the ground just in front of Varac. There, glowing with Elcaronic power, lay a stone just like those the six friends had received at the start of their journey.

'It is for you Varac,' came the message from Elcaro. 'Take it and keep it with you always. It will help you and your young leader to overcome the problems you face in changing the lives of your people.'

They had all understood Elcaro's message and automatically the six friends withdrew their own stones from their pockets and held them on outstretched palms where all glowed as brightly as ever before.

Varac bent down and, lifting the seventh stone, he too held it on the palm of his hand and his gaze moved once more to the top of the mountain. He was deeply moved and with great emotion welling up from the depths of his being, the simple

226

words, 'Thank you,' breathed through his lips.

The others watched as Varac lifted the seventh stone high above his head as if to show to the whole world that he had accepted joyfully the help and guidance of Elcaro. They moved until they encircled him and, thrusting their hands towards his at the centre of the ring, brought all seven stones together in a brilliance matched only by the tip of the mountain itself.

As they stood there in complete harmony, Elcaro spoke again. 'You now know that the secret of life lies not in understanding how life is brought into being. Suffice it to know that it exists. It is much more important, as you have all found out, to live that life to the full, to enjoy using your talents, not for yourself alone but for the welfare of others. See and revel in the beauty of nature, the material world, and most of all the relationships between peoples. Use wisely what you have and what you discover, and you will continue to learn more and more of the secret of living life to the full.'

There was a pause during which the seven friends exchanged glances, which indicated that they had all received Elcaro's words. Gradually they lowered their arms as Elcaro brought them back to earth.

'You must go now. Your parents and friends are waiting for you,' he continued in a much more matter-of-fact manner. 'Goodbye, we shall meet again. Goodbye.'-

'Goodbye,' echoed round the mountain as they all responded.

They stood silently for some while, gazing at the mountain peak as it slowly became less bright and then disappeared altogether as if covered by a cloud. Then their precious gifts from Elcaro were returned once more to their pockets.

Varac took charge again. The transport re-absorbed them and the next thing they knew was that they were standing on the plain where the Androphine family had started their momentous journey.

A car was approaching and, as it got nearer, Oj recognised it as their family vehicle. Together they ran to meet the two men who scrambled out, and were immediately smothered in the embraces of the two fathers. Tears of joy flowed freely and all the two men could say was, 'At last, at last – all safe and sound!'

Varac stood some way from the joyful group, vicariously

enjoying the happiness of the reunion of his friends and their fathers. Everyone was talking at once in excitement, but at last the storm of delight subsided and Aggorine led them all to where Varac waited.

'This is our friend, Varac, from beyond the mountains,' she said introducing him to the two fathers. 'Without him we should not be here today. We owe him so much.'

'No, no,' interjected Varac, as he took the proffered hands of the two men in his. 'It is I and my country who are in the greatest debt to these six brave and talented young people. It is a great honour to meet their fathers. But now I must leave you. You have so much to talk about and I would not wish to intrude.'

'Please don't go yet,' pleaded Yma. 'Our mothers would wish to meet you and, in any case, we should like to show you where we live.'

Varac did not take much persuading and, amid another babel of questions from all sides, none of which were capable of being fully answered in the highly charged happy atmosphere of the reunion, they squeezed into the Androphine family's eight seater, and were soon speeding their way across the plain towards home.

Aggorine and Shimah had been delighted, and not a little surprised to find their father had been there to meet them. On the way towards the Androphine's home he explained that there had been some publicity in the national press when two groups of young people were overdue from an expedition to the mountains, and he had got in touch with the parents of the group of four, so that plans to search for them all could be co-ordinated. Since then the two sets of parents had become very close and had spent a great deal of time in each other's company. He said that, as soon as possible the two fathers had themselves penetrated the foothills of Mount Tarara but had had to give up because the way became impassable following a massive rock fall. Since then they had made the trip every day to the two places where they had last seen their children, and each time they returned with heavy hearts, but were never willing to believe the worst had happened and that they would not see their children again.

Hoping against hope, they had set out once more that morning, – the morning of the fortieth day of the children's

228

disappearance. They had travelled in silence towards the foothills as they always did, not wanting to risk expressing their fears to each other, yet inwardly knowing that, as each day passed, the chances of the families ever being reunited were smaller and smaller.

But this day was gloriously different from all those other days. They were together again. What had happened while they had been in the mountains was, for the moment of secondary importance. Aggorine and Shimah on either side of their father, with their arms through his, were deliriously happy. Ecila, just in front of Shimah was happy just to be near him in a safe and familiar situation. Occasionally he would run his fingers through her straw-coloured hair and she would turn and smile broadly at him, her eyes just a little bit misty! Yma, Lekhar and Oj, sitting alongside, or just behind their father kept up an incessant chatter and all he could do was smile and listen, trying to sort out some sense from the cacophony of voices. Eventually Shimah started to sing. His heart was bubbling over with joy and out it had to come! Immediately they all followed his example. And so they proceeded bellowing joyfully, if not melodiously, until they reached the outskirts of the town. Even then they didn't stop, but made their noisy way through street after street until they approached their destination where two anxious mothers awaited what they expected to be the return once more of two dejected fathers.

The people in the streets knew before the mothers did. Hearing the singing and recognising the car and its occupants, they had joined in the celebration and soon the news was spreading:

'The children are back – the children are back.' The whole town rejoiced.

Only when the house came into view did the singing stop. The two mothers were in the front garden, weeding the beds and tying up a few wayward blooms in a very desultory fashion. Their sad minds were elsewhere and they were waiting for their men to return. But this time there was no need for words of consolation nor of an embrace of shared grief and disappointment. A blast on the horn made them lift their eyes and in that moment happiness was reborn in their hearts.

Tumbling out as fast as they could, the children surrounded their mothers, embracing them and being embraced. Tears flowed freely as their happiness was given full rein. Words, words, words were flying back and forth with no expectation of replies. Varac, the last to leave the car, stood by, drinking it all in and treasuring the still unfamiliar emotions.

Somehow they gradually made their way indoors. Oj and Shimah lifted their mothers high in their arms and led the way, amidst unbounded laughter and not a few screams from the two women. The others followed and the fathers brought Varac with them, to make sure he felt most welcome.

When eventually a little peace was restored Yma and Aggorine introduced Varac to their mothers, telling them, as they had their fathers, how they would never have been able to return alive had it not been for their friend. He in turn emphasised how much he and his people owed to the young folk and how they had been instrumental in ridding his country of the evil influence of the tyrant Haon.

'They will tell you the whole story, I'm sure,' he said, 'but for the moment let it suffice to say that their mission was wholly successful. My country now has a new young leader who is dedicated to peace and the peaceful uses of scientific knowledge. I hope you will all meet him in due course.'

The four parents were desperately anxious to hear the account of their children's journey but the excitement of the reunion was still running too high for them to expect any coherent tale at the present moment. After a meal together, perhaps they would be more settled.

By now it was late afternoon and high tea was announced by the two mothers. How comfortable and homely high tea sounded to the travellers, and sitting with their parents and their friend Varac around the table, each one realised that their journey really was over at last. At the end of the meal Varac declared that he must now return, and though they all pressed him to stay, they realised that they could not detain him longer.

'We shall miss you,' said Aggorine.

'And I shall miss you too,' he replied, 'but I am sure we will keep in touch regularly and we must arrange for you and many more of your plainsfolk to visit our country. Equally I trust there will be many visits in the opposite direction. We will be friends and will continue to learn from each other, to everyone's advantage.'

They all escorted him to the door and when he was offered a lift in the car back to the foothills he smiled and said, 'Thank you all the same, but I have my own transport,' and he winked at the children, saluted them by pressing his hand to his breast pocket where the seventh stone nestled, and was gone.

'How on earth will he get back?' queried both fathers together.

The children smiled. 'We'll tell you all about that and much more,' they chanted. 'Let's all sit down.'

'You'll never believe what we have to tell you,' began the logical Lekhar. 'If I were in your shoes, I know I wouldn't believe it! – but it happened just as we are about to tell you – I assure you!'

And so the whole story unfolded, each one taking up the story as and when it seemed appropriate. No-one thought of sleep until the early hours of the next morning but at last everything had been told and it was time for bed.

The table was still uncleared and the girls started to put things on the sideboard.

'Leave it all until morning,' said Yma's mother and took the plates from her and then put them herself back on the table. As she did so she noticed an unfamiliar packet at the place where Varac had been sitting for his meal. She picked it up and read out loud what was written on the wrapping:

'To my new-found friends, in the hope that, in the future, you too will only be a thought away from visiting us in the mountains.'

Inside the packet they discovered detailed production plans of the wonderful nuclear powered thought-transportation system which had been one of the most jealously guarded secrets of the Haonic scientists.

There was also a card which said, 'I myself have asked Varac to give this to you and your people. We owe you so much and this is but a token of our gratitude.'

And it was signed 'Haonson.'

'Some token!' breathed Lekhar.

Yma had wandered towards the window which looked across to the east and when they heard her say, 'Come and look,' they joined her there.

In the far distance the tip of Mount Tarara was glowing a brilliant white and they knew that Varac would be looking at it too. All was very peaceful.